BEARHEART

GERALD VIZENOR

BEARHEART

THE HEIRSHIP CHRONICLES

University of Minnesota Press

Minneapolis

Published by the University of Minnesota Press
111 Third Avenue South, Suite 290, Minneapolis, MN 55401-2520
http://www.upress.umn.edu

Printed in the United States of America.

The characters in this novel arise from the author's imagination;
any resemblance to actual persons is purely coincidental.

Third printing, 2001

Library of Congress Cataloging-in-Publication Data

Vizenor, Gerald Robert, 1934–
    [Darkness in Saint Louis Bearheart]
    Bearheart : the heirship chronicles / Gerald Vizenor.
        p.   cm.
    First ed. published as: Darkness in Saint Louis Bearheart. 1978.
    ISBN 0–8166–1851–8. — ISBN 0–8166–1852–6 (pbk.)
    I. Title.
    PS3572.I9D37   1990
        813'.54—dc20   90-32974

The University of Minnesota is an
equal-opportunity educator and employer.

He looked like a white Indian. . . . He had a slow walk like a somnambulist enmeshed in the past and unable to walk into the present. He was so loaded with memories, cast down by them. . . . He saw only the madness of the world. . . .

This fatalistic man, emerging from the depths of his past with intolerably open eyes, offered the world first of all an appearance of legendary elegance. . . . He himself passed invisibly, untouched, unattainable, giving at no time any proof of reality: no stain, tear, sign of wear and death coming. It seemed rather as if death had already passed, that he had died already to all the friction and usage of life, been pompously buried with all his possessions, dressed in his finest clothes, and was now walking through the city merely to warn us.

Anaïs Nin, Under a Glass Bell

¶ Letter to the Reader

The bear is in me now.

Not since the darkness at the federal boarding school and the writing of this book, the heirship chronicles on the wicked road to the fourth world, has the blood and deep voice of the bear moved in me with such power.

Listen, ha ha ha haaaa.

We raise the secret language of bears in the darkness, stumble into the fourth world on twos and fours, and turn underwords ha ha ha haaaa in our visions. Bears are in our hearts. Shoulders tingle downhill on dreams. The darkness moves in ursine shivers, moves in the maw.

Measure most of our lives in darkness, the bear is with me, and count in silence our faces on the dawn, our service in the wars, turning out tribal heirship chronicles at government desks, under the slow motions of federal forearms. We dreamed about the omens and grave heirship stories we told on the future of the tribes at war with evil and words.

We are finished with the third world now, and we wait here in the darkness, less than one month from federal retirement. Our last words into the fourth world winter solstice. The heirship stories are hidden in a metal cabinet with other tribal documents. Bearheart at his words, but who would read our heirship documents now?

We are locked in darkness with wicked words.

Bearheart, bearheart, bearheart, bearheart at his words.

Listen, ha ha ha haaaa.

The voices of the bear spoke through me for the first time when the boarding school superintendent cornered me in a narrow dark closet on the reservation. For a time we moved our memories with hatred, alone in the darkness with our picture memories on thunderclouds, crows in the cedar. We were cornered three times as crows and then the bear opened his maw and took me into his heart. We moved federal school time in our wild darkness on the winter solstice.

Listen, ha ha ha haaaa.

We were twelve years old then and had run from that federal school four times, once in winter. The moons were wild, and the government agents were waiting, waiting, waiting for the heirs at the treelines, waiting for the defeated tribes to stop running from the uniforms and closets. The agents, colonial hunters hired by the government, captured me once as me, three times as a crow, and ran me back four times from dreams in the sacred cedar.

The first time, to teach me a lesson not to run with the tribes and our memories and visions of birds and animals, the agents forced me to wash floors and clean toilets for two months at the federal boarding school.

The second time back, from the sixth grade then, the superintendent, and a cruel teacher, bound me in hard uniforms, oversized shoes, and pushed me into the classroom. The crow was in me, and we were beaten over a desk for our avian dreams.

The third time we were captured at a swollen river. We were leashed by government agents and marched back to the classroom, and we were chained at night to a stone in the cowshed.

We survived as crows and bears because we were never known as humans. Those cruel teachers never heard our avian voices, they never roamed with us at the treelines. We dreamed free from our chains.

Listen, ha ha ha haaaa.

The fourth time back to the boarding school we were chained and bruised, the last time as a crow, and we learned to outwit the government in the darkness. We were pushed and punched, cornered in a narrow closet by the superintendent. We were the heirs he would never tame, and his promotions were measured by our assimilation, our tribal death.

We could hear the harsh sounds of the superintendent and teachers through the ventilator hole in the ceiling of the closet. We could smell the bitter poison smoke from his cigars. The bird in me was tired, we were weakened in the darkness, no water, no trees but our interior landscapes.

Listen to us now great bears, old bearmen, bearhearts in the stars on the winter solstice, we are here once more in the darkness, we are praised in the darkness.

Listen, ha ha ha haaaa.

There are new tribal evils with us now. The crossbloods and wicked skins dressed in animal hides and plastic bear claws are down around us here in the heirship documents. The aimless children paint hard words on the federal windows in their material wars, and the words are dead, tribal imagination and our trickeries to heal are in ruins.

The heirship rooms were hot and humid. We roamed in the darkness and remembered the treeline in the cities. The superintendent died one month into his retirement, but he was never buried, now he wanders late at night with the skinwalkers and torments the tribes in dreams. He was there in our heirship documents, in our stories, and touched our laughter, our seasons.

Listen, ha ha ha haaaa.

The Bureau of Indian Affairs hired me to dance in the darkness on the cabinets and to remember the heirship documents, the crossblood tricksters at the treelines. We laughed, no one in the cities would believe that we were related to animals, that we were bears in these stories.

Someone beats on the door.

Stand against the wall, old man, she says.

She is nervous. Her voice wavers. She has little white chickens in her heart, they thrust their feathered decorated heads around the door. The halls outside the room are dark. The government cut the electrical power when the militants seized the building. She flashes her light on the animals, our bear faces.

Listen, ha ha ha haaaa.

You the hairship man? she asks.

Down in the darkness.

Where are the hairships?

Our tribal heirdom no place now.

Hairdom?

The white lies that would be our tribal inheritance.

You nuts old man, she says.

Never rush darkness and the bears with chickens.

What bear?

Listen, ha ha ha haaaa.

Some bear, she says and mocks the laughter.

You pose as a warrior with chickens in the third world, the best comes closer to the end. The bear, bearheart in his words, our heirship documents are in the fourth world.

The revolution has changed that now, she shouts.

Revolution with plastics.

We speak for the people, she insists.

Then we must be the enemies of ourselves in the darkness, rushed to hold our praise, our vision in the fourth world. Did the people lock us in this room?

We are the warriors of freedom.

Whose freedom?

The people, freedom to our people.

This must be your federal boarding school, freedom in the darkness once more. Freedom, freedom, and what are your dreams and visions. We are bears, not the painted riders in the cities.

Who is this we here?

The darkness and the bear in me.

What bear?

Bearheart, ha ha ha haaaa.

Never make fun of our sacred religion.

What religion?

The bear clan religion, she answers.

You would be a word bear, your religion a word pile.

She shouts and slams the door closed. Now she opens the door again. Little chickens are so nervous around bears. She beats her *turquoise ring on the metal door. She must be on television in the darkness.*

What is the hairship?

Who is asking?

The American Indian Movement.

But you are a chicken.

We have occupied this building in the name of the tribes and the trail of broken treaties, she says, and the government will answer all of our demands or else we have come here to die together for freedom. She smiles, proud to hold freedom in terminal creeds.

Their freedom is your suicide.

She sneers now.

The bear moves closer to her, bearheart the old colonial bear, closer to the chickens in the cage, and the bear says to the chicken, Would you tell us good stories about our people and the revolution in winter words before we die?

You old white bastard, she shouts.

Now the bear has you in the darkness, our darkness, we hold your mouth and watch you listen, ha ha ha haaaa. See how sudden we die, the word wars end at the mouth in freedom.

She wears bear claws.

Paws down old man, she says.

Plastic bear claws.

The chicken feathers are stained with words. The muscles on her neck are tense. Mouth warm on the word, under paw, chicken woman in the paws of the old bear. She seems passive, lonesome, less tense in our maw.

She moves down in the darkness, down on the cold floor. She smiles, now she shoulders our paws, moist thighs.

What is your name? asks the bear.

She moves her tongue.

Touch your name on our cheeks, word to word.

Never, she traces.

Who would be never? asks the bear.

Neverwhiteindian.

Listen, ha ha ha haaaa. Once in a boarding school we were locked in the darkness. The enemies turn but the visions are the same, the bear is with me now.

She trembles under his paws.

On the seventh morning in the closet at the boarding school the bear came to me in a vision, our sacred time, our dreams in a secret language over human word wars into the fourth world.

What is hairship?

She moves her tongue and listens. The names of the tribal people who were bears, who would own the land if tribal land could be owned, and if those who had died owned the land. The government held our reservation land in trust so the timber could be cut and minerals mined. She moves in silence.

What is your name? asks the bear.

Songidee migwan.

Fearless feather, a sacred name?

What else?

Who would reveal their sacred name?

White Indian, she shouts.

Sagima, you are the one who moves without shadows, says the bear, sagima, those with sacred names would not wear plastic bear claws, sagima, the one who shouts but does not dream with grand medicine.

White, white, white, bear, she shouts.

You must hate men, old men the most for their darkness.

She is silent.

Bearheart turns in the darkness, we are bears in the Bureau of Indian Affairs, says the bear. The others are outside, lost memories in the word wars and we are here with the bears. Warm chicken, show bearheart the road back to the tribe.

Songidee, she is passive.

Tender breasts in the darkness.

Listen, ha ha ha haaaa.

White Indian, she shouts and unbuttons her leather blouse.

Who would your we be songidee?

My brothers in the American Indian Movement.

Mouth warriors, says the bear.

We took this building for tribal people, for our past and future on the reservations, says the bare chicken. We are the new warriors out for tribal freedom, but you old fuckers sold out to the white man too long ago to understand the real movement.

Stomach, moist fur, ha ha ha haaaa.

White Indian, hate me, hate me.

Touch me, we are word bears in our book.

What book?

One word at a time, the heirship documents and bears on the road to the _fourth world_. Proude Cedarfair, the old shaman, our bearheart on the winter solstice. We are there now, in our own documents.

Someone beats hard on the door.

She moves on the old bear in silence.

Outside, someone curses the government, the weather, darkness, and hails freedom in the Bureau of Indian Affairs. Freedom in a word comes to prison. The movement would turn to a government word hospital to heal their broken promises, the church of last names.

Where did you come from old man?

Listen, ha ha ha haaaa.

You got nuts ideas about skins, she says.

Trickster liberation, says the bear.

Weird skins, man.

Bears see memories, not our bodies tuned to concepts.

Whose speech are you in now?

Mouth on the bear.

She moans and shudders.

Bearheart, ha ha ha haaaa.

What is your book about?

Sex and violence.

Show me the hairship documents.

Would you read?

Yes, but where?

There, our heirship in the closet.

White Indian on me in the darkness, tells me this book shit,

hold the bear in me, finish us old bear, harder old bear, she says,
you never wrote no hairship book on bears.

Listen, ha ha ha haaaa.

Harder old bear.

Proude Cedarfair and our terminal creeds.

Harder old bear.

Proude Cedarfair and the evil gambler.

Harder old bear.

Proude Cedarfair on the winter solstice.

Harder old bear, harder, harder to the last word.

The leathers on her back hold their sweat in the darkness. She
rises, opens the cabinet in the closet, opens the bound
manuscript, and reads out loud sections in the heirship
documents. Songidee reads under the bright beam of her
flashlight.

The federal man leaned over and touched her muscular calves.
. . . She stumbled out of her clothes. His short blunt penis was
wobbling like the neck of a dead sparrow. She leaned back on her
elbows over the cedar fronds and spread her legs open to the
federal man. . . . He missed more than half his frantic earthbound
thrusts, leaving her spread and moaning, falling through
cloudless space, out of time and green paper, plastic flowers, part
thunder and poison rain.

Bearheart, ha ha ha haaaa.

THE HEIRSHIP CHRONICLES

Proude Cedarfair
and the Cultural Word Wars

Saint Louis Bearheart

I am like a bear,
I hold up my hands waiting for the sun to rise.

Pawnee song, translated by Frances Densmore

¶ Morning Prelude

The last full moon of summer slumps alone through the palmate shadows of the cedar night and then stretches out over the dark river water into morning.

Proude Cedarfair is a ceremonial bear. He dreams in sudden moods and soars through stone windows on the solstice sunrise. The clown crows trail his luminous breath and thunder voice ha ha ha haaaa from his magical directions into the fourth world.

The earth turtles emerge from the great flood of the first world. In the second world the earth is alive in the magical voices and ceremonial words of birds and the healing energies of plants. The white otter is the carrier of animal dreams in the new hearts of humans. The third world turns evil with contempt for living and fear of death. Solemn figures are slashed open on the faces of tribal dream drums. In the fourth world evil spirits are outwitted in the secret languages of animals and birds. Bears and crows choose the new singers. The crows crow in their blackness. Ha ha ha haaaa the bears call from the sunrise.

Cedarfair circus in the morning. Clown crows. Incense from moist cedar. Time turns under the warm figures of breathing. Moths and the sound of dew coming down the fern and pale waxen faces on poplar leaves near the river.

Proude Cedarfair determines his thoughts from morning dreams and moves through the trees in whispers. Seven clown crows crow in gentle spurts at his walking in horizontal flight fastened step over step through the first light. In his sacred tribal name, *tagwagig nessewin*, autumn breath, the last old man of the cedar nation stops at the tender center of the *migis* sandridge which parts the sensuous mouth of the *misisibi* from the lake like a mythic smile.

The *migis* is the sacred shell tribal people follow inland from the great salt seas. The *misisibi* flows from the west into the red cedar and then south through pollution storms to the desert. From *tchibai* island the evil spirits and creek devils hiss and groan with the distance of the shadowless and the wandering dead.

Proude draws the figures of four turtles in the sand. Cool dew covers his dark flesh. He chants ha ha ha haaaa and then walks into the silent water as his fathers have done for more than a thousand new tribal moons from the same sacred place. The red cedar water is heaped high with morning brume. The clown crows wait in the trees.

¶ Cedar Celebrants

Four Proude Cedarfairs have celebrated the sacred cedar trees. The first was named by the missionaries who admired his stubborn courage and stern pride. The first refused their religion and would not remove himself from the fair cedar wood to the grim reservation.

First Proude claimed a large circle of cedar trees which bordered the *misisibi*, the great river, on one side and lake *miskwawak nibi*, the red cedar water, on the other. He built houses of bark in the circle there, loved two women, one a pale mixedblood, and praised his seven children and four brothers in their sacred names.

Three Proude Cedarfairs have defended their sovereign circle from national and state and tribal governments, from missionaries, treekillers and evil tribal leaders. Seven sons have died defending the sacred nation. One son in each generation has survived to protect the dominion of natural cedar.

First Proude moved from the north near *anishinabe nibi*, the water of the first tribal families, searching for a place to live in the sacred cedar. On the shores of the *misisibi* and *miskwawak nibi* he built a small house. The cedar became his source of personal power. He dreamed trees and leaned in the wind with the cedar. In the winter he stood outside alone drawing his arms around his trunk under snow. He spoke with the trees. He became the cedar wood.

"We are the cedar," he told his sons. "We cannot leave ourselves . . . We are the breath and voice of this woodland."

Nineteenth century frontier politics favored the interests of the railroads and treekillers and agrarian settlers who were promised ownership of the earth. The excitement of the furtrade had passed leaving the tribes to their failing cultural memories and dreams, woodland apostates, while the new voices of the woodland cracked with harsh sounds. Whitemen possessed trees and women and words. Violence eclipsed the solemn promises of woodland tribal celebrants.

A small detachment of surveyors and federal officials passed through the cedar woods marking trees. The cedar shunned the intruders. The crows were raucous. First Proude greeted the whitemen but they were rude. He was told the trees were being marked for cutting to build houses in the cities.

Proude retraced the crude path of the detachment through the cedar. He spoke to each tree, moved with them, and removed the death markers on their trunks. When the officials returned with treekillers the next morning they found the cedar had been posted in a wide circle from the river to the lake: The cedar circle had been declared a sovereign nation. The longarms would not enter the circle to cut trees. They were mixedbloods and suspicious.

"What is the meaning of this?" one official asked, poking him with a leather tube of maps and charts. "We have the power of the federal government to cut these trees."

"You do not believe our words," said First Proude looking into the woods. He would not let the agents of the government know his eyes. "This is our sovereign nation. These trees are the families of the earth here ... You will not mark them for death ... You will not cut them down ... There is nothing more to my words."

"If you interfere with the work of the government you will be removed with force and charged with treason," said the government official cracking his map case on his thigh.

"But you are the treacherous one," said Proude turning his back on the official and walking toward the *migis* sandridge at the mouth of the river. When he reached the tender center he stopped and turned toward the white detachment with a smile.

"Seize that man," ordered the federal official. His hand trembled as he pointed and yelled. "Seize that goddamn black savage ..."

Proude drew a deep breath and exhaled in a slow whistle. Then he raised his head high like an animal scenting his enemies on the wind, expanded his chest and growled with the great power of the bears. The sound was deep and wild. The federal official and the detachment turned and ran from the cedar circle.

First Proude tumbled into the water laughing. The clown crows crowed and circled overhead. He plunged his head beneath the water and growled again in his bear voice. The crows crowed and laughed. He squatted just over the river and farted into the surface water. The crows laughed.

One of the surveyors, who had not departed with the government officials, was sitting against a cedar tree near the *migis* sandridge watching the crows laughing and laughing.

"Who is that laughing at the bear?" asked Proude.

"An explorer, I am one of the surveyors from the detachment," he replied, rolling back in the coarse shore grass and laughing again.

"Who are you laughing about?"

"You, you must be a clown bear."

Proude shook and stroked the water from his dark flesh. He farted again. The surveyor told him he wanted to share his courage and defend his sovereign cedar nation, and beginning with words, he named the circle in the cedar a circus, a civil and sacred parish, a circular arena of cedar wood, "a fine place to name the whole world," he said.

First Proude Cedarfair was at war with the federal government and the treekillers. The battle lasted for several weeks while the trees were cut all around the newborn circus. Proude lost all but one of his sons. Two of his brothers were killed defending the cedar. One of his wives, the mixedblood, was raped by whitemen. Her blue eyes were burned with hot coals. Her flesh was pinched and torn. The soft brown hair on her pubic arch was cut and stuffed into her broken mouth by officials of the federal government.

The explorer was captured during the night near the end of the cedar war. While his captors were sitting around a fire and drinking near the border of the cedar circus, the surveyor loosened his bonds and ran through the stumps into the darkness of the cedar. He was shot nine times in the back, three in the head and impaled on a cedar stake facing the circus. When the cedar war ended he was buried near the *migis* sandridge.

The cedar was cut and cleared around the circus. The cedar stumps spumed under the bright sunlight and moaned and screamed during the night. Proude had won the cedar war and preserved his sovereign nation in the circus. The cedar trees at the edge of the circus had turned brown and died from the violence. The circus was enclosed with a row of brown cedar ghosts. The spirits of the dead cedar wandered at night near *tchibai* island.

Proude had become a warrior, praised for his visions. Tribal people came to visit him, to share his courage and to tell him stories about the summer bears and thunderbirds from the mountains and deserts and plains. He laughed over in the water. The federal government ignored him, treekillers no longer needed him and politicians honored his courage and pride, telling the new voters of the state that he was a true patriot, a true and honest man defending his rights. Tribal leaders on the new federal reservation surrounding the circus, coveted the power of the cedar and the man who spoke and acted from his heart. Proude told the leaders that he would recognize no government but his own, no nation but the cedar, and no families but his own blood. We are sovereign from all tribal and religious and national governments, he told the leaders, and we will listen to nothing more about the future. That settles that, said the old tribal leaders, but his words were misunderstood and his sovereign circus was misrepresented as a selfish possession. When new trees began to grow over the stumps surrounding the cedar circus other tribal families following the example of Cedarfair declared themselves sovereign circuses. Tribal leaders were disturbed by these declarations.

The warriors of evil, the religious oppressors, the leaders from tribal fears, envied places of peace and personal power. Proude contradicted their blackhearted energies. He and other families exposed the evil of tribal governments and taught people to control themselves and not to fear the political witching of shamans from the evil underworld and *tchibai* island.

The clown crows were late one morning. It was warm near the river. First Proude was sleeping in the sun on the *migis* sandridge. He was dreaming of turtles and dewfish and swimming underwater with the fish when an evil tribal fisherman split his chest open with an axe. The blood from his fissured heart burst upward with the sound of a roaring bear and blinded the evil fisherman. The second blow of the axe severed his head. The smell of blood and death absolved the evil hissing from *tchibai* island that had possessed the fisherman. The hissing stopped but still blinded with blood the fisherman stumbled into the river. He thrashed his head underwater until he could see again. Turning toward the *migis* sandridge he saw the dark eyes of the first Proude Cedarfair staring at him from the sand. The fisherman emitted a high pitched moan, took the head by one braid and hurled it into the deep red cedar water. First Proude Cedarfair looked back while he tumbled and soared alone in silence. In his dream his lungs filled until his chest burst beneath the water of the great salt seas.

Second Proude Cedarfair turned the sovereign cedar nation over to the women of the circus when he enlisted to serve in the first white world war. His burdens had grown from the expectations of his father to protect the honor of the cedar nation. Second Proude was drunk when he called the women together to hear his proclamation.

"Because of circumstances beyond our control," he said in his drunken falsetto voice, referring to the wars of the whitemen, "I have been called as a leader to serve another nation threatened by evil aggressors." His long pause did not produce the desired responses from the nine women of his tribal dominion. No wailing, no moaning, no fear expressed for his life, so he continued speaking. First he cleared his throat with hard booze distilled from wild rice and bread. "Our father trusted this cedar nation to all of us," he said sweeping his arms so wide he stumbled out of balance. "We must protect our families here ... now I have made myself drunk again ... you know the reasons I am leaving," Second Proude said, leaning forward and almost whispering. His voice wavered. "I am a failure here ... there are no wars for me here. This nation has become the good work of women and I must pass between these circuses to become a warrior ... I drink to smile when I should dream, to give me laughter and grace, to give me the wings of courage I must bear ... I can no longer soar ... I am afraid of death ... the wars of the whiteman will be my good wars until I find myself again." The women turned to avoid his weakness and his pleading words and eyes.

Second Proude, burdened with the image of his brave father, walked to the *migis* sandridge where he spread himself out on the tender center and beat his head against the sand. Small cumulus clouds passed overhead like a great fleet of white warships. He wagged between them bearing the flags of sovereign nations. Bearing the green and white and red flag of the cedar circus, a cedar tree against the great sunrise with two white otters and two black squirrels.

Second Proude in uniform. He returned in two years from the white wars limping and drunk. He sang new songs and drank for the next two hundred new moons. The women continued to govern the circus in the traditions of tribal families, the values of shared consciousness until the patriarchal whitemen rewarded the tribal men as chiefs and rulers. Meanwhile reservation governments were gaining new powers and new generations of evil politicians were seeking control of the sacred cedar. The Indian Reorganization Act created constitutional governments on reservations. The constitutions were designed by white anthropologists and the elections of tribal people were manipulated by colonial federal administrators. Men of evil and tribal fools were propped up in reservation offices to authorize the exploitation of native lands and natural resources. The cedar nation and all the sovereign circuses surrounding the cedar wood resisted all government controls, federal and tribal.

Second Proude stopped drinking to save his cedar nation. He was not romantic about the trees but he was moved with the new challenge to defend the values and beliefs of his father and the creation of the cedar circus.

Second Proude, in uniform for the second time, organized the circuses surrounding the cedar nation into a common defense league. He developed survival plans and warrior societies on each circus. When he declared war on evil and corruption in tribal government, the elected tribal leaders laughed and mimicked his limping gait and stiff neck and authoritarian speech. But when Second Proude ordered the arrest and detention of government officials who had violated the sovereign sanctions of the circuses, the tribal leaders issued similar orders that the circus clowns would be institutionalized if they were found wandering anywhere on the reservation. The tribal government considered the circuses to be within the original colonial boundaries of the reservation, the boundaries created in treaties with the federal government, which meant that the tribal circus families were in violation of the orders wherever they lived on the circuses.

The word wars and humor ended in the spring when circus warriors detained a federal vehicle and three tribal officials. The officials had been drinking and thought it would be an adventure to chop down a cedar tree in the middle of cedarfair circus. The sound of their chopping and their grim laughter was heard for three months. Second Proude, bored with organization and eager for conflict, declared war on the tribal government. He announced the aggressive position of the circuses on hand printed broadsides in the colors of the cedar nation.

WARNING
Declaration of War
Against Evil
Oppressive and Putrescent Officials
Federal and Tribal Governments

By
ALLIED TRIBAL CIRCUSES
Cedarfair Circus
Fairbanks Circus
Hole in the Sky Circus
Fineday Circus
Beaulieu Creek Circus
Ironmoccasin Circus
Bungo Circus

ALLIED CIRCUS COMMANDER
Proude Cedarfair

Several small battles were staged during the summer months. Prisoners were taken on both sides. The three tribal officials caught cutting cedar trees were tried as criminals in the cedar word wars and held as prisoners.

Justice department officials from the federal government were not able to convince the corrupt tribal leaders that they should honor the sovereign nations by declaring them political reservation districts from which representatives would be elected to serve on the tribal council.

The war ended when the president of the reservation government and two council representatives were kidnapped by circus warriors. The tribal government collapsed and the allied circuses declared themselves the provisional reservation tribal government. Circus candidates were elected and controlled the reservation government for the next two decades. Second Proude Cedarfair retained his title as allied circus commander, but bestowed responsibilities for the

13

cedar nation on his son, Third Proude. The women smiled. Third Proude was their child, sensitive and determined, from their secret visions. Second Proude had won his war, he had fought in the word wars of the whiteman and for the sacred dominion in the cedar. With no more wars to know he started drinking for pleasure rather than from shame. In the summer he slept on the *migis* sandridge, swam across the red cedar water and drank wild rice wine with his warrior friends from the circus wars. In the winter he ran with the circus animals and howled at night under the full moon. He wrapped himself in ceremonial cedar boughs and would sit for hours singing in his sweat bath house.

Second Proude disappeared in the spring. It had taken him three weeks to walk to Wounded Knee in South Dakota where the American Indian Movement had declared a new pantribal political nation. In sight of the radical encampment, coming out of a cold wash on the prairie and over a rolling hill, the second old man of the cedar was stopped by a tribal government policeman. When he began singing in the deep voice of bears and continued walking toward Wounded Knee the policeman shot him in the face and chest with a shotgun. The blast knocked him down but the old man, blinded with his own blood, lifted himself to his feet and started walking again. The policeman shot him a second and third time in the back of the head. Second Proude fell forward on the stiff prairie grass and moaned his last vision of the bear into death. There were no witnesses but dreams. A decade later in a state mental institution the policeman confessed to the crime. He had been committed for his suspicions and overwhelming fear that his friends were becoming bears and would devour him during his sleep.

When Third Proude questioned the policeman about the death of his father he was told that the old man would not stop walking toward Wounded Knee. It took three shotgun blasts to stop the old fool, the policeman said. Third Proude told the policeman that he had killed a powerful tribal shaman. The bones of the allied circus commander were returned to the cedar circus and dropped in the red cedar water near the head of his father First Proude.

Tribal people tell of seeing four white crows soaring near the water ghosts of the two old men of the cedar.

Third Proude Cedarfair was a warrior diplomat. The women

taught him to seek peace and avoid conflicts. He abhorred violence more than evil and corruption. "Evil men," he once told his children, "can be outwitted but never eliminated . . . listen to the sinister sounds from *tchibai* island . . . The ghosts of evil men who have died through violence indict the living for their revenge . . .

"Outwit but never kill evil . . . evil revenge is blind and cannot be appeased by the living. The tricksters and warrior clowns have stopped more evil violence with their wit than have lovers with their lust and fools with the power and rage . . ."

His daughters asked if the ghosts of good people join with the peaceful living after death. Peace must be as strong as evil power and more clever, her father said. "Peace has no revenge but trickeries. Beliefs and traditions are not greater than the love of living." Third Proude debated in gentle moods the meaning of living without evil. He was killed while swimming near the graves of his father and grandfather in the red cedar water. Thunder clouds gathered overhead and he was struck with two powerful strokes of lightning.

Fourth Proude Cedarfair, the last leader of the cedar nation, avoided word wars and terminal creeds. He convinced himself that through political and religious interdependence he could protect the sovereign cedar nation as well as did his diplomatic father who abhorred human violence. Fourth Proude saw his cedar nation existing in the minds and hearts of the living, he did not feel he needed to prove the endurance of sovereignties. The cedar circus was recognized by several governments, which he used to protect the image of independence. Fourth Proude saw himself as a ceremonial diplomat. He learned from his father how to please with silence and smiles. He honored those politicians who respected the cedar nation and avoided direct contacts with evil tribal leaders.

Fourth Proude provided cedar ceremonial objects to tribal governments and cedar incense to tribal shamans and pantribal religious leaders. His ceremonial cedar products were considered sacred because they were made from sovereign native cedar. With each package of cedar incense a printed legend of the cedar circus was enclosed.

The sense of peace at the cedar nation endured for more than a decade. The demands for cedar incense grew as interests in tribal religious ceremonies increased and radical revivals stimulated new retreats from the machines of the cities. Tribal religions were becoming more ritualistic but without visions. The crazed and alienated were desperate for terminal creeds to give their vacuous lives meaning. Hundreds of urban tribal people came to the cedar nation for spiritual guidance. They camped for a few days, lusted after their women in the cedar, and then, lacking inner discipline, dreams, and personal responsibilities, moved on to find new word wars and new ideas to fill their pantribal urban emptiness.

Fourth Proude gave more time to being alone. When his four daughters left the cedar nation, three marrying professional white-men and one moving to the mountains to live with a mixedblood shaman, he gave less and less time to preparing cedar incense for false ceremonies. Substitute tribal religious movements were satisfied with substitute cedar incense. Pantribal people were less drawn to visions than to ceremonial entertainment.

Fourth Proude and Rosina Parent were married with the spirit of the cedar. Now their voices were distant. Her daughters were gone and she watched her husband turning to the cleverness of crows and the visions and ceremonial powers of the bears. All their lives have passed through two small rooms in a cedar log house without running water or electrical power. For as long as she has lived with him, he has risen before the first morning light to walk in the cedar wood with the bears and crows. When he returns, he starts a small fire with cedar sticks in the cooking stove and then walks to the *migis* sandridge in the river where he swims over the head and bones of his grandfathers and the water grave of his father. Seven clown crows circle overhead while he swims. In the winter he cuts a hole in the ice near the graves and splashes his face with their water.

Rosina lives alone with her memories. During the autumn when she walks in the cedar woods her breath takes her beneath the damp leaves where she inhales the first sacred earth. She pushes her face into the leaves and brushes her cheeks against the cool moist earth.

¶ Migis Sandridge

Fourth Proude Cedarfair emerged from the water. The seven clown crows circled overhead, swooped through the dewclouds and then landed on all sides of the *migis* sandridge. Proude followed the clownish flight and roared like a bear. The crows were silent.

Perfect Crow, the smallest of the seven, opened her wings on his shoulder, stretched her black iridescent neck, polished her beak and listened to his flight as she rode through the cedar.

"One day, " he told the crows, gesturing toward six black marks in the trees around him, "you will circle the *migis* and the old man will not return from the water." His braids dripped down his back as he walked.

Proude learned to walk alone when he was ten years old. His father taught him to live alone in the world. "Cedar warriors should never be dependent ... From the sounds of your silence," Third Proude told his son, "you will learn not to measure yourself through others." Fourth Proude lived in his own silence, with the sounds of his heart and breath, for seven nights in the cedar woods when he was ten. In that time he followed a black bear for two nights. He understood the language of cedar and learned to trust the voices of the crows. He became the rhythm of cedar trees and birds. Silence and languages of animals gave him power.

Returning to the cedar cabin he smiled to his wife who had placed an open copper pan of water on the wood stove to heat for their morning tea. He hung his wet shirt behind the stove and sat at the small split log table with his back to the fire. His bare skin was tight from the heat.

"The crows are restless," she said, turning from him to look out the small window near the door of the cabin. The clown crows were calling to each other from the cedar. "Do the crows tell that the owl ghosts and creek devils took the cedar overnight?"

"Not the owls."

"What then?" she asked, turning from the window to face him at the table. "The crows have tormented the other birds all morning . . . even the dogs are restless from their harsh voices."

"Seven warning crows . . . *windamagosiwin*," spiritual warning, he told her holding the warm cup of tea with both hands. "The government wants the cedar again, not for closets and beams now, but for official firewood."

Rosina was silent.

"The crows followed from the *migis*," he continued, smiling and touching her hands. "Soaring through the dewclouds over the lake. I did not hear their warning at first so they went after the other birds and the dogs, stirring them up so we would not feel relaxed or unprepared for our meeting soon with the government." She asked him when and he said, "Before the weather changes." She knew she would soon be leaving the cedar nation. Her cheeks were warm.

The clown crows bounded and bounced from tree to tree scolding the mongrels while the old man cut wood. Proude knew the cedar so well that he never raised his axe higher than was needed to split the sticks with gentle blows. He chooses his thoughts from morning dreams. He often thinks about his children saved in memories and dreams. Seldom does he think about the future, but on this morning,. responding to the voices of the crows, he was thinking about the government. The clown crows scolded him while he split cedar sticks. He thought about what he would do when the government came to claim the cedar. He saw himself listening to their official voices and then he heard the roar of the bears in his memories.

¶ Green Machines

Sentence, subs, verb, object.

| we see black blotch

The clown crows were raucous. Two officials from the federal government were riding through the sovereign cedar nation on dark green fenderless machines. The government had issued pedal machines for official transportation when gasoline was no longer available for automobiles. One of the pedalers was a young woman dressed in a coarse turtleneck sweater. The second pedaler was an older man with short blunt fingers. It was a warm afternoon in late summer. The sun was drawn in deep angles through the cedar trees.

Fourth Proude walked into the woods with the mongrels when he heard the government pedalers. He watched from a wilding distance. The woman pumped her government machine over the soft cedar earth to the log cabin. She stopped near the woodpile, leaning her machine against a tree. Her legs were muscular. The older man had dismounted and was walking his machine through the woods. His stamina had been altered in automobiles. The woman waited for him, smiling, with one hand on her hip and the other resting on the top of her firm buttocks.

The clown crows were swooping and flapping after the federal man. When he reached the woodpile and the woman the crows retreated and waited in the trees. Black blotches in the cedar.

"Government service ratings should be based on stamina," the woman carped at the breathless man. "No wonder our government fell apart with weaklings like you sitting behind desks and using up the gas driving three blocks to lunch." He ignored her, but smiled in agreement as he had learned to do in interpersonal service training, and then, when the subject of his weakness had passed, he made historical reference to his honorable and dedicated service to past federal programs and administrations. Their laughter was strident and mechanical. The dogs nudged each other. Proude, waiting in the distance, looked over to the crows. The clown crows yawned and poked at their black claws.

"No one seems to be home," said the federal man, after knocking three times on the open door of the cabin. "Jordan Coward at the tribal headquarters said the old cedar man never left the place." The federals called into the cabin. The woman squinted through her blue tinted glasses.

"The door is open ... there can be no harm in waiting inside," the federal woman said, stepping into the cabin and pulling out a chair near the wood stove. Rather than sitting, she moved around the small cabin, looking and touching personal objects with her fingertips. "These people own so little ... there is nothing here but little shrines."

Proude circled around the cabin through the cedar trees. The dogs and clown crows moved with him in silence. Rosina was stretched out on her back near the shore of the lake watching the thin clouds pass through the cedar boughs.

"The government people are here," he said as he sat next to her. "They wobbled through the cedar on their slow machines to tell us the government wants the circus."

Rosina rolled on her side to watch his face and eyes as he spoke. Sometimes his words were so distant. "What did you tell them?" she asked.

"They said we would not mind if they waited for us in the cabin ... They are there now comparing their lives with ours for the afternoon."

Proude told his wife he did not wish to speak with strangers now, he did not want to know what official words would be told until he knew more about their insecurities. He would be a clown, he said, a compassionate trickster for the afternoon, a bear from the cedar. When his voice and personal energies changed with the thoughts about trickeries the clown crows cocked their black heads at each other.

Rosina walked around the cabin to the western boundaries of the circus where the federals had entered the cedar woods. She rested against a tree and waited.

Proude circled around the cabin on the eastern side, stopping at the *migis* sandridge where he dipped his face under the water and opened his eyes. The pebbles and sandgems cracked in the angular iridescent sunbeams. He wiped his face with his blue shirt and strode into the woods toward the cabin. The mongrels moved with him. He stopped near the cabin on the north side, the winter side, the sunless side of moss and fern, the side of moths, the hoarfrost side, and roared ha ha ha haaaa four times as a bear.

The dogs ran off in five directions, circling each other near the cabin, yelping and howling. The clown crows crowed in shrill voices and swooped on the cabin. When the federals ran out of the cabin to see what was the matter, the crows swooped again and cawed at them. The dogs ran into the woods howling.

Proude moved to the west side of the cabin next, the black side, the sunset side, the direction of the thunderbirds and summer storms, and the side the federals had entered. The mongrels and clown crows waited out of sight. Proude roared ha ha ha haaaa again and snarled four times. The dogs howled in the distance and then, when the federals ran out of the cabin the second time, the crows called in their loudest voices while hopping and flapping from tree to tree in front of the cabin.

The federal man was so unnerved by the sounds of bears and harsh crows that he picked up his machine and started running, not pedaling, in the wrong direction out of the woods. The federal woman stopped him and encouraged him to return to the cabin. She reminded him of their responsibilities as elite employees of the federal government.

Proude circled to the south side of the cabin, the summer side, the flower side, yellow and green, and snarled and roared four times again. The dogs howled and the crows flapped again. When the federals came out of the cabin for the third time, Proude snarled several more times with his deepest bear voice. The federal man could not be stopped the third time. He ran out of the woods in the right direction with the federal woman following on her machine. Pumping with her stout legs the federal woman was the first to reach the brown cedar ghost border of the circus. Exhausted and near heart failure, the federal man slumped out of the cedar woods, vowing never to return to the wilderness with bad news.

The federals pedaled their machines down the dirt roads on the reservation to the tribal center where they told Jordan Coward, elected president of the reservation government, about their harrowing experiences with the bears in the cedar. Coward first laughed and then his mood changed and he cursed them, calling them louts, addlebrained, beefwitted, and sapheaded federals, while he paced back and forth on the squeaking oak floors of his office in the old federal school building. Spume from his hostile words gathered on his bulbous purple lips.

¶ Federal Humanoids

Jordan Coward drank a full bottle of gin before he stopped cursing the cedar circus and dropped numb into sleep. Each night his wife, ignoring his evil, abandoned him on the kitchen floor where he slid from a chair twitching and groaning like a reservation mongrel. He snorted at the demons and slobbered in his drunken sleep about the foolish federals who had failed to claim the cedar.

When the federal officials arrived with an executive order reserving half of all the timber on the reservation, Coward attached the cedar nation to meet the demands of the government. Through political and executive nonfeasance the national supplies of crude oil had dribbled to nothing. Paralyzed in its own political quarrels the executive and legislative branches of government were not capable of negotiating trades or developing alternative fuels. The nation ran out of gasoline and fuel oil. Electrical power generating plants closed down. Cities were gasless and dark. Economic power had become the religion of the nation; when it failed people turned to their own violence and bizarre terminal creeds for comfort and meaning. New families were made from aberrations.

In desperation, and to be sure that the interests and comforts of federal bureaucrats were protected, the government attached half of the standing timber in the nation. The federals were each given sticks of woods as fuel rations according to their rank. Coward, possessed by evil revenge, dreamed of the cedar nation being cut into little sticks and burned in the federal offices of the bureau of public remorse.

In the morning he blamed his problems, his whole tribal skin and gin puffed face and hands on the stupidness of the federals. His flesh was creased from sleeping on the floor. The muscular federal woman was disgusted with his drunkenness and verbal abuses. She had expected more wisdom and magic from the mouth of a tribal person. She warned him that if he did not stop his cursing she would have him removed from the world.

"But first you will remove that last cedar faggot from his circus and cut down that goddamn crusading nation into little sticks," Coward smacked. Elected tribal leaders are numb from exposure to repeated promises and threats and have developed immunities to federal messages of limitation. His own needs for revenge put him in agreement with a federal executive order for the first time in ten years. He would have thrown the federals off the reservation with their order but half the standing timber within the boundaries of the reservation was on the cedar nation.

Jordan Coward entered the circus with harsh words. The clown crows were silent and waiting like black blotches in the trees around the cabin. Proude was splitting cedar sticks.

"*Anishinabewish* ... you goddamn crusading savage," Coward screamed, waving his arms and spurting spittle and word spume three feet around his mouth. His face and lips were swollen and purple from gin and evil. "You should be shot and stuffed like the goddamn dumb bear you are ... Who the hell do you think you are scaring off the government with that goddamn bear talk and walk shit? Who do you think you are being here ... You goddamn stinking bear.

"This cedar nation shit is done," Coward hollered in a febrile rage. "Pack up your goddamn circus crusade and leave our reservation. You have never been welcome here. The government is going to split this goddamn circus into little sticks and burn it for paperwork ... bear shit.

"If you are still here in the morning we will have you shot for treason," Coward growled out of breath. His evil fathers spoke through him with revenge. "The laws have changed and you will never find a crusader to help you in a hundred miles ... You and your goddamn incense ... even the religious fools have given up on you and this sacred cedar crap."

Coward lost breath as the clown crows dropped from the trees and one by one in crude black formation pecked and hacked at the back of his huge fat head. Coward covered his head and face with his fat arms but the crows clawed at his closed fists and the dogs jumped against him knocking him down. He was twitching on the ground, one leg, his eyes and his cheeks jerking out of control. The dogs growled and poked their noses at his creased face. The federals were frightened by his rage and when the crows attacked they moved away from the scene and stood near the cabin door.

Proude motioned for the dogs and crows to leave and then helped the twitching tribal leader to his feet. The crows flew back to their blackness in the cedar trees. Coward wiped his face over and over again with his huge fat fingers until the twitching stopped. Then he snarled like a crazed mongrel and waved his fists. The cedar trees shunned his evil energies.

"We will not leave . . . we will not leave the dreams of sacred cedar," Proude said looking up at the trees. "We will be here tomorrow in the morning waiting for your peaceful death."

Seven clown crows dropped from their blotches a second time and swarmed and flapped at Coward cowering under his fat arms and fists. First the crows pecked and clawed at him and then circling over his head one by one they shit on his head and shoulders. Waving his arms and fists in febrile madness he ran from the cabin through the cedar woods and out of the circus. His head and shoulders were steaming with white crow shit. When he stopped to clean his spattered glasses the crows attacked him again. They soared over him until he was beyond the circus and on the road to the reservation tribal offices.

"He does not speak for the government," the muscular federal said. "If we could have a minute of your time we will complete our business here and leave you to your peace and . . . your problems."

The clown crows returned. The two federals were watching them with caution while the crows settled again like blotches in the trees around the cabin.

The federals opened a plain green federal envelope, the same color as their uniforms, and recited the executive order attaching the cedar circus trees. First the federal man read a phrase in official federalese and then in turn the muscular woman read a phrase. Their voices differed in timber and volume but the tone and gestures in their speech was the same.

Proude, who had been soaring with the slow moving clouds, told them to stop speaking like machines. When they continued their grim alternating recitation, Proude turned from them and walked into the woods toward the *migis* sandridge. The federals continued reading the subsections while following the old man of the cedar and bears through the whispering trees to the river.

"I will not listen to you speaking as an institution," said Proude. "Fools listen to the voices of the government . . . and the fools are lost and starving in the cities. When you speak as individuals in the language of your dreams I will listen, but I will not listen to that foolish green paper talking to me."

"The government will have every citizen understand that half the national trees are being protected as a federal resource," said the federal woman.

"Minnesota is your place but we are not citizens."

"But sir, in a realistic sense, we all live on this great earth in the same nation," said the federal man running his blunt fingers over his wide nose. "Come now mister cedarfair circus, mister cedarfair, you must understand the meaning of being a citizen."

"This is a sovereign nation," Proude said walking toward them with his chest expanded. "These trees were the first to grow here, the first to speak of living on this earth . . . These trees are sovereign. We are cedar and we are not your citizens . . . We are the cedar and the guardians of the sacred directions into the fourth world . . . Can you see and feel how we shun your indifference to our lives."

Proude drew his braids forward onto his chest. His black hair was turned with red ribbons. His dark eyes were blazing as he spoke. The dogs kept their distance. The clown crows were silent. He drew a turtle on the *migis* sandridge. "Our families have lived in this circus with these cedar trees for more than a hundred years. People in our families have died defending the rights of these sovereign trees and now you come to tell me from green paper about citizenship and government responsibilities," said Proude. "You speak in the language of newspapers and false pictures. Your speech has nothing but words to see what you have said. I did not read or listen to the words that spoke to you from that green paper," he said in a softer voice. "We will not listen to your possessive voices. We will not bring harm to our visions and dreams with your word wars . . . if you choose to speak with me alone in your personal voices then I will listen."

"You can go first," said the federal woman.

"Well, we should do this together," said the federal man with hesitation, "but so long as we speak from the same executive order we can trust our individual contact ... We must keep in mind, however, that our superiors would not approve of this personal procedure."

"Perhaps you would prefer to pedal your fat ass back for their approval," she said, flexing her cheek and neck muscles. Her blue eyes were turned down to a fine bead. She was a career government bureaucrat, one of the possessive elite, but she disliked weak men with short hair and fat lips.

Proude walked through the woods to the shore of the red cedar water. The federal man followed. The lake was brushed with a light breeze. The federal talked about urban social models of personal affiliation. Being personal he told about his one night a week in the model of silence and loneliness. "Loneliness feels good at the right times," said the federal. "My father once had a summer cabin on a lake like this, but the tribal government took the land back and the old man never returned to another lake or reservation the rest of his life. He died in a highrise death house hating the world because he lost his reservation lease."

"Was he evil?" asked Proude.

"No not evil, he was a gentle man."

"Then was his hate in good humor?"

"You are a strange person ... What is this model of evil in your experience?" the federal asked. "Have you ever been away from this place, this circus as you call it?"

"Through visions from these cedar trees ... this is our place in the world," Proude said.

"This seems like a limited model."

"We can see the whole world from here."

"Was President Coward serious?"

"He is possessed with evil," said Proude.

"What did you mean when you told him that you would be waiting here tomorrow for his peaceful death ... what did you mean?"

"The meaning of his power does not come from his evil threats. We will not confront him because he is evil," said Proude. His eyes were distant. "But we will outwit him and his evil in the morning."

The federal stretched out across the coarse grass and fell asleep. The noise of his snoring was unnatural under the cedar. Proude returned to the cabin. Rosina had been talking with the federal woman about life in the cities. She was concerned for her three daughters who lived in large cities. She learned that there was no heat or power. In some places, she was told, people crowded around the owners of portable radios to hear the censored government news reports. The federal woman told her that without gasoline fine automobiles were abandoned in the streets.

"Do people sleep in the cars?" asked Proude.

"Yes, sometimes poor families, whole families, will pretend that they are rich and live in a big new car for the weekend," the federal woman explained.

"Some tribal people have made cars their homes on the reservation," said Proude. He clapped his hands on his thighs. The mongrels raised their heads from the floor. "At last, near the end, the nation has become a tribal reservation."

"Do you fear President Coward?"

"Not him, but his evil we avoid."

"His threatening voice . . ."

"He will not harm us. If we are gone he will have no use for these trees . . . will you pretend these trees do not exist. Three generations have defended the cedar circus, but to defend the trees now we must not defend them again."

"This is an executive order."

"Do those phrases you were reading from the green paper, those words, have more power than the lives of these native cedar trees? Can you sign away the lives of these first born cedar trees?"

"That is not my decision."

"Then you have lost your heart."

"I am an independent person, thank you."

"Do you fuck that federal man with the blunt fingers . . . do you fuck him in the same way you speak together from that green paper?"

"What is this . . . ?"

"Do you fuck with words?"

Her face turned deep red with embarrassment and rage. She turned and stumbled out of the cabin. Outside she called to the federal man in a demanding voice. He did not respond. She called again. The federal man stumbled through the woods toward the cabin. His face was creased and turned into a dumb smile.

"We are leaving," she demanded, her muscular hands squeezing the plastic grips on her green machine.

"Is there something wrong?"

Proude was standing near the machines. Perfect Crow landed on his shoulder and flexed her wings and stretched her neck. The other clown crows were hopping around the two federals and their machines.

"Yes there is something wrong. I asked her if she fucked you on these trips," said Proude in a casual voice and looking toward the federal man.

"Well ... as you can see," the federal man began to explain, "we dress the same to avoid sex determination and lustful thoughts about other employees ..." The federal woman pedaled her machine through the woods before he could finish his sentence. "These are strange times," he added as he mounted his machine and wobbled off behind her through the cedar.

The federals stopped at the brown border of cedar ghosts. Breathless, the two dropped their green machines into the grass and rested next to each other on the same tree. The federal woman cursed the old man of the cedar for his arrogance and rudeness. She was hostile for being deceived by expectations of his wisdom and offended by his profanity. She hated him for his crass assumptions and under no circumstances, she emphasized in her thoughts, smacking her right fist into her left hand like a shortstop, would she show favors to the cedar nation. "Cedar nation or no cedar nation," she told the federal, flipping her fingers into the air, "the government will have these trees with no exceptions."

"You are beginning to sound like President Coward," said the federal man. "Punishing the cedar for the values of men."

She made circles in the air with her fingers. The muscles in her huge jaw were flexing as she ground her precious teeth together and frowned. She was determined to preserve her rejection of the old man.

"Did you hear me?"

"No," she responded.

"But it is such a beautiful place," the federal man seemed to chant. "There are few places like this remaining in our whole ravaged nation ... either the government or corporations have taken the trees for one important use or another."

"Those should not be the words of a federal servant," said the federal woman, admonishing her partner by raising her dark eyebrows and looking around to see if anyone was listening.

"Nor is your hatred."

"He has no right to emphasize our sexual differences."

"No," the federal man responded with hesitation. He turned toward the federal woman and noticed the deep color in her cheeks. Her lips were dark and moist. "But we should do it in this beautiful place before we leave here ... How do you feel about it? Just here, now, right now ..."

She did not respond. Her memories were floating with the clouds. It was warm and she thought about the smell of the earth. "In this beautiful place," he emphasized. "Now, right now ..."

The federal man leaned over and touched her muscular calves with his blunt fingers. The federal woman closed her eyes to avoid thinking about his potential slack and lack of vigor. He stroked her wide set crotch with his thick yellow nailed finger stubs. She moaned to meet his animal needs and slid down from her position against the tree. The earth was warm.

His lips were thin, lifeless, those of a small woodland animal, and his fetid breath burned the tender nerves in her earth nose. With her eyes still closed she touched his loose testicles through his green trousers. He stood on his knees, ripped the zipper tape, opening his green trousers and exposed his oversized green undershorts. She stumbled out of her clothes. His short blunt penis was wobbling like the neck of a dead sparrow. She leaned back on her elbows over the cedar fronds and spread her legs open to the federal man.

Their lust sounds passed through the cedar trees. He punched his penis stub between her muscular legs, so eager to come under the cedar trees. He missed more than half his frantic earthbound thrusts, leaving her spread and moaning, falling through cloudless space, out of time and green paper, plastic flowers, part thunder and poison rain. His thick white semen slid down the stiff hair over her crotch like wet snow over the cedar boughs. She could smell the earth beneath her, rising between her legs. She tipped him over and wiped her crotch hair with her hands and rubbed the semen over her hot red cheeks. The semen smelled like salt cedar and drew her skin tight when it dried on the wind. She thought about bears and crows.

In the morning while she was washing her muscular limbs and brushing the coarse hair on her pubic arch, she finished, in silent thought, her official report, never mentioning the existence of the cedar trees. Her thighs and breasts tingled. She still smelled of semen and cedar.

¶ Fires in Jordan Coward

Proude was sitting in the center of the *migis* sandridge. The rising sun tumbled over the wind on the red cedar water. Fern and late summer flowers opened and closed on his travels from the cedar circus through dream cities. Proude raised his head with the moon and the sun fell behind the trees.

The moon climbed over the red pines behind *tchibai* island and trembled in deep columns on the dark water.

Seven clown crows were walking in a circle around the *migis* drawing their claws over the turtles and luminous ribbons of wet sand and thrusting their black beaks at their black reflections on the whole white water drums.

Insects dropped near shore. The creek devils and *tchibai nopiming*, woodland phantoms, hissed on low witchingwheels from the pale cities of the dead and shadowless.

Seven clown crows followed Proude on foot through the last cedar night back to the cabin. Rosina was sitting at the log table when Proude entered with an armful of cedar sticks. He shaved four small sticks with his knife and placed them in the black iron wood burner. The fire lighted the room and their faces in the center of their circus world.

"What is this bundle?" Proude asked. In the corner of the room near the door was a round bundle with cloth bands attached to both sides.

"I made that more than ten years ago," she said without lifting her face. "I am prepared to leave this cedar circus and the distance between our memories."

"We will leave in the darkness of morning," he said while he placed several more sticks on the fire. The smell of cedar incense filled the cabin. "Coward will believe we are here when he sees the fire and our sleeping shapes ... Our sleeping shadowless shapes will suffer his violence."

Proude slept at the table most of the night. The cedar circus night passed in solemn silence under the late summer course of the moon drums. When the shadows had shifted from the west to the east, he moved through the cabin in the darkness gathering objects for their travels from the circus. Two tribal medicine bundles, his smoking pipe, the flag of the cedar nation, seven small bundles of cedar incense, a spirit catcher, two small carved cedar spirit figures, his knife, dried meat, berries, vegetable roots, wild rice, several cloth packages of dried plants and healing herbs. Proude placed his pack beside the door and walked outside. He rode the last shadows of the moon through the trees back to the *migis* sandridge. The seven crows followed. He removed his clothes and for the last time swam through the brume to the water graves of his father and grandfathers. He circled their graves in the cool cedar water and then slid beneath the surface and dropped thirteen feet to the soft bottom. He could feel the pressure on his head and heart. He roared beneath the water ha ha ha haaa. His heart was pounding as he swam back to the *migis* sandridge. The clown crows were waiting in the trees near shore.

Rosina was awakened by the sound of his roaring bear voice. She walked through the trees toward the *migis*. The sound of his roaring voice echoed across the lake and up the river past the boundaries of the cedar nation. Standing naked on the *migis* he roared ha ha ha haaaa and roared until the eastern night turned deep blue. Proude dressed, waved to the seven crows and walked with his wife back to the cabin.

In silence they stuffed their bed with their shadowless shapes and built a cedar fire to last through the morning. The clown crows flew to the western border and waited with the brown cedar ghosts for the reservation leaders.

Jordon Coward had awakened before the first morning light. His head was clear for the first time in months. Clear from the fine white flames of evil violence and thoughts of revenge. When he heard the voice of the bear roaring up the river, he gathered his followers and set out for the cedar circus.

The seven crows saw them coming and flew back to the cabin. Proude locked the door from the inside and climbed out through the small window. Rosina shouldered her pack. The dogs nudged each other and the crows flew off to curse the reservation leaders.

Proude smiled to his wife and together they walked south through the *gijik gwanatch,* the beautiful cedar, for the last time. They waited and listened with the brown ghosts on the southern border of the circus. In the distance they could hear Jordan Coward cursing the crows and banging at the cabin door. The sound of his wicked banging echoed through the trees. The clown crows crowed and crowed. Coward yelled to his friends that he could see them in their beds in the cabin. "Burn those goddamn cowards . . . burn those cedar savages out of there!"

Coward ordered his assistants to gather brush and cedar boughs and pile them against the cabin. Stepping back from the door he growled his final warning: "This is your last chance to come out or we will burn you out . . ." He waited a few minutes and then commanded his followers to start the fire. His eyes blazed with revenge while the flames licked at the side of the small cedar cabin. The surface of the logs burned black but the cabin stood against the flames, until the fire was banked against the walls near the windows. The frames and the roof burned through and the fire dropped to the inside of the cabin.

Coward collapsed out of breath against a tree. His face had turned pale from the exhausting pleasures of his evil. The four log walls of the cabin remained standing, but inside the shadowless shapes had burned to white dust and sifted through the metal bed springs to the earth.

Fourth Proude, the last old man of the cedar circus, listened until evil and the fire had died in peace. Tribal leaders were not honest enough to bear the dreams, he said, and then he turned the past under when he passed through the brown cedar ghosts on the border of the circus. The cedar would be alone for the first time in four generations.

¶ Scapehouse on Callus Road

Benito Saint Plumero, dressed in his finest blue satin ribbon shirt and suede leather trousers bound from the ankles to the knees in red velvet, hailed them at the bright orange door. The crows recognized the guileless face of a clown. His greeting gestures at the door were twice his actual size. Proude and Rosina, tired from their walk from the circus through the woods to town, nodded to the clown at the door and entered the humid scapehouse of weirds and sensitives.

Animals were asleep on the floors. Cats were poised on the shelves and mantlepieces. Birds were perched on the thousand plants and trees and hundreds of rails and posts and roosts in the fragrant demigreen house. Insects sounded from the potted earth. The birds and animals and the people were all silent for a few minutes, time to feel the ethereal energies about the bodies of the strangers, and then Saint Plumero thumped and snapped into the room breaking the silence with his demanding voice and gait.

"Bigfoot is my name," he said, turning on his heels to spread his huge feet and folding his arms across his chest. The cats licked themselves with indifference and the birds cawed, croaked, chirruped, and peeped on their roosts, when he gestured and spoke. Saint Plumero was given his descriptive name in prison where he was sentenced for stealing a bronze statue from a park. "Find your perch in the plants," he said smiling and then thumped out of the room.

Proude first met Sister Eternal Flame, one of the most sensitive sensitives living in the scapehouse, while she was gathering herbs in the cedar circus. When he first spoke to her deep in the woods near the river, she smiled on him and hummed a little tune. One morning late in the spring when she was gathering mushrooms he slipped through the trees in front of her and roared in his best bear voice, but she was not distracted, unafraid she went on gathering and humming.

The humid room was peaceful. It was the first time Proude and Rosina had visited the scapehouse, their first experience with domestic plants and animals. "The outside is inside," said Proude.

"Idle machines are the work of the devil," said Bigfoot, thumping into the room again. He often announced himself with peculiar bromides when he entered a room. The social habits of shortened clowns, the sensitive women once explained. "Flame is in the garden awaiting your arrival," he said. He was a little person, but his feet and the measure of his footsteps were twice his visual size.

From the lush demigreen light of the living room the cedar couple passed through several worlds of plants and birds and animals and insects on their course to the garden behind the house. Sensitive women were working in the rooms where they passed. The women were weaving and potting and painting and sculpting. Two women with long white hair were sitting at a table facing each other and writing poems in different directions on a ten foot piece of narrow orange paper. Near the end of the house the smell of plants and paint and clay mixed with the odors of baking bread. In the kitchen there were three women singing their whole grain breads into firm brown loaves. There were two rooms near the kitchen. One was a bathing room with a great sunken pool and hanging ferns. The last room in the house was a glass enclosed solarium and winter garden with long rows of vegetables and edible flowers. The smell of mint and onions followed them into the garden outside.

The four level frame house, once the residence for railroad officials and their families, was situated on a hedgelined block in the center of Cache Center. The scapehouse faced Callus Road between a church and a row of pastel public houses.

The scapehouse was organized and founded during the first national energy crisis when the price of gasoline and heating fuels soared and people were building wood burners in their houses in the cities. Thirteen women poets from the cities obtained state and federal funds to develop a survival center in a rural area. The poets chose Cache Center because it was remote, the giant house was inexpensive and residents of the town were not surprised by peculiar people. Cache Center, located on the Red Cedar Indian Reservation, was settled and named by a mixedblood treekiller. The town has grown to several hundred permanent residents, but in the summer the campers and tourists crowd into the little town for sundries and pleasures. Tribal people once danced, sold handmade oriental beadwork and baskets, and freebooters extracted an unofficial territorial toll from whitepeople crossing the reservation boundaries.

The thirteen sensitive women were seldom noticed until it was learned through breastworld gossip that the women were eating the cats and dogs and birds and fish that lived with them. The women soon became known as the weirds and sensitives. With their original grant the women set out to know the world around them through their precious poems and to live through barter and on what could be grown in their garden during the summer. The local tribal people thought the women poets were strange but less evil than common whitepeople. The farmers, retired rockhounds and fishingpeople thought the women were dangerous witches.

Cannibalism was practical in the scapehouse of the weirds and sensitives. The women agreed that their bodies would be their food. The women eat what is known, what and who is part of their lives in the scapehouse, the plants and animals, and so their lives are continued in the cellular consciousness of the living energies in the scapehouse.

"We grieve that you were forced to leave your circus," sighed Sister Eternal Flame. "But we are so pleased that you have come here to stay with us." She smiled and rubbed her hands together. She had been scraping the inner bark from willow boughs for medicine. Her face was distorted with comical stretch marks from her constant expressions of happiness.

"We are secure here," said Eternal Flame, who was the oldest scapehouse sensitive and one of the six remaining from the original women poets who founded the house. "We no longer need the cash and carries, the power and energies of the outside world."

Bigfoot shifted and turned on his huge heels in the grass. "We are trapped in hope when tomorrow is more likeable than now," he said. "But that was two months ago . . . Flame is the softest of the toughest, or is she the hardest of the softest. The new women are the hard ones, but this place will soften even the hardest from the streets."

"We will leave soon," said Proude, flicking his eyebrows toward the clown who was turning on his heels. His feet moved in the grass like huge rodents. The circus mongrels were panting and bumping into each other. The clown crows flapped their wings in the hedges surrounding the scapehouse gardens.

"But not before tomorrow."

"We are walking," said Rosina, "it will take us months to reach the warm desert ... we have never walked on hard roads through the cities."

"We will toast the hard rocks and ride the cushions to dinner," said Bigfoot smiling and nodding toward Sister Eternal Flame.

"This little man has three oversized things about him," said Sister Flame, cupping her breasts with both hands. She was wearing a loose white diaphanous dress. Two dark nipples were turned upward from her breasts. "Neither his brain nor his heart, but his nose, and, and, his superlative president jackson ... and his feet as you can see, all in proper proportions, should belong to a man ten times his altitude."

"His president jackson?"

"His glorious uncircumcised president jackson penis," responded Sister Flame. She rubbed her hands on her thighs. Bigfoot turned on his heels to show his feet, turned his head to show his nose and cupped his leather crotch with his right hand. The seven clown crows flapped and crowed from the hedges.

"But the grandest of all is this heart," said Bigfoot, bounding through the garden thumping his chest.

The women poets consented that no man should enter the scapehouse as the sex object of a single woman, but rather, all men were shared with all the women. Men were not exclusive.

Benito Saint Plumero heard rumors about the scapehouse rules which aroused his sexual fantasies. While passing through Cache Center earlier in the summer he knocked on the orange door and asked if he could share a meal and spend the night.

"He must have been put together from broken clowns," said one sister. Thirteen women negotiated and examined the short mixed-blood with huge feet before rejecting him. Slumping to the grass in front of the scapehouse he beat his fists and moaned from his deep loneliness. The dogs and cats and birds of the scapehouse came out to watch him. Pure Gumption, the glowing female dog and healer of the animals, sat near the little man who had buried his face in the grass. Bigfoot felt the sensuous warmth and power and thought it was a woman. When he looked up he was face to face with a brown and white dog with long ears and sad brown eyes. He saw a soft blue aura around the animal.

"You are beautiful," said Bigfoot.

"He has fallen in love with Pure Gumption," said Sister Flame, who was the first to discover the length and breadth of president jackson. The women of the scapehouse speak of the male organs of copulation with the names of presidents.

The thirteen weird and sensitive women have never known a chief executive to stand so tall and last so long and to be so proud as president jackson. It was not uncommon for six or seven scapehouse poets to spend the long nights lusting with the namesake president. So overwhelmed with love and pleasure was he that during the first weeks there he could for the first time in his life accept death. Because of his intense survival instincts he responded with selfish panic whenever he faced thoughts of death, but in the orgiastic arms and legs of the weirds and sensitives he sighed that death, waiting in the space between lips and legs, could take him whenever she found him a place to ride high. In the morning, pleasures done, he was tense again thumping and curving his words like a circus clown. Weeks later, after he had touched all thirteen bodies in the scapehouse, mouthing dozens of nipples and thrusting through the creases of the universe, he was again drawn to the fantasies of new experiences in heart and hand.

The five circus dogs nosed the air and nudged the women in the garden. One was Sister Jacinth, the hand washer, whose cellular perfumes bewitched her lovers but whose skin was sensitive to animal hair. She flushed at Private Jones, the most inquisitive of the circus mongrels, when he sniffed and nudged her thin legs through her long pilgrim dress.

Rosina returned to the scapehouse. For the rest of the afternoon, until dinner, she worked with different women in various parts of the house. The women asked her questions about identities, her dependencies, her sexual and political responses to men, and her rituals as a person, to which she did not have abstract answers. Her life was visual and personal. She did not see herself in the abstract as a series of changing ideologies.

The oldest woman of the scapehouse, Sister Willabelle, the survivor, was bathing in the deep pool. "Sister Rosina," she asked, "have you tested your instincts of survival?"

While she paused to consider the question, Sister Willabelle next asked her to rub her back and neck. Rosina complied, but when she saw the deep scars, rippled and discolored flesh on her neck and shoulders, she was uncomfortable.

"Do the scars disgust you?"

Rosina did not respond.

"When I was young" Sister Willabelle began, "my body was smooth and desirable . . . I still see myself in the mirror without scars, but dark little fish and savage insects and worms and leeches devoured me.

"Somewhere down that dark river, in that jungle, the fish and worms have reproduced millions of me, millions more with bits of my flesh. The flesh of my sexual attraction. The insects have my cheeks and lips and forehead . . . sucked my smile off . . . The black razor fish have my soft thighs and shoulders, leaving me a stiff tight cover over my bones to offer my lovers."

Rosina forced herself to touch the scars. She moved her hands across the rough hard flesh. Sister Willabelle moaned. The skin was so tight in places that it turned white when she moved her arms and neck.

She continued telling her stories about the plane crash in the jungle while Rosina massaged her neck and shoulders. Willabelle was nineteen and traveling with her mother who had deserted her father because he would not accept her ambition to become a lawyer. The plane crashed during a thunder storm. When she regained consciousness she could smell perfume and heard birds singing. The perfume was from a broken bottle in a suitcase. She was still strapped in her seat.

"My wrist was swollen from a broken bone," she said. "Blood trickled into my right eye from a gash across my forehead where my head struck the seat in front of me when we crashed. The insects were swarming around my head and dipping their mouths into my blood. Thousands, millions of them were taking my blood into their bodies. Parts of bodies were dangling from the trees and vines. The insects and worms were feasting on the flesh of my mother. Her head was gone.

"I spoke to her dead head," said Sister Willabelle, with her hand lowered near the surface of the water. Her words rippled. "I shook every body part, but there was no life left for me to tell how scared I was of the sounds and animals in the jungle . . . I was the sole survivor and followed the rivers for more than two weeks before I was rescued.

"Worms covered my body and fed on my tender parts. The worms wormed through the openings in my ears and nose and vagina. I could feel them crawling inside of me ... Then, when I crossed the river to a tribal village on the other side, hundreds of fish grabbed at the worms and took parts of my flesh with their razor teeth."

"Do the sounds of the birds here remind you of the jungle?" Rosina asked. She stopped massaging Sister Willabelle's shoulders and waited for an answer.

"No, not now ... I am never alone here because we are survivors protecting ourselves from our fears and past memories," she responded as she lifted herself from the water. Her breasts were marked with hideous scars. Worms and fish had eaten her nipples.

Rosina removed her clothes. The women touched hands and then together slipped in silence beneath the warm fragrant water of the scapehouse pool.

¶ Scapehouse Ritual Feast

There was a circular parade of humans and animals and birds in conversations from the kitchen to the scapehouse dining room. Sparrows and bluebirds and crows fled down the halls between rooms and rode back on the heads and shoulders of the humans bearing food to the tables. Birds sang in the parade, humans hummed, crows crowed, the animals barked and moaned, hissed and sniffed from the food pens. The scapehouse smelled of chicken and kitten and fish, nettles and yams, dumplings, carrots and greens, and several shapes and colors of breads.

When darkness settled on the windowsills the plants leaned from the windows toward the candles and conversations at the table. The faces of fourteen women and two men wavered in the light at the edge of great green shadows. Sister Flame sat at one end of the table, and Sister Tallulah, the bogus barrister, sat at the other end. The birds perched on the green plants surrounding the table. The dogs waited near the opened doors and the cats were hunched over the mantelpieces and chairs around the room. The animals flared their wet nostrils to savor the remains of dinner.

"You haven't eaten the stuffed kitten," said Sister Tallulah to Proude, who had eaten breads and vegetables. "It was hard for me to eat them at first too, but touching them with indifference and realizing our dependencies on precious pets changed my attitude and appetite." The oil on her chin and cheeks sparkled from the candle light. She sighed and chittered and then wiped her hands on her dress. She was a law school graduate but could not face men in a courtroom without giggling like a little girl so she concentrated on interior litigation and the ideologies of feminism and fell in love with women.

Now she practices herb gardening at the scapehouse. She talks on herself in small rooms and dances for the split leaves and smells of dill and basil. Her half closed eyes drift upward and her head drops to the side when she smiles.

"These lives were not praised," said Proude.

"Tell us Mister Proude what it is in life we should praise," asked Sister Dimetria, the cardinal. When she spoke the sails of white flesh around her eyes stretched open and exposed blood streaks in the great white rings. She is a former nun and wears a red cap and soft red dancing shoes. She walks on her tiptoes through the streets of Cache Center.

"Praise for the living."

"What he means," said Sister Jacinth, the hand washer, "is that he is not a barbarian feeding on whatever pet he can strangle for a meal." Sister Jacinth resisted the consumption of the cats and birds in the scapehouse. She was humored because she suffers from terminal cancer. The cancer was caused by chemical preservatives in food. As a student she lived on cold luncheon meats. She is also humored for her pure speech and pure habits of washing her hands after touching people and places. Believing she is allergic to the finger salts from perspiration she washes her hands after touching doorhandles and arms of chairs.

"We do not eat ... meat which has not been praised," said Rosina. She was leaning against the table with her hands folded over her plate. She had drunk two cups of wine and her voice came in short spurts. "We celebrate . . . what we will eat and praise . . . ourselves . . . Death comes in gentleness to deer and bear and kittens when we exalt their flesh through our spirit . . . These kittens are screaming with the shadowless for our praise . . . Their death was a cruel surprise."

"Never knew what hit them," smacked Sister Caprice the scapehouse butcher. She chops off the heads of chickens and kittens and housebirds with a short axe on a blood soaked cedar stump in the garden behind the house.

"We all know when our time comes," said Sister Sophronia the rock freak. "We know the animals know because when we are looking for our dinner the wise ones hide. The dumb ones know we are their end."

"Our uncelebrated end," mocked Bigfoot as he slumped down in his chair clutching his neck and chest. "Spiritual indigestion comes from unpraised kittens," he mumbled and then climbed under the table. The dogs found him on the floor and licked his smiling face.

"We appreciate the same things," Sister Sophronia insisted. "We cannot understand the secrets of living so we demand some explanation ... some praise for death and our witness." When she spoke she cocked her head. She collected hats and for dinner she wore her tall sandman hat with lace streamers floating down her back. "Even praise at our executions should soothe our primal cells and expel the evil from our quick breath."

"Death is death and food is food," said Sister Caprice. "The cells of kittens are poised no more from fear of the chopping block than from games on the kitchen floor." Sister Caprice was a hard and bitter person when she first came to the scapehouse. She was laughed at most of her life because of the way she walked, the way her feet wobbled and landed in different directions with each step. She is bald and has wailed that no man will run his hands through her hair. "It is not a matter of celebration or praise, but rather it is one of surprise ... The meat tastes best when death is a surprise, when the owl swoops out of the darkness on the mouse.

"The birds and kittens love surprises ... we all like surprises," she said, lifting her hair and exposing her bone white bald head. Sister Dimetria stretched her eyes, the clown crows crowed about the evil owls. Sister Flame, who had been licking her bright lips, drew Bigfoot into her crotch under the table. There he rubbed his nose in the soft hair and brushed the stubble on her legs with his hands. The dogs were nudging him under the arms. Private Jones sneezed.

The women of the scapehouse were moaning under the lips and tongue and fingers of the clown. Proude and Rosina moved to the corner of the room next to the windows where they waited with the cats and birds and watched the orgiastic scene unfurling near the table. The women were moaning and touching each other. Bigfoot climbed out from under the table and was standing over three women on the floor. The women were unwrapping the red velvet leg bands and pulling down his leather trousers. When the leather fell from his buttocks his penis lifted like a proud president. Sister Flame whistled hail to the chief as he kneeled between her legs and pumped her until she trembled in a deep orgasm. Then president jackson penetrated the other women in turn in a circle on the floor around the table. While the president ducked through slick lips and hair other sensitives sucked his tight testicles until the president throbbed and spurted.

"These are the survivors," said Proude.

¶ Zebulon Matchi Makwa

The moss covered double doors over the cellar opened like the wings of a mammoth moth in the first frail light of morning. The patron saint of transit was waiting in the subterranean darkness.

"The last of a fine breed," whispered Sister Flame. "He has a full tank, no registration . . . but if the inspectors find him here we will be charged with the high crime of possessing precious national gasoline."

"Who owns this machine?" asked Proude.

"One of our rich friends," said Sister Flame, "who died in the scapehouse . . . an ecstatic passing."

"Between the legs of flame . . ."

"Never complained . . ."

"The state claimed his remains," Sister Caprice, the butcher, continued, forcing the words between her thick lips, "but no one came for the car. All but new, so we rolled him down here with a full tank waiting for the right moment . . ."

She was a beautiful silver cabriolet with a deep red leather interior. The last of the fine convertibles equipped with an expensive electronic combustion engine. Sensuous and plush chaise. Her meters and dials were recessed in natural wood. With full power she could raise and lower and place the amorous motorist in his most desired and upstanding positions. Saint Plumero whistled once and then took his bearing behind the wheel. Activating her circuits the engine started, hesitating at first, but when she warmed she began to hum and purr with contentment.

"The longer we idle here the farther we will have to walk on the other end," said Bigfoot, poised behind her at the wheel and eager to drive. He had not been at the wheel for more than a year, and he had never driven such a luxurious automobile.

"This is the last call for the south," he announced and then backed the convertible out of the moist storm cellar. The eastern horizon was turning deep blue.

"But we will be seen," said Rosina.

"I hope so," responded Bigfoot. "But who will dare catch us on the road? No one has a full tank of gasoline, not even the police . . . We can wave past them on their pedal machines."

Proude and Rosina climbed into the back seat where their thin bodies were taken into the plush leather cushions like herons wading in a marsh. The dogs took their places in the front and the clown crows perched on the wide padded dashboard.

The scapehouse women surrounded the convertible. The sensitives were waving and touching and laughing as the automobile began to move. With Pure Gumption in her arms, Sister Flame walked beside president jackson telling him how much his upstanding member would be missed and then she dropped the glowing animal next to the others in the front seat. "Take care of our Pure Gumption," Sister Flame said as she waved with both hands. "Someone would eat her here . . . praise her soul."

The silver convertible turned down Callus Road and streaked through the darkness out of town. The dogs were smiling and bumping their noses on the window glass. The clown crows were thrusting their black heads at each other and poking at knobs and instruments on the wooden dashboard. Bigfoot drove without lights through Cache Center but on the open road he turned on the high beams. The animals came out from the woods to catch in their eyes the last passing lights.

Bigfoot turned on the public radio band and the signal tracer selected the national station. Proude and Rosina never owned a radio or a television set. There had never been electrical power on the cedar circus. The officious voices coming from the radio announced new government restrictions and regulations on travel and the use of fuels. All citizens will be issued bionic residential identification cards during the coming month. No citizens will be permitted to travel without government authorization. Citizens found cutting or selling federal timber will be executed.

"We are not citizens," said Proude.

Bigfoot adjusted the climate and cruise controls and leaned back in the ecstatic comforts of technological power, the last memories of national material indulgence, which the pilgrims from the cedar had never known living in the cedar circus.

Bigfoot was so relaxed behind the wheel that he did not see the person standing at the edge of the road until he had passed. Who would be hitchhiking? He stopped and waited for the tribal person to reach the convertible, out of breath.

"Drinking ... has shown me ... some strange and beautiful worlds," said Zebulon Matchi Makwa, puffing over his first words. His breath smelled foul with the metallic stench of reservation gin. "But I never thought ... I would ever see a moving car again ... I have been walking these naked roads for weeks now ... thinking about the good ... times on gasoline ... Whose dream are we in now?"

"This is a cruel world if we never take new comrades and goodfellowship as a surprise. Grab a seat with the animals," said Bigfoot in the falsetto voice and gestures of a chauffeur clown. "This chariot has been in hiding. The couple in the back are heading for the desert."

Zebulon Matchi Makwa, named after the explorer and a wicked bear, a talking writer and drunken urban shaman, settled in the deep leather between the dogs and sighed and smiled in rare comfort. "This is some reservation on red leather." His fetid breath and unwashed smell tingled in the nostrils of the sensitive clown crows flapping and cawing into the rear seat. The dogs sneezed and turned toward the hitchhiker with their wet noses.

The riders introduced themselves and spoke of the immediate past. Matchi Makwa said he was once invited to the scapehouse for one night but was not fortunate enough to have a woman there. Traveling most of his life with thumbs and stories, he told the pilgrims about the cities and the people in their futures. In Saint Paul, he said, the downtowners are like owls and old winter coats. Whole blocks are claimed in the names of weirds and aberrant categories of people. The retarded have the block around the old bus depot. The poor drunks have the brick piles near the mission while the rich drunks have taken all the mansions on the hills with the feminists and high pretenders. Rich and privileged people moved from private business to government service when the fuels were down and the moving was the best.

"In Santa Fe," said Matchi Makwa, who has been there twice as a tribal consultant when the government was still subsidizing the tribes to convene, but he was drunk and his lessons and views on the southwest and most of the rest of the world were creative assemblies from travel brochures and passing gossip, "people are less predictable." His migrant stories are interesting because he describes peculiar people he has known. He places people he knows in cities he knows nothing about. The listener remembers the person but learns nothing about the place. Reservation gin, he believes, alters spatial recognition and recollection.

"In old Santa Fe," he continued, "I met an old tribal titleholder from the reservation ... He was a cripple, lost his leg in a drinking accident, how else, he once said ... and explained that a logging train ran over him in the woods. When I first saw him he had been drinking at a lavish little place up the hill in old town ... When he left the bar he hopstumbled to the door with one hollow pant leg ... A yapping little mutt followed him and stood up inside his phantom leg. So I asked him what happened to his leg, first he said 'nothing, it looks dressed enough to me' but when I nudged the dog out of the pant leg he told me the whole time of the accident, six views over and over ... Listening as long as I could, I told him I meant what happened to his wooden leg. He looked around the room and said 'that one over there ... that gentleman in the blue suit bought my leg about an hour ago now' and hopped out the door. The leg buyer was one of them curatorial hustlers from old town who drank that flaming chartreuse and sat there with the wooden leg on the chair next to him ... The wooden leg was covered with signatures and travel decals from tourist traps across the nation ... On the outside of the leg near the ankle was a plastic covered identification card holder with a return address ... So I asked the slicker in the blue suit how come he bought a wooden leg off the titleholder and he smiled and said the old man left his leg for a drink ... Real or wooden the old fool could not stop giving up his legs for drink ...

"He was a brush savage ... But the old town attracts fascinating people with or without their legs ... The titleholder knew no one would keep his leg for long, never had before, because the return postage was paid by a liberal foundation ... But most of the time someone would show sorrow and deliver his leg in the morning ... Santa Fe artists once celebrated his wooden leg during the feast of the patron saints of foolishness. His wooden leg is known across the nation ... Bears the signatures and initials of famous writers and politicians and artists ..."

The eastern horizon was turning pale. Pools of brume flowed across the road near the marshes. Since the end of gasoline, weeds were growing over the asphalt roads. Tough flowers crept over the unused shoulders of the road and sprouted from cracks and potholes. Bigfoot avoided the late summer flowers and green weeds down the center of the road. In time trees would take root and turn the cement and asphalt to dust again.

In the distance, around a low rising curve the silhouette of Big Walker emerged on the horizon. Bigfoot announced for the first time that he was stopping in town to pick up a friend who has been waiting for several months to leave for the cities. "She lives alone in an abandoned house on the old school hill road, a few blocks up from the main street ... on the shortcut."

¶ Last Attraction

Big Walker was named in honor of the founder, Thomas Barlow Walker, a true antisalooner and capitalist treekiller who in good conscience raped the cedar and red pine on virgin woodland reservations. He ripped the trees and shipped the beams and planks to the cities for house building. When he was an old man he gave part of his vast timber fortune to found an art center which still bears his name.

The pilgrims rounded the curve near the vacant lumber yard which had been picked clean. Even the sawdust had been sifted as fuel.

Big Walker was silent. The three service stations stood bare, their islands and pumps like phantoms of a civilization past. Stores were closed, stripped clean of combustible materials. Windows were broken. The movie theater which had served the fantasies of the hard drinking whitetown for three generations was unharmed. The paint was peeling on the marquee and the broadside announcing the last show was stained and faded. Spiders had taken over the show cases. The last attraction was a film about ceremonial violence and death, starring a cast of evil whitefamilies convicted for the ritualistic murder of tribal people. The members of the evil families were released on parole to the film producers through an arrangement with correctional authorities. It was a new effort to raise funds for treatment when the public and conservative legislatures became more punitive about corrections. The public did not mind the cost of admission to a motion picture about ritual violence, supporting the power of entertainment, but would not approve an increase in taxes for treatment of violent people and their victims. Because of the contracts between prisons and entertainment companies the public paid less in taxes to support institutions. Meanwhile, various state institutions competed for the care of those convicted for committing sensational violence. Several famous murderers were given special accommodations in prison because of their value as actors and entertainers.

One famous filiation of ritual assassins lived in Big Walker in an old mansion on the lake. There were thirteen residents in the evil bloodline, the sons and daughters of whitepeople who had lost their leases on reservation lakeshore properties. The racist filiation killed dozens of reservation drunks when the tribal government canceled the leases. The drunks were pulled apart between automobiles. When the end of gasoline came, the violent filiation used knives and forks and spoons in their ritual assassinations. The dark eyes of tribal victims were popped with spoons and heel tendons were severed. While the victims struggled to escape, crawling on hands and knees with images swirling from each dangling eyeball, the whites stabbed at the victims with sharp forks. Before death came to most of the tribal victims their ears and lips and genitals were removed. Hundreds of tribal people were murdered before the leaders of the evil filiation were brought to trial, convicted and sentenced to serve ten years in prison. Members of that filiation performed their violence on film for public entertainment and the profits subsidized the construction of a new cohabitation center at the state prison.

Big Walker was covered with debris. Several buildings had been burned for the insurance. Bigfoot eased the silver convertible around the corner near a gutted supermarket and started up the school hill road.

Matchi Makwa told about armed tribal people coming into town in small groups. The white merchants complained to the police that tourists and their customers were frightened, too many dark tribal faces on the white streets.

"The local sheriff, a pigface from the cities, convinced the town government to enact a law against more than three tribal adults, or two parents and five children, from gathering in shops or on the streets in Big Walker," Matchi Makwa explained.

"Who are those people up there?" asked Rosina, leaning forward in the back seat. She pointed toward the old courthouse which was surrounded by a tall fence. Inside the fence were stacks of logs and cords of split wood. The dogs were nervous. The crows were sitting in the back window.

No one answered. "We are not known to them ... We should be walking now," said Proude. More than a dozen whitepeople were standing near the fenced entrance to the courthouse. The sound of a moving automobile startled the whitepeople who stopped talking and moved toward the street.

"When in doubt panic with good humor," said Bigfoot as he increased the speed of the convertible. The whitepeople were standing in the road holding their rations of firewood.

"Make up names, make up names," demanded Bigfoot, waving and smiling while he lowered the convertible top. "Wave at them, smile, make up all the names you can think of when we pass ... this is a parade." The top lifted like the clipped wing of a bird. The clown crows flew out of the back window. The dogs cowered.

Matchi Makwa stood on the front seat with one hand on the windshield. He waved and threw kisses to the whitepeople standing on the road. Bigfoot honked the horn and chanted that the parade had just begun. Pure Gumption was standing with her front paws against the dashboard and howling, her glowing head thrust backward.

"Join the parade," yelled Matchi Makwa. "Join the parade for good gasoline and freedom from the cords ... Vote for the best woman in the shop ... Fetch those mass murderers back to town for their last acts."

His mistake was in slowing down to avoid hitting the curious whitepeople standing on the road with their arms loaded with firewood. When he slowed down they enveloped the car and demanded rides home in the parade. Several threw their firewood into the car and climbed over the doors expecting to be driven to the top of the hill. More and more whitepeople climbed into and onto the silver convertible. Bigfoot could no longer see the road over the bodies on the hood. The car moved at a slow idle while more and more whitepeople from the courthouse joined the parade.

Rosina and Proude climbed out of their plush red leather seats and slipped down over the trunk. The cedar pilgrims were unnoticed in the eager crowd. The crows crowed overhead and swooped down on the whitepeople. Pure Gumption was pressed close to Bigfoot under piles of whitebodies but Private Jones had jumped clear of the car and ran ahead up the hill. When a whiteperson opened the door on the passenger side, where Matchi Makwa was sitting three dogs slipped across the floor and through the legs of those in the convertible.

"Vote for the white pigs ... send the lean white pigs to market," Matchi Makwa shouted as whitepeople bumped against him climbing into the car. His bad breath was a natural defense.

Whitepeople were fighting with each other for control of the wheel. Matchi Makwa seemed to grow taller and taller in his seat until he stepped over the windshield onto whitebodies on the hood and slid down whitebodies to the road. Bigfoot had been pushed down to the floor where he covered his head with one hand and held Pure Gumption with the other hand.

The silver convertible continued creeping up the hill. So loaded with bodies and firewood, the rear tires exploded. The sound seemed to panic the whitepeople who started cursing and fighting. Several whitepeople used sticks of birch and oak as clubs to beat a path to the red padded wheel. Faces and ears were crushed under the blows of firewood. Slivers were sticking from the heads of whitepeople. Noses were broken and teeth were smashed. More and more whitepeople tried to pile onto the convertible. The rear tires flapped against the asphalt. The rear bumper was dragging and the plush seats were torn and broken.

Bigfoot and Pure Gumption managed to crawl through the whitebodies struggling for the wheel. The tribal pilgrims ran ahead of the car up the school hill road. The seven clown crows flapped and hopped from tree to tree following the mass of whitepeople beating each other for less than half a tank of gasoline.

When the car reached the top of the hill near the school the wheels snapped and the tires flapped beneath the fenders. The frame was dragging on the asphalt when the last tire exploded. The convertible stopped but the powerful engine continued to turn the rear rims. Blue and white sparks illuminated the dark wheels wells. Whitepeople stopped fighting when the convertible stopped. They stood around laughing at the sparks darting from the rear wheels. Then the whitepeople started beating the car with their fists and with firewood.

Meanwhile, three whitepeople had torn up the trunk floor and severed the spiral gasoline line. When the three started a siphon flowing the sparks from the churning rear wheels ignited the spilled gasoline. The whitepeople turned to run but the tank exploded in a giant red ball of swirling flames. Flaming whitebodies were hurled against the curbs and poles and trees beside the school hill road.

Others skidded and rolled across the asphalt. Whiteskin peeled like the bark from winter poplar trees. The flame flickered, whitepeople moaned and cried, the metal creaked and snapped from the changes in temperature and then it was silent. Rosina reached out to the smouldering whitebodies. Hairless mounds of flesh slipped through her fingers like spring river slime.

The clown crows flew over the hill into the trees. More whitepeople were gathering near the courthouse at the bottom of the hill road. The explosion and flames and black smoke had awakened the whole town.

"We must leave," Proude insisted. He turned toward the flight of the crows. "We will be responsible for these deaths . . . the woods will protect us until darkness."

"Into the darkness with the crows," snapped Matchi Makwa, whose mood and humor had not changed with the violence. Even the stench of burning hair and blood did not overpower his fetid breath.

The automobile exploded near the small house where Belladonna Darwin-Winter Catcher, the person the pilgrims turned up the hill to find, had been hiding. She watched the crowds and followed the tribal people when the convertible exploded. She shouldered her personal possessions and circled through the trees.

"*Apissin agawateon* . . . violet shadow maker," exclaimed Bigfoot as he turned toward the poplar trees. "And you remembered, you remembered my beautiful umbrella." Belladonna came through the trees bearing his violet umbrella. She smiled and the tribal people greeted each other while the bodies of whitepeople burned on the road. Crowds of whitepeople started up the hill. The pilgrims ran into the warm morning colors of the late summer trees. The crows crowed in their blackness and then disappeared.

¶ Gay Minikins

The circus pilgrims followed the clown crows for four nights through the *shingobee* woods and the foothills pine forest and over the shallow creeks to *nisswi,* three, the summer vacation town.

"Our women were poisoned part white," Matchi Makwa wailed through the poplar and pine. "Part peeled at night ho ho ho ho buried deep down where the dead turn around."

"Our women were poisoned part white . . ."

"His mother married a mountain *makwa* bear," Proude told Belladonna during their walk through the foothills. "But Matchi Makwa never speaks with bears . . . Matchi Makwa was taken with the evil word sorcerers."

"Living on names."

"Terminal names . . ."

"Our women were poisoned part white . . ."

The clown crows landed on the black roof of a cream colored house with chartreuse shutters and a white cross on the front door, situated on the western poplar side of a thin clearing near *nisswi* three tribal haunts. White smoke was trailing from the brick flue on the house. Matchi Makwa approached the house while the others waited under the trees.

Pure Gumption and Private Jones were standing with their front paws on the low sills and noses on the windows.

Inside three men moved with grace over the white carpets in the spacious rooms and halls. The men were former priests who chose to leave their diocese to establish the Sacred Order of Gay Minikins. The minikins assume number names following sacred oral initiation rites. First Minikin Father, the wrinkled one who met Matchi Makwa at the door, was the founder of the order and the author of several celebrated homosexual litanies.

"Our order is a house and haven of familiarities," said First Father, pressing the graceful sounds of each slow word over his tight lips. He was thin and appeared weak from malnutrition. Matchi Makwa whistled and signaled his pleasure to the circus pilgrims under the trees and then entered the house of minikins.

"Without gasoline we have been alone for most of this year ... our neighbors stole our food cache, emphasizing that we were immortal and had little need for food, leaving us to our pure splendor," First Father continued, gesturing with graceful hand movements. Matchi Makwa slumped in a plum colored chair near the fireplace.

"We are the last to live in *nisswi* with our habits and our hunger ... The government has ordered us to move before winter and live in a public school with hundreds of common families," said Father Sixteen, who limped over the white carpet to meet the hesitant pilgrims. "Neither the government nor the church has recognized our sacred order."

"We do not fear death because we share our final sounds, our speech, our litanies, we celebrate our lives and sacred bodies together in grace and splendor," chimed Father Nine. The voices of the minikins were harmonious.

"Living through the flesh makes a man thin and wise," said Bigfoot with a wide smile. He moved from father to father and passed the back of his hand across their cheeks. "Now tell me doctor," he said to First Father, "what could be worse than starving to death in the arms of two queer old priests?"

Father Sixteen and Father Nine wagged the whiteskin hanging from their chins and turned from the pilgrims to leave the room. Father Nine dragged his feet as he walked.

"If you must know, my little queer clown saint," responded First Father with a hostile sweep of his hand, "we have suffered less in the hands of ourselves and other men than in the wicked arms of church women ... Our mothers were manners and creases and androgynous fantasies, but our fathers were ecstatic survivors."

"Mind fucking whitemothers," snapped Matchi Makwa.

"Immaculate deceptions," said First Father.

"Fear of our fathers..."

"The insecurities of fear are precious acts of survival ... Fear is grand but dependencies on mothers are poison ... poison ... poison."

"Our women were poisoned part white ..."

The circus pilgrims were invited to share the food of the generous minikins, their last meal, with three lighted black candles. Small macaroni elbows, stewed tomatoes, dried cheese, slices of coarse meat and green beans were counted and sorted in even piles and rows on eight red plates. Five green beans and three elbows of macaroni and one brown apple, the last indivisible portions of their survival food, were set aside, in good humor, for the teller of the best stories.

Proude and the three minikin fathers were the last to finish their meal, nibbling and savoring each elbow and length of green bean.

"I have never shared last meals," said Belladonna.

"All meals are the last."

"The last in taste," said Father Sixteen.

"Save the splendid taste of the last bean, the last curd of cheese," said First Father over his steaming cup of herb tea. "Bring up our memories, this last meal is a greater pleasure than all the meals before us now ... Better than the second or third to the last ... Taste was never clearer ... Our hunger has been released. When the rabbit is caught in the claws of the hawk, the imminence of death is ecstatic."

"Ecstatic rabbit talk from a nonrabbit," said Matchi Makwa. "We are the words that keep rabbits numb and dumb with fear and no less dead."

"We escape the final moment ... all the same in rabbit word worlds," said Proude. He leaned forward when he spoke and rested his arms in front of him on the table. "Few humans struggle and twist against the claws ... The end comes soon enough without struggling. Small honors struggling against the fear of death when death is certain."

The three priests were watching the hands of the old tribal pilgrim while he spoke. Proude spread his graceful fingers out on the table, moving them like shaman animals through the tender fern. His fingers became turtles and touched his spoken words. Words came before him on the wind.

The wind tossed leaves against the windows. The animals were groaning in their sleep and the clown crows crowed in the distance. Proude was asked to tell one short tale before leaving the house. He began in a gentle voice, introducing the characters: a shaman crow, a child girl, a mongrel and four puppies. The place of the tale was a tribal village near the river on the prairie.

Through uncommon dreams the child girl visited different worlds at night ... Her visions separated her from the people in the village where she was born. She moved in the magical flight of shaman crows and the languages of tribal animals.

One night while her favorite mongrel was sleeping at her feet she dreamed that the animal had become a man ... She traveled with him and made love with him on the warm banks of the river.

Soon her parents discovered that she was pregnant. The people in the village began to gossip that she had given herself to an animal ... She was alone and did not suffer from the gossip but her parents depended on the praise and acceptance of other families in the village.

The common father of the child girl was preparing to sacrifice his daughter to save his image when the shaman crow warned her in a dream ... She escaped into the darkness while her father set fire to the house of reeds where she was living with her mongrel lover ... Her lover died in the fire and the families abandoned their familiar summer village near the river.

The crows taught her how to live with herself, how to make fires and how to gather food and build a shelter for the winter. In the spring during the night of the first rainfall the child girl gave birth to five puppies ... She was pleased that the love of her mongrel lover would continue in other lives ... She named one pup for her lover and the others for the colors of the four directions.

The mongrel children puppies grew and became more independent. Two were deceived with too much attention from strange humans and killed and roasted. The child mother was so upset that green and black had been eaten that she turned cold and taught her two remaining mongrel children to kill humans ... She stole through dozens of villages at night removing the hearts of sleeping humans. The villagers were terrified and called upon the owls and the wisdom of the shaman crows to save them from the powers of evil.

Proude paused for a moment with his hands resting on his chest over his heart and then continued. Evil humans sleep with their hands over their hearts like this. Private Jones twitched in his sleep near the fire. Pure Gumption sat near the front window watching the clown crows in the poplar trees.

The shaman crows told how cruel the tribes had been to their mongrels ... Then evil came upon them because the people shunned the love of animals ... The evil and deception in their lives had been drawn from the monsters of their ritual past. Their own past devoured their hearts during the night. The shaman crows told them that the people must purge their tribal blood and praise their animals to save their hearts.

The humans changed and began to celebrate and worship their animals. Their new obsession with animal love turned families against themselves ... Humans died of hunger while mongrels became fat ... Humans gossiped about each other and sacrificed those humans who did not live and show love for their animals ... The mongrels became spoiled and selfish like the people.

The shaman crows were discouraged with the terminal creeds of humans ... In visions the crows spoke with the child mother of the mongrel children. She was still mourning the loss of green and black but she agreed that if the crows could gather the powers to turn her mongrel children into human forms she would return to her human families and teach them to love both animals and themselves.

She returned to her village and her families became known to all the tribes of the prairie and the woodland as the people of love ... The people who love animals and themselves.

But when she was old and wrinkled and her mongrel sons and daughters were themselves peaceful parents, the whitemen arrived and poisoned the families with selfishness ... The whitepeople killed animals without praising their lives. Tribal people were weakened with hunger and the mongrels turned against humans again ... When whitemen removed tribal families from the prairie and woodland the shaman crows turned tribal children into mongrels because white-people would not eat them. Pure Gumption is a healer and cedar shaman. Private Jones is a tribal clown and trickster.

The black shaman clown crows turned some humans into other animals to survive during the slow death coming to the hearts of whitepeople. Whitepeople love domestic animals but so hate themselves that evil takes their hearts at night.

"Our women were poisoned part white ..."

Proude drew seven circles with his fingers.

"This was our last meal," said First Father. "The last of our food, the last of our friends, the last of our good lives and loves ..."

"But others will pass," said Rosina.

"You are the first in three months who were not thieves and hostiles," said Father Sixteen. Whitefoam gathered on the thick rim of his bluish lips as he spoke.

"We will live a week or two more," said First Father, "but on the road we would suffer in the hands of evil ... We would die a worse death in loneliness."

"We must share our hunger and our death here," said Father Nine. "We have shared the bodies and souls of four fellow minikin fathers who have died before us here in this house."

"You have shared the last of their sacred minikin flesh with us during this meal," First Father said as he stood up from the table and waved the sign of the cross with his trembling hands. Father Nine and Father Sixteen stood with him and chanted their strange homosexual litanies of the minikins.

Proude moved from the table in silence, shouldered his pack and opened the front door with the white cross. The afternoon wind was warm. He did not speak. He did not thank the minikin priests but nodded from a distance to them as he walked out of the house.

Matchi Makwa and Bigfoot embraced the three thin minikin priests before leaving. Rosina and Belladonna exchanged praise and messages of good fortune with the priests before the door closed behind them. The clown crows were crowing and flapping in laughter through the trees ahead of the pilgrims. Proude has eaten human flesh. The circus was on the road again.

¶ Dead Birds for Lindbergh

The circus pilgrims followed fourlane roads eighteen miles south, crossing over open fields and circling small lakes behind the clown crows to the confluence of the *kagagi migwan,* crow feather, and the *misisibi* rivers. Following the shores of the dark *misisibi* the pilgrims passed the island and buried villages of the old tribes. The clown crows were silent in the scrub oak trees. The brown palmate leaves rattled ho kwi ho ho ho on the wind over the sand hills from the past.

"*Tchibai* winds ... ghost winds and wandering spirits over the hills," said Proude. *Wanaki, wanaki,* a place of peace, he called, and then walked south in silence. The leaves rattled.

"Where are we?" demanded Matchi Makwa. "What are all these tanks and armored cars doing here?" The pilgrims were crossing the Camp Ripley Military Reservation. Trucks and combat vehicles were abandoned at peculiar angles. Doors and hatches yawned open over the shifting sand hills and stiff weeds. Gophers watched the circus from their dark tunnels.

Bigfoot broke the silence when he dumped his shoulder bundle and umbrella and bounded toward the river. His huge feet thumped on the sand. Climbing on a tank he slammed the hatches shut and then pressed his ear on the cold steel to listen. Inside the dark turret he heard the muffled thumps and cries of frightened birds.

"Roast birds for dinner," said Bigfoot.

The animals and clown crows circled the tank barking and crowing. Matchi Makwa and Bigfoot danced on the turret celebrating the catch. The other pilgrims rested on the sand banks and watched the bird catchers.

While Bigfoot opened the command hatch a thin crack Matchi

Makwa caught the escaping little birds and whacked their heads on the steel cannon. The two clowns had killed several dozen bluebirds and spirited sparrows. Bigfoot climbed into the turret searching for the last survivors. He found several nests and skeletons but no living birds. He opened all the hatches and summoned the others to share a moment in his fantasies of the great wars. Bigfoot flapped his motor lips and cranked the cannon down the river to liberate the innocent women of the villages. Blasting the cannon and machine guns he killed the demons and saved three women who were forever his war prizes. The women rode in the turret with him and worshiped his courage.

"Fuck the war games," snapped Matchi Makwa.

The bird catchers gathered the dead birds. Their beaks were dripping dark red blood. Walking south down the river Matchi Makwa spread a soft trail of brown and blue feathers pulled from the bodies of the little birds. Less than a mouthful featherless and roasted. He dropped one bird for each crow and animal and stuffed the remaining bodies into his large coat pockets.

The pilgrims crossed the *misisibi* on the bridge near *kakabika*, the place where the water falls over the rocks, and stopped to rest in the town of Little Falls. People hungered like rodents down the streets from house to house. Faces were hidden. A column of white smoke was rising through the trees down river.

"Oak smoke from an indoor fire," said Proude.

Shouldering their bundles again the pilgrims moved through the woods near the western shore of the river. The sun had set and the wind was silent.

"Must be government business," said Belladonna.

"Grass trimmed with scissors."

"Too neat for humans."

"We can ask for food."

The smoke was rising from a large stone chimney on a green and white frame house. The clown crows circled and then swooped through the small unscreened front porch. The crowing crows brought a woman to the windows and then to the door. The pilgrims waited behind the white pine down the hill from the house near the slow flowing *misisibi*.

The animals sniffed the steps and splitstone foundation and bumped against the front and side doors. The woman ran from window to window again and then threw open the porch door and emerged with a small shotgun swinging from her right hand. The crows flapped a secure distance from the house. The animals ran back to the river.

"Look at that red hair," said Bigfoot.

"Animal fires," said Matchi Makwa.

Scintilla Shruggles, a new model pioneer woman and keeper of the Charles Augustus Lindbergh house for the Minnesota Division of Historic Sites, leaped from the porch with her thin legs spread, threw her long red hair back over her broad shoulders and dashed down the lush green bank to the river. She raised the shotgun with one arm, slapped her other hand on her narrow hip, thrust her breastless chest out, and shouted at the tribal pilgrims who had taken cover behind the white pine. The clown crows swooped and crowed at her flaming red hair.

"Call back those damned crows and mongrels before the shooting starts," she shouted. "The rest of you animals come up to the house." Proude waved the crows back into the woods and then walked toward the woman.

Scintilla touched their hands, nodded, smiled wide, creasing the freckles on her cheeks. She tossed her hair back over her shoulder several times and ordered the pilgrims up the hill and into the house. The circus clowns nodded back, smiled wide, shrugged, hesitated, and then entered the house under the strange personal power of a pioneer museum keeper.

Inside, she ordered them into the large kitchen where she lived and worked. There was a neat writing table and eating place near the windows. The house was heated with an old cast iron cooking stove. Matchi Makwa hung his leather coat on a peg behind the stove.

"I live in the kitchen and play games in the rest of the house," said Scintilla, offering the pilgrims herb tea. The coming winter will be the second alone here since the state closed all historic sites. She could not leave the house. Charles Lindbergh was the first perfect man she learned to love.

The pilgrims sat near the stove and listened.

"This is the second house on this foundation," she continued as she dipped the bundle of herbs into the hot water. "Built more than a century ago by Charles Augustus Lindbergh."

"Who is this person?" asked Bigfoot.

"One was a lawyer and congressman with a mouth full of rough words and backwoods idioms and the other was a famous aviator," she said as she handed the pilgrims postcards with a picture of the house and a few nostalgic words from the daring transcontinental aviator.

"... I spent hours lying on my back in high timothy ... watching white cumulus clouds drift overhead. How wonderful it would be, I thought, if I had an airplane — wings with which I could ... ride on the wind and be part of the sky."

"Terrific ... so much for gasoline," said Belladonna.

"Heroes with machines," moaned Bigfoot.

"If he was alive now he would be dreaming the same thing but he would be flying on something other than gasoline," said Matchi Makwa.

"Interesting."

Rosina poured the tea. The pilgrims watched the fire and drank in silence. The oak coals from the opened wood stove illuminated the room. Belladonna prepared the fish she caught in the river. Scintilla made bread.

"When did you last wash?" Scintilla asked Matchi Makwa. She pinched her nose while she spoke. Bigfoot rolled over on the floor in laughter. "You smell worse than a spring bear."

"He is not the bear," said Proude.

"Take this and wash," said Scintilla, throwing a wrinkled bar of abrasive soap to Matchi Makwa. She opened the door and waved him outside, still pinching her nose. "You are some woman," he said, standing on the threshold. She pushed him out.

Matchi Makwa stumbled through the darkness toward the river. The animals nudged him with their wet noses. Before he dunked himself in the cold water he stretched out on the grass and flew from star to star. Then he opened a small metal flask and drank wild rice wine.

Inside, Proude opened his bundle and removed a handful of cedar incense which he placed on top of the stove. The heat of the metal caused the cedar to smoulder and the incense filled the kitchen. Proude inhaled the cedar smoke from the circus. His breathing filled the room. Then he walked out of the house and down the grass slope to the *misisibi,* the same sacred river which flows through the cedar circus. The same river that flows over the bones and spirits of his grandfathers and father. He removed his clothes and slipped into the dark cold water.

Proude swam upstream and then floated with the slow current on his back watching the stars and ghosts behind the trees. When he drifted back to where he had entered the river he saw the shape of a head in the water. He floated past the figure and then stepped out of the water and roared in his bear voice in the four directions.

"What was that?" asked Scintilla in the house.

The clown crows called in a low voice from the dark trees. The animals listened. Matchi Makwa was humming to himself and sloshing in the shallow water near shore. Ghost lights bounded across the northern horizon behind the trees.

Belladonna stepped out of the water. Wiping her shoulders and breasts and thighs she walked up the slope and stood near Proude in the soft grass. She reached out and touched his cheeks and then drew her fingers across shoulders. When she pressed her head against his chest he lowered himself into the grass. Her dark hair was wet and cold against his stomach.

"Will you keep secrets?" she asked.

Proude did not answer.

"I am pregnant."

Proude did not respond.

"Three months pregnant."

Proude touched her shoulders and breasts with the tips of his warm fingers. Her energies rushed to his silence and gentle touch.

"Please listen ... I must tell you this."

Proude did not speak.

"Three whitemen made me pregnant."

Silence.

"Three whitemen raped me and raped me until I could not walk ... I crawled through the streets but no one would help me ..."

Proude was silent.

"Crawling through Big Walker alone ... Saint Plumero found me near the courthouse and carried me home."

Proude did not respond.

"But he does not know what happened to me ... No one else knows about the whitemen ... three evil whitesavages."

"Evil does not give life," said Proude and then he moved down the grass slope toward the *misisibi*. She followed him and while she dressed he touched her dark hair and told her to return to the house.

"Did you wash yourself?" Scintilla shouted while Matchi Makwa was drying his long tangled hair near the stove. He turned to defend himself but she sniffed past him like a cat to his leather coat hanging on a peg.

"The birds ... the dead birds."

"What birds?"

"The birds we trapped in the tank this afternoon," Matchi Makwa explained while he emptied his pockets. "Thirteen dead birds for dinner ... but now their little guts and hearts have gone rotten in the heat." He pitched the plucked bodies out the door to the animals.

Following their meal of bread and bitter river fish and herb tea the pilgrims bundled themselves together in wool blankets on the floor around the stove. Matchi Makwa told stories about peculiar people in strange places.

Rosina was awakened during the night. The animals were howling and she heard breathless whispering near the stove. Scintilla was crouching and moving her mouth up and down on president jackson. The upstanding president throbbed and spurted in the pale golden light from the oak coals.

In the morning the pilgrims toured the museum house. There were fine linen and thin oriental dishes and a floral beaded pouch from the colonial tribal leaders of the past. In the basement, under glass, there were two automobiles the aviator owned. But more valuable than all of the mundane memorabilia belonging to the pioneer avaitor was a warped flatbottom wooden boat hidden in the rafters. The pilgrims were ecstatic over their uncontested discovery and claimed it in the name of the inland naval circus. The cracks were plugged with pitch and shredded inner bark before the circus punt was soaked in the *misisibi*.

"If I had a choice I would rather have birds than airplanes," said Matchi Makwa mocking the thoughts of the famous aviator.

"Or a river boat."

"The citizen is not true to his country unless she criticizes ... and does her best to improve things," said Belladonna. She was quoting with new pronouns the words of Charles Augustus Lindbergh while the pilgrims checked the punt for leaks. "Look where it got the radical old legislator," she said, sweeping her arms open. "Little more in his memories than dead birds and a house full of mixedblood river clowns."

¶ Umbrella through the Hostiles

Scintilla Shruggles shoved the watersoaked circus punt into the morning brume on the dark river. The slow current turned the pilgrims around and around until Matchi Makwa raised the oars and started rowing slow with the flow down toward the evil cities. Seven clown crows perched on the bow of the punt.

The first strokes of sunlight burned through the leaves on the oak and cottonwood river trees like *tchibai nopiming* woodland phantoms dancing over the faces of the passing pilgrims.

The pilgrims took turns at the oars rowing into the darkness before coming ashore for the night at a low dam near an abandoned paper plant.

Proude was rowing the next afternoon when the pilgrims approached the first bridge over the *misisibi* in the town of Saint Cloud. The animals were restless.

"We have nothing to fear but people in the cities," said Bigfoot turning in the front seat. "Look at all those goddamn whitepeople on the bridge."

Hundreds of whitepeople were cursing the puntload of pilgrims from the high bridge. Bigfoot, whose words and their meaning lasted no longer than the time it took the words to speak through him, could not resist the hostile audience. He stood up in the front of the punt and waved to the hostiles. The hostiles waved back and then started throwing stones at the pilgrims passing beneath the bridge. Bigfoot pounded his huge feet on the front punt seat in a strange dance mania, while he sneered and wriggled his fingers and cursed at the hostiles above. Stones dropped around him.

Proude pulled harder on the wooden oars. Stones splashed in the dark water near the circus punt. Evil whiteflesh eaters, whitesavages, *windigo wabishkiwe,* whitecannibals, he growled as he rowed through the hostiles. Private Jones panicked when the first stone hit the punt near the bow. He leaped into the water to escape. The stones splashing in the water drove him toward the western shore of the river near a state college where hundreds of starving whitestudents were waiting to catch an animal for food. Pure Gumption stood in the bow and howled until Private Jones paddled back to the punt. Matchi Makwa pulled him out of the water by his ears. The clown crows crowed and flapped and bounced in flight beneath the bridge to distract the hostiles.

The second bridge, down river from the college, was closer to the water. The hostiles and whitestudents were waiting with enormous boulders for the pilgrims to pass beneath them.

"Give me your little white hostile hands," chanted Bigfoot. "Give me your wretched blond whitewomen to push ashore and fuck with the team. We were hoping against hope that no one would see our little boat." He threw kisses to the hostiles while he danced on the bow seat in his red velvet leggings. Some of the hostiles and whitestudents began to laugh at the short clown with the huge feet.

The clown crows were flapping up and down as avian escorts ahead of the punt. When the punt came within stone throwing distance of the bridge, Bigfoot, still dancing on the bow, popped his wide violet umbrella and whirled, wheeled, shunted and wriggled like a tulip in the clenched fist of a child. The punt dipped and took on water but the pilgrims passed beneath the hostiles in humor and without harm.

Between Saint Cloud and Saint Paul Bigfoot popped and danced and chanted and wriggled and twirled his violet umbrella seven times through whitehostiles.

"Where did you find that thing?" asked Matchi Makwa.

"It has magic power ..."

"Bought it at an estate sale in the cities," Bigfoot answered. He closed the umbrella and returned it to its leather case. Little did he know when he found it that his alleged great great grandfather, the hotheaded political exile and bigfooted explorer, Giacomo

Constantino Beltrami, had carried an umbrella with him when he paddled down the sacred *misisibi* through hostile tribes. Beltrami made the hostiles laugh with his red umbrella on the river road to old Fort Snelling.

¶ The Cathedral Tunnel

Inawa Biwide, the one who resembles a stranger, was standing under the lintel stone over the Vanutelli Portal of the Cathedral of Saint Paul dressed in his white surplice and waiting for more tribal pilgrims to arrive from the river before he closed the doors for the night.

The stranger was sixteen. His black eyes, like the dark apsidal chapels, absorbed the pale light from the ceremonial candles. He was an orphan rescued by the church from the state and the spiritless depths of a federal reservation housing commune. He works for his rescuers and respects his religious masters.

Inawa Biwide had been waiting in the cold portal for more than three hours. The stone building obstructed the flow of warm air over the gentle river hills and trimmed the wind quick and cold through the door. The stranger waited with his back resting against the portal staring into the darkness toward the river at the bottom of the hill. He filed his thumbnail on the rim of a coin while he waited.

Bishop Omax Parasimo, one of his religious masters, wearing the metamask of a redhaired woman with the same facial features as Scintilla Shruggles, had gone to the river caves to meet the new pilgrims from the tribes. He was obsessed with the romantic and spiritual power of tribal people and told his radical tribal friends that he would contact pilgrims near the power plant and river caves and lead them to secure underground shelter. Citizens were not permitted to enter the cities without authorization and tribal people were banished to reservations. Two weeks before, he found Sun Bear Sun and Little Big Mouse in the caves. During the same week the masked redhead escorted Justice Pardone Cozener, the tribal lawyer and one of the new prairie bigbellies, and Doctor Wilde Coxwain, the arm wagging tribal historian, through the federal mercenaries protecting the cities to the secret cathedral tunnel. Improper tribal travelers in the cities were removed to reservation work camps as laborers of the state.

The old elites had become the new state.

"Cities take the mind and then the stomach and at last the heart. In the name of the father and the other holies, give me good signs in our own sacred safehouse," said Bigfoot as he passed through the portal with his umbrella and shoulder pack. His voice and thumping echoed through the chapels. The candles flickered from the sound of his huge feet. "Our safehouse from the brutalities of the new state."

The other pilgrims slipped out of the darkness and passed through the portal. Pure Gumption moved close to the marble walls. Her nails ticked against the cold tiles and her quick sniffing breath echoed in the domed space. She illuminated the black chapels where she walked.

Inawa Biwide was drawing the doors closed when the seven clown crows swooped through the portal and into the great hall of the angels. Startled, the stranger called to his religious master. Bishop Parasimo pulled up his metamask and shouted at the crows to leave the chapel. The clown crows swooped and flapped and crowed in their blackness at the long red hair on the metamask. The animals yawned and sneezed. Matchi Makwa bounced down the marble walls in laughter. Bishop Parasimo lost control over his emotions and leaped up and down, shouting and screaming and pulling the hair on his metamask. The crows flashed past him in their blackness once again.

"Get those damn birds out of here . . . out now!" he raged while he waved his short hairy arms at the crows. He feared that the birds would take his vision. "Get those black devils out of the chapel before they drink the holy water and shit all over the high altar altar altar!" Bishop Parasimo and the pilgrims stood in a circle with their heads raised and watched the crows soar in wide circles through the frail pastel figures on the walls and dome of the chapel. Private Jones barked twice. His voice bounced through the candle lights and echoed through the chapel. Proude waved to the crows. Swooping over the candles the clown crows landed on the sacred statues.

"The crows are with us," said Proude.

Bishop Parasimo pitched his metamask over his shoulder by the hair, exhaled, wiped the sweat from his balding dome and said nothing more about the crows. Inawa Biwide, the stranger, told the others to follow him through the shrines of the nations to the statue of Saint John the Baptist. Behind the patron saint the stranger lowered a panel on the base of the statue which opened onto a narrow stairwell leading to the cathedral tunnel. Bigfoot, having been that way once before, was the first to descend the winding stairs. At the bottom the pilgrims followed a narrow corridor to the old streetcar tunnel which had been filled in on one end and closed with steel doors on the other end.

The five new tribal pilgrims and two animals came upon the others sitting around a small fire in the tunnel. The air was damp but clear, the smoke was vented through the church flues. The faces of the pilgrims were illuminated by the fire. Bigfoot thumped past the fire to the end of the tunnel where he climbed into the dark opening of a giant carbo trailer and pulled the doors closed.

Lilith Mae Farrier was tugging at the short leashes on her two brown boxers. The animals growled and lunged at Pure Gumption and Private Jones. Lilith Mae hushed them but the boxers pulled her across the floor with erect tails. When the boxers growled, showing their perfect white teeth, Private Jones looked down and then rolled over on his side. The boxers were poised for battle. Their nostrils were flared and their lips twitched above their teeth. Private Jones sneezed. Pure Gumption raised her head and moved with ceremonial steps, paw over careful paw in slow motion, toward the growling animals. The boxers tugged at their leashes. Pure Gumption illuminated the tunnel with a morning light as she moved closer to the boxers. Her paws and nose and brown coat seemed to flow within the green and blue aura around her shape. The boxers dropped their tails and turned toward their mistress. Sitting at her feet they rested their blunt noses in her crotch. Private Jones pranced off, looking back several times, sniffing corners of the tunnel. Pure Gumption turned in her aura and followed Inawa Biwide to his place near the fire.

"Inawa Biwide has the old nights in him," said Proude to Rosina. "He knows the darkness and how to live alone." He turned toward the fire and examined the faces of the other pilgrims.

Lilith Mae Farrier, the horsewoman of passionless contradictions, the child hater and mistress of two boxers, had been a teacher in a tribal round house on the White Earth Reservation. The old women on the reservation called her *animosh, abita animosh,* the woman who is a dog, half dog. But fairminded Lilith Mae, with her expressionless eyes set wide on her angular face, thought the old tribal women meant that she was a person who loved and cared for dogs. Keeping up to this mistaken impression she was feeding most of the mongrels on the reservation. She was fired for having sex with several members of the tribal school board. The wives packed her belongings into her van one afternoon and shunned her off the reservation. She came to the tunnel to confess her sexual sins, hoping to recover passion in her passionless emotions. Bishop Parasimo subscribed her to the therapeutic underground and the grande tribal caravan to freedom.

Sun Bear Sun, the three hundred pound seven foot son of the utopian tribal organizer Sun Bear, and Little Big Mouse, who was sitting in his enormous lap, were found in a cave near the river. Little Big Mouse was a small whitewoman with fresh water blue eyes. She forgot her birth name but took names from the shrines she made from random things. She moved through her visual and tactual worlds on the surfaces of things, touching walls and banisters as she walked, holding to corners, in constant touch with linear surfaces. Sun Bear Sun carried her most of the time in foot holsters attached to his waist.

Justice Pardone Cozener, illiterate law school graduate and tribal justice, fulfilled the expectations and aspirations of his unschooled father who knew nothing about law but moral rights and wrongs and pardons. His father blessed him with his first name. Pardone was short with small feet and was overweight. He waddled from side to side as he walked. His thighs were so thick that he could not walk far without spreading his knees. He was one of the new tribal bigbellies, those overpaid tribal officials who fattened themselves overeating on expense accounts from conference to conference. Pardone was in love with Doctor Wilde Coxwain, the tribal historian. Coxwain resisted, having a fine reputation as a woman lover to defend, until the two of them fell into bed drunk one night. The two have been sleeping together since. Coxwain is the name a prairie reservation religious teacher and naval fanatic gave to his grandfather. Wilde comes from the birth name of his whitemother who was a school teacher on the reservation. Coxwain earned a doctor's degree in tribal histories and directed tribal studies programs at several universities before the government stopped funding the education of radicals and idealistic separatists.

Pio Wissakodewinini, the parawoman mixedblood mammoth clown, was ashamed of his visible decline as a woman. So ashamed that he shuns the full light of the flames on his face. Neither man nor woman, Pio cowers from the fire holding back his face and hesitant to be seen or heard. He was twice convicted for raping whitewomen, charges he has denied, and was sentenced under the new penal code for double sex offenders to become a woman. The determinate sentence for two convictions on rape was a sex change, no prison time, but transsexual surgery and freedom on hormones. Pio, who was an enormous and simple man, became an aggressive woman and found a place in the leadership of the liberation movement. His punishment to become a woman became his enlightenment as a person until economic conditions turned foul, fuel supplies expired, the government fell dumb and numb back to the elites, minorities were shunned and medical and pharmaceutical supplies were limited to emergencies. When Pio could no longer fill his prescriptions for female hormones her pendulous breasts shriveled, his beard returned and her voice wavered and vibrated. The mammoth parawoman clown seldom spoke now. He joined the grande tribal caravan in search of a special tribal herb which would bring back to him her new woman dreams and voices.

¶ Kitchibiwabik Osidaman

Pure Gumption circled the fire, stopped behind each pilgrim, and then walked to the dark end of the tunnel. Inawa Biwide followed her glowing lissome shape to the cargo trailer.

Music from old showtunes sounded from the trailer. The stranger opened the door wide enough to see Benito Saint Plumero dressed in a white linen shirt and dancing in candlelight in front of a beautiful bronze statue of a woman. Pure Gumption barked until the door was pulled open.

''Tell me good stories and you will hear the secrets of our lives like the plucked string on an old guitar,'' said Bigfoot, gesturing with one hand extended and poised on one huge foot in the same dancing position as the female statue. The stranger lifted Pure Gumption into the trailer. His hands seemed independent of his mind and muscles when he touched her warm aura. Climbing into the trailer he touched his warm hands to his cheeks.

The bronze figure was mounted on a swivel base. When Bigfoot danced around the statue she pivoted from side to side. Her breasts were large and she had sensuous calves and thighs. Her feet were huge.

"Tell me stories," said Bigfoot.

There was silence.

"Tell me stories," he repeated.

"There was an old tribal trickster who left this world," said Inawa Biwide, still feeling the warmth in his hands. "The old trickster left this world and became a cedar tree . . . Will you become your statue?"

Bigfoot lifted the arm on the ancient windup phonograph and placed the needle on the scratched record. He danced around his statue, around and around, twirling the bronze figure from side to side. Then he stood on the base of the statue, his cheek against her breast, and turned with her until the music stopped.

"I am a fool," he said, leaping from the figure. "I am a fool, but not so foolish that I must live in loneliness and unhappiness ... I am in love with a vision ... She is a personal vision and caring gives me good time."

"What vision?"

"*Kitchi osidaman*," he answered, pulling his short fingers through his hair. "It means big feet, *kitchibiwabik osidaman*, big metal feet," he said pointing to the large bronze feet of the statue. "*Ikwe kitchibiwabik osidaman*, woman with big metal feet ... she is my vision."

"Is that her name?"

"*Ikwe kitchibiwabik osidaman*," he answered, looking down at his own feet. He turned them apart on the wooden trailer floor and laughed. "We come from the same foot maker."

"But where did you find her?"

"In Rice Park," he answered. "In the park downtown, but it was not until I saw her in a vision that I knew I was in love, in love like a great fool ... In love with a woman on big bronze feet."

"Alonzo Hauser was the sculptor ... I saved her from her terrible isolation in the park. She was alone there all summer and winter ... Standing alone in a fountain pond waiting for someone to love her. I took her from the drunken admirers in the park and gave her love and a descriptive name in the world."

"You must be a fool."

"Foolish I am, but not uncertain, not unkind," said Bigfoot and then his mood changed. "Never unkind, but I did kill a man to save her from sexual abuse and loneliness ... We do not live without visions."

"You killed someone for her?"

"Well," he began, with sudden hand gestures, "I killed for passion ... I killed a man who had deliberate plans to hurt me and to deprive me of my vision and love. A whiteman who wanted me to live in his loneliness."

Inawa Biwide lowered himself to the floor and leaned against the side of the trailer. He drew his legs forward against his chest, folded his arms, and rested his chin on his knees. He was waiting for an explanation. Pure Gumption sat next to him. When the stranger lighted another white altar candle, Bigfoot began to tell his vision stories.

"It was the second year of the full time paid juries," he said. "The judge read the verdict from a television screen . . . redhanded killer, guilt and eternal shame on you. But then she mitigated, I told her that was a nice word, citing the new television guidelines in the up to the minute criminal code, and sentenced me to serve about, she said *about*, two years working at home, which was what the court thought was a prison then. Prison sentences at home, the last word in community based corrections. About two years at home, she said, because I killed a man, a whiteman at that, for love and passion rather than killing for no good reason at all.

"Amazing you say, two years at home for cutting the head and cock from a whiteman? True, but judicial folks were downright pleased to meet an old fashioned passion killer, a killer who made sense, because most of the killings going on are reasonless now. Random living and random loving and random death. New generations with no causes and no effects in their machine minds. When the judge read the sentence the jurors one by one came up to shake my hand and congratulate me for having passion and determination. Strange people. What the jurors will never know is that the woman, the object of my love and passion, whose honor I defended, is made out of public park bronze.

"No matter, he said, because the new mental hospitals are also located at home. Going home is real punishment in a mobile world. Well, bronze she is, but not in real life. In the real life of my dreams and visions she is a soothsayer, a pioneer representing the sources of rivers and thunders and the snow and sunshine. She is the curve and color of the earth and the breath of our lives.

"But at first, he said, I was just a common drunk and she was just a common Saint Paul statue standing in a pond. Then I had a vision and we both changed. She fell in love with me and I carried her away in a pickup truck. Not your average love tale . . . let me back up for a minute. I met his white anthropologist who I fed a lot of traditional bullshit to about old ways and he said right back to me that I was full of tribal shit. So I laughed and told him I was a trickster clown, sort of a new contrarion down on my luck, and he said right back again that I was drunk down on my visions and he gave me some magic vine leaves that he mashed up and we drank it together in his mansion up on the hill near here. Well, let me tell you what happened. That mashed vision vine stuff changed my life. *Kitchibiwabik osidaman* was no longer a bronze statue and I was no longer a common drunk and alone. I saw colors and places I have never known before, spiral worlds of blue and green and yellow and I flew through the trees and the eyes of insects and summer clouds with my friends and enemies. The most amazing thing was hearing the thoughts of strangers, sharing common thoughts and feelings without words. I knew what people were thinking by looking at them. I swooped down like a crow and listened to strangers thinking thinking, people hating and making love. I heard women in bed with one thinking about another. I learned who were my friends and enemies, swooping in on them to leave thoughts about myself with them and then listening to what they thought about me. It took the insecurities out of friendships and romances. No more trusting the kind words of whitefaces when tics of hatred took over their faces. I could locate my enemies and protect myself and I learned how to focus on tics and tell the meaning. I learned how to read muscles and sounds and I could speak several languages. Imagine that, I could speak languages without studying them, just like that. I spoke with my distant *anishinabe* and Italian relatives like *gijig oshkinjigoma*, sky eyes, and old Giacomo Constantino Beltrami, who was exiled from his native land and traveled alone with tribal people in search of the source of the *misisibi*. He found one source, he told me, because he asked tribal people where it was located and they told him. Other whitemen named a different source the source because they never asked the tribes. I saw old Beltrami and talked with him in my vision. He told me how he paddled down the river without problems because he popped his umbrella in the presence of hostiles. He was surprised when I told him that a county was named in his honor. Surprised because he thought the namers could have given him more than one county.

"But you would rather hear about our love somewhat, he said. I was aroused, the vision vine turned me red, my cheeks were flaming and my cock turned to blood stone. I was mister lust with an overnight erection. Have you had a woman yet? Never mind for now. Well, when I flew down to the park and saw what I saw, she was no longer a bronze statue with big feet, she was a perfect love, my soul woman, earth mother, my dream keeper and she has been with me ever since, except the time when this whitedude, may the evil shaman flick shit in his underworld face, stole her, and then the time I have been traveling in the past few months. She was with me when I was in prison at home in the woods on the reservation.

"Well, you may ask, how did he steal her? How did the whitedude take *kitchibiwabik osidaman* from me? I will tell you how he did it and how I found her and killed him with a piece of steel wire.

"I drove her up north to the reservation, after I rolled her out of the pond, and built a shrine for her deep in the *mishkwawak*, cedar woods. She was beautiful there, standing on one big foot like the earth mother dancer under green canopies. The most beautiful shrine in the whole wide world. Sunlight fell through the cedar on her face like the smiles of clowns.

"I was with her every day. Eating, dancing, singing, we sang old showtunes together, and sometimes I stayed overnight at our shrine. Well, on with the story about this cheap creep Orrel Hanson the whitedude who followed me into the woods one night and found our shrine. He never talked about it and I never saw him following me, but when he started joking around about how I had fallen for a hardgreen coldheart woman, I got the feeling that he knew about the shrine, so I followed him. Did you get that? I followed him following me and sure enough he found her and was climbing all over the earth vision woman under sacred cedar. He was jerking his pecker stub with two fingers and shot right in her face and mouth. All over her breasts. He came right in her mouth and it ran down her chin and breasts and over the tight folds on her dress. I would have killed him there and then, then and there, but I did not want her to see violence in the cedar shrine ... and , well, the truth is, she understands now, but for some reason the whole episode turned me on with a new lust and madness. I just stood there and got turned on watching the whole thing.

"The next day I moved her to an even more secret shrine and never said a thing all summer to the whitedude. I was planning my revenge. I thought of poison and castration, but the more I thought about it the more satisfied I became with the punishment through violent thoughts. So, by the winter I had forgotten about it and told him so, without revealing that I saw him at the shrine. I said, Orrel, I said, you cocksucking whitefaggot, if you ever go near her again you can count yourself dead. He laughed. I could tell something had happened from his laughter, and the way his face twitched. Later that day, through a snow storm, I trudged out to the shrine. When I got there she was gone and the tracks of where the thief had taken her were covered with fresh snow. My eyes felt like they would explode so I squeezed the lids down to slivers of light to keep them in my head. I went straight to his house and waited outside until he came through the door. I grabbed him from behind and pressed my knife against his throat. Tell me where she is, I demanded, but he just smiled and said if I cut him he would never tell me where she was hidden. I pressed the knife deeper into his throat and asked again. He said nothing so I drew the blade across the front of his neck leaving a long shallow cut. The blood oozed from the cut and ran down his neck and soaked into his shirt. He wailed and then clutched his hands to his throat and screamed that he would never tell me where he hid *kitchibiwabik* fucker. I lunged at him with my knife but he jumped aside and ran through the woods leaving drops of blood in the fresh snow.

"Well, I watched him and followed him for several weeks, waiting for him to lead me to *kitchibiwabik*. When he led me nowhere I threatened him again and then offered him money, thinking once I found her I would kill him and take the money back, but he said nothing. When he told me to forget about her I knew he was planning to sell her to some art collector in the cities.

"I was driven with loneliness and started drinking again and then I remembered the white anthropologist. I went to the cities looking for him and more of his vision vine so I could fly back and locate my enemies and *kitchibiwabik*. I waited for several weeks at his mansion but he did not return. Meanwhile my loneliness grew and grew into a fine white flame of hatred for Orrel Hanson who was keeping me from my vision and love. So I returned to the reservation late in the winter and planned to kill him. I watched him for several days, tracked him like an animal, recorded his behavior, his movements, his times and places and who he visited. I wanted his death to be a surprise.

"Late in the morning he skied down a steep hill near his house to the lake on his way to the village. I measured the point of greatest speed and the exact elevation of his neck as he came down the hill and then I strung a single strand of fine steel wire across the hill. Next morning he fastened on his skies and poled to the hill. He came down faster and faster. The wire caught him in the mouth cutting through his cheeks. The tips of his skis lifted from the hill and dangled seconds before the wire broke. The sound of the snapping wire was mixed with his high pitched scream and then he dropped backward. I walked toward him and told him to tell me where she was, but he shook his head. The wire had cut through his flesh from his cheeks to his temples exposing his upper teeth. His eyes had popped out of his head and were dangling on either side of his nose. His jaw was twisted and gaping to one side. His breath gurgled with steaming blood. I asked him again where he had hidden *kitchibiwabik* and he shunned me with his hands. So, without hesitation, I slit a hole in the crotch of his pants and cut his cock and balls out and stuffed them in his mouth. The medical examiner testified at my trial that even though the wire had sliced the hard palate, severing the optic ganglion, and penetrated the brain, the whitefaggot died of suffocation.

"Imagine that. Well, you know the rest about the trial and home sentence so let me tell you how I found my love the next summer in the water. The white anthropologist had disappeared and I could not find anyone with a supply of the vision vine to help me locate *kitchibiwabik*. I waited and waited and then one fine morning in the summer I was canoeing on the lake near where I had killed the white-faggot when she appeared before me like a vision in the water. I thought I was dreaming or throwing her figure ahead of me in my loneliness. There she was, resting upright in about eight feet of clear water. I slipped off my clothes and dove down to be with her. You may not believe this, but I wept with her under water. She drew me to the lake that morning, I knew that, when the water was still because if there had been a slight wind I would not have seen her under a rough surface. Well, what happened was that the whitefaggot had hidden her in an icehouse and come spring when he was dead and the ice melted she slipped into the water and waited there for me to find her. Well, there you have it, our love stories. Except this, when the white-faggot was waving his hand, just before I cut off his cock, I thought he was shunning me with a negative answer, but he could have been pointing to the icehouse on the lake at the bottom of the hill."

Bigfoot slapped his leather covered thighs. The smack flickered through the altar candlelight. From his pocket he presented a thin flat metal cosmetics case which he said contained his traveling supplies of the vision vine. "Never be without it again . . . enough here for all our friends," he said.

Pure Gumption had fallen asleep. Inawa Biwide was still cupping his chin on his knees. He stretched his legs out and turned his head toward the bronze statue. His dark eyes flashed in the candlelight. She was a beautiful woman, he thought.

"Will she travel with us?"

"She will and she could teach you the meaning of love too," Bigfoot answered. "She could give you a vision to live without loneliness."

"Loneliness is not evil."

Bigfoot stepped up to *kitchibiwabik osidaman* and took her outstretched bronze hand. Then he walked with her in a circle and embraced her resting his cheek on her cold breasts. He hummed to himself and shifted back and forth with her on her swivel base. The stranger watched them. He thought he saw her smile. He thought he saw her eyes and hands move in the gentle manner of angels and prairie dream dancers.

The silence was broken by the sound of thumps and clanks outside the trailer. Inawa Biwide opened the double trailer doors and found the other pilgrims examining the truck. The tires were hard and the two tanks were filled with precious gasoline.

Bigfoot and Pio had stolen two government postal trucks the year before. The two clowns backed one into the tunnel and after siphoning the gasoline from the second truck ran it down the hill in neutral. The truck crashed through a guard rail and plunged into the river.

"When do we leave?" asked Sun Bear Sun in a deep rumbling voice. He was supporting Little Big Mouse on his right hip. She stepped out of his arms into the trailer. Moving on the edges of shapes through space, touching the walls of the trailer at all times. She admired the bronze woman. When she was near the statue she let go of the wall and swam across open space to *kitchibiwabik*. She touched the huge feet of the figure.

"Tomorrow night we leave," said Doctor Wilde Coxwain. "Under the blazing darkness of the new autumn moon," he added, waving his arms to emphasize his words. Justice Pardone Cozener, waddling near him in his wide moccasins, smiled wide and pushed his rimless glasses back up on his small fat nose.

Little Big Mouse touched the heel tendon and giant bronze toes of *kitchibiwabik* and looked up to the swelling dark green breasts. "She has warmed to my touch," she whispered.

¶ Abita Animosh

Lilith Mae moved from the fire to the front of the tunnel where the truck and trailer were parked. With the care of an old woman, while her boxers watched with their tongues dangling from the sides of their mouths, she climbed in and spread her handwoven ceremonial tribal blanket on the hard trailer floor. In the center of the blanket, which she received from a pantribal fusion of female sorcerers, there were five figures woven in an even row and circled with a seven color rainbow. The tubular bodies of the figures were similar but the faces changed from a smiling child on one side to part animal child becoming a savage beast on the other side. The beast resembled the visual crossing of bear and dog and child. The colors changed with the features and expressions from white and cool blue to the beast in black and harsh blood red. The beast had deep set necrotic gray eyes. Next she unrolled a quilt decorated with constellations and androgynous celestial human and animal signs over the blanket. She slept with her head over the animal children and the beast. Lilith Mae was protected during sleep from the evil and erotic hostilities of men who would otherwise invade her dreams with foul smelling penises. When she rolled out the quilt she swung her arm back and clipped the snout of one of her boxers.

"You dumb bastard," she said.

The boxer sneezed and blew drool across the trailer. The second boxer licked the face of the first one and then squirmed up to Lilith Mae and pushed his wet nose under her breasts. She held the boxer by his short ears for a few minutes while he snorted and rubbed his nose against her nipples.

"Not now," she said through her teeth. "Not now you dumb

bastards." She pushed them both away when the second boxer moved his wet nose against her crotch and snorted through the thin cotton. The boxers moved back from the ceremonial blanket. Lilith Mae removed her soft leather shoes and let the boxers lick her bare feet while she wriggled her toes against their cold blunt noses.

Inawa Biwide was watching the boxers.

"My feet perspire," she said while the boxers moved up her legs. She put her feet on their noses and pushed them back. "When I am nervous my feet perspire and the boxers love the salt."

When Inawa Biwide looked into her wide green eyes she became nervous and uncomfortable. He knelt near the end of the blanket. The boxers slobbered over her short toes. She pushed them back several times when their noses climbed her legs.

"You are strange," Lilith Mae said with a nervous smile. She looked into his dark eyes for a few seconds and then turned toward the constellations. She stretched her neck and cleared her throat.

"Silence is not strange," he said.

"Where did you come from?"

"I am with Bishop Omax Parasimo."

"Now I remember, yes, I did see you there ... you were there lighting the candles while I was confessing," she said with less stress in her voice. "But I mean, where did you come from?" she asked again, as she spread four fingers over the quilted zodiacal constellation of Pisces. She touched the four stars of her birth sign. "Did you come from the reservation to live here?" The fingers of her other hand walked across the quilted heavens to the constellation *kitchi animosh,* canis major.

"Do you like your dogs?" he asked.

"No, I hate them," Lilith Mae answered, snapping her fingers at the boxers. Their huge jaws were resting on their front paws. The animals looked up at her, lifting great wrinkles of flesh over their eyes. "Look at them ... the dumb bastards remind me of my slobbering father."

"But the animals love you."

"So did my rotten father ... What is your birth sign?" she asked in a high falsetto voice while she pressed flat the folds in the constellations.

He pointed to the ram of Aries.

She ignored his response and continued talking about stars and time. Inawa Biwide lighted a white altar candle and placed it between them near the blanket while she talked about tribal people and reservations.

"The tribal women made fun of me," she said. "For two years they made fun of me, calling me *abita animosh,* half dog, the woman who makes love with dogs and then telling me it meant I was a person who was kind to dogs and loved to feed them. The women made fun of me on purpose. They made a fool of me for two years and I will never forget that. Never. They made a fool of me just like my stepfather did when I was eight years old. He took me on a camping trip and told me that all fathers and daughters share a secret and then made me suck the head of his fat purple penis until it spit all over me. It was awful, just awful, but I never could keep a secret. Never. That much is a good thing for me because I told my mother when we got back to the house. We were sitting at the dinner table, my mother and stepfather and two older brothers, when I told them all in vivid detail how he made me suck his penis. My brothers snickered and looked into their laps. Stepfather choked on a mouthful of food. His neck and cheeks twitched while he told me not to talk like that at the table, and where did I learn such bad words. But mother would not be fooled, no——woman should be fooled by a penis. She turned red, so red she began to perspire. Then she began to whine like a frightened animal. The whine turned into rage. First she threw things at him and then she threw him out of the house for good. Later mother joined a group of twice divorced women and we got along fine without an evil man lurking around for a place to put his foul smelling penis.

"Just fine. I finished college and went to work on the reservation teaching in an experimental school and the women there made a fool out of me. *Abita animosh, abita animosh* half dog, they shouted to me when I fed the dogs. *Abita animosh* and then laughed at me. I thought they were amusing people and loved what I was doing there. I had no idea they were evil and laughing at me because I had not learned the language. Of course, you know about reservation mongrels. I started feeding two or three mutts at first. They hung around the school to be with the kids. I was living in the teacher house right across the road and it became a habit. I fed two or three school mongrels when school was out in the afternoon. As the weeks passed, more and more dogs came to school, not for school but to be fed when school was out, you see. It was plain and simple that it was getting out of hand when two dozen dogs were hanging around my house waiting to be fed every afternoon. So I hit on the idea of filling the back of my travel van with dogfood and driving around the reservation feeding the dogs. I would drive up, ring a small dinner bell I found at an antique sale, and then lower the ramp from the rear doors of my van so the dogs would walk up and in to eat. And they sure did eat. It became a full time job after teaching all day, just feeding all those mongrels. The women would shout at me when I drove up, *abita animosh abita animosh*, and then holding their swaying stomachs in laughter. They laughed all the time while the dogs ran up the ramp into my van to be fed. They laughed and I thought they were thanking me for being so generous to their goddamn reservation mongrels. They must have thought I was making love with all those dogs. For a whole school year they made a fool of me at my feeding stops when I rang the dinner bell. Ding ding ding ding ding ding dingaling. Look at the boxers perking up their ears, they remember when. They remember how I hated them. How I cursed at them and would not permit them to eat in my van with the other dogs. I hated them because they reminded me of my stepfather. I would have nothing to do with them. But they followed me everywhere. Always begging for food. Ding ding ding ding ding ding dingaling. I never gave them even a smell of food. They were the only dogs I refused to feed on the reservation. The only two, and now like a noose around my neck I am leashed to them forever . . . forever. What ever happened to innocence, the first recess in school? Never let me hear you say that my life has gone to the you know whats.

"Listen to the last part which has some humor even though I was run off the reservation in humiliation. But then a fool is never at home. Run off the rotten reservation, as if I cared. Those bastards. It was the best thing that even happened to me. I might still be there taking all that crap in. Taking in that idealistic shit about the humble people so close to mother earth. Close to my ass. Nothing honest about those school board members who came into my hotel room at an education conference and violated my body several times. I could have appreciated the attention, but they were drunk and three is a bit much for a green beginner. I was willing until they told me what *abita animosh* meant and then they made jokes about me doing it with all those goddamn mongrels in the back of my van. Then they forced me into all sorts of things. Enough of that, the point is that their wives found out and while I was teaching one afternoon the women who had made fun of me loaded up my van with all my belongings, including several hundred pounds of dogfood, and when school ended for the day they told me to get moving and never come back. There was nothing to do but hit the road, so I climbed into the cab, started the engine, turned the van around, gave the women the finger and roared out of the school yard. The dogs saw me leaving and thought it was time to eat again, so they all came out to the road and ran after the van. Hundreds of mongrels were running after me by the time I reached the highway leading off the reservation. Hundreds of yelping mongrels.

"It made me sad seeing all those dogs who believed in me, not the people mind you, they made fun of me, but all those dogs who trusted and appreciated me. They never made fun of me. It made me sad and I was crying. One by one the mongrels dropped off the chase until only the two boxers were running behind the van. They must have run more than ten miles so I stopped and let them in the back to eat. I was still crying and lonely and they were so grateful that they could finally eat from the van that they have been with me ever since. They know how to take care of me now, but I still hate them because they do remind me of my stepfather ... I have said enough. You must have something to say. Living in this tunnel for the past week has made me lose track of time. But I have myself ready to leave whenever we leave. Tomorrow. Flick, flick, how I hate you fatherfuckers, how I hate you and love you at the same time."

She flicked the noses of the boxers with her finger and then pulled the constellation quilt up around her shoulders. Her passionless eyes gathered the pale light from the candle. She sighed. The boxers dragged their bodies along the floor with their front feet until they reached the edge of the blanket.

"I lived with the mongrels on that reservation," said Inawa Biwide. "Grandmother told me stories about a woman who loved all the dogs on the reservation."

"Foolishness becomes tradition."

"Foolishness but not fools become tradition ... Grandmother told me about a child who gave birth to five mongrel pups. It was their custom that animals sleep at the foot of their beds ... but one dog became a dream man during the night and made love with the child."

The seven clown crows swooped into the trailer from the tunnel and cut the darkness with their blackness. The candle flickered their enormous shadows on the walls. The crows crowed and perched on the head and shoulders of *kitchibiwabik osidaman*.

Lilith Mae was closed in her constellation blanket like a prairie flower under the moon. The boxers moved closer and huddled on the changing child blanket. The boxers watched the clown crows on the statue.

"Her father and mother were shamed," he continued. "They burned their possessions, killed the lover mongrel and left the pregnant child alone to die.

"But the crows knew of her love for animals and directed her to a place where she could find fire and warmth. The crows brought her food and sacred objects from the woodland and prairie and helped her care for the five mongrel babies ... But the crows are not just good to people. The crows are cosmic clowns ... wisefools and tricksters. When the mother went out to gather food near the river the crows brought the mongrels into human form through humor and taught them to dance. One day the mother caught them laughing as humans and scolded them until the babies were ashamed and turned back into mongrels. The crows became hostile and swooped down on her for being so mean about humans. Mother was so ashamed that she praised her mongrels back to human form, burned their animal blankets and taught them how to be good hunters. The mongrel humans became great hunters like the crows and when the frightened villagers, the ones who had left the mother to die, were suffering from famine the mongrels brought them food. The tribes gave them the power of their lives. The mongrels and their mother were honored but no one told the secret of their birth. The crows know which of our lives are birds and animals and humans."

Lilith Mae smiled. Her nose wrinkled and her eyes closed. The boxers nosed her breasts. One boxer caught her nipple, hard beneath her thin dress, in his blunt wet nostril. She lowered herself on the blanket and caressed the chests and stomachs of her animals.

Inawa Biwide watched the boxers snort and drool over their mistress in the candlelight. He pinched the flame on the altar candle. The rear doors were open and the fire at the other end of the tunnel filled the trailer space with a shadowless copper aura.

Lilith Mae unbuttoned the top of her dress. She touched the genitalia of the boxers while they nosed her firm breasts, holding her nipples in their nostrils. The boxers moved down her soft stomach and thrust their blunt wet noses against her vulva. She sighed and raised one knee. The boxers touched her bare vaginal lips with their cold noses.

When the boxers mounted her knee and thigh Lilith Mae pushed them aside, opened a small canvas case and pulled out four soft leather thumbless mittens which she tied to the front paws of the boxers. The leather mittens protected her from paw scratches. The boxers raised their paws in ceremonial expectations until the mittens were tied. Lilith Mae removed her dress and leaned forward on the blanket with her face next to those of the changing faces of children and animals. Her buttocks were elevated and glowing in the copper aura. The first boxer mounted her with his leather padded paws around her waist and began his sexual motions near her glowing cheeks until his penis bloomed like a stiff flower and slipped between her wet and waiting vaginal lips. The second boxer licked her shoulders while she sighed and moaned and dreamed of falling through sensuous secrets on a warm wind with her wide lips opened.

The first boxer ejaculated in powerful bursts and shuddered against her buttocks. The band of muscles on the head of his penis bulged and throbbed between her contracting vaginal muscles. She tossed her head from side to side on the blanket faces. Then the second boxer mounted her and thrust his flaming penis into her vulva. The sound of her deep animal moaning and the motions of the panting boxer padded through the trailer and tunnel. Conversations stopped near the fire. Proude Cedarfair raised his head in front of the fire, closed his eyes, spread his arms, and moaned in a low voice ha ha ha haaaa.

¶ Watering at Lourdes

Past midnight on the night of the first new moon of autumn after the democratic government had failed and fuel supplies were exhausted, Sun Bear Sun pressed the accelerator several times, turned the ignition switch and started the truck engine. The engine hesitated, popped and then howled in the tunnel. The huge steel doors at one end of the tunnel were pushed open. The cool moist air rushed into the tunnel and mixed with the nose pinching stench of the engine exhaust. Sun Bear Sun pulled the shift lever into gear and the bicentennial red white and blue postal truck and trailer moved out of the tunnel and through the weeds like a howling reptilian ghost. He turned right down the hill and across the *misisibi* on the new federal bridge. The mercenaries waved them on never questioning the postal service. There was enough precious national gasoline in the truck tanks to drive to What Cheer in the middle of Iowa.

Little Big Mouse, Bishop Parasimo and Private Jones rode in the cab of the truck. The other pilgrims rode in the trailer with *kitchibiwabik osidaman* and the animals and seven clown crows. The truck bore through the night heading for Waterloo and south down the old roads through Buckingham and Montezuma. The grande caravan of tribal pilgrims would reach What Cheer before morning.

"Why what cheer?" asked Little Big Mouse.

"Gasoline gasoline gasoline precious golden gasoline," chanted Bishop Parasimo three times, his trine word habit in speech. The dashboard lights flashed like beads in his agate eyes as he gestured with his hands and face. "In What Cheer is a man known as the evil gambler ... He is evil and has gasoline for sale, enough perhaps perhaps perhaps to reach our new world paradise in New Mexico."

The roads were rough. Weeds and small trees were growing through the cracks and seams lifting the black asphalt. The cab of the truck thumped and shook over the holes and rubbish on the road.

"What do you have in that neat black case there?" asked Little Big Mouse, moving her short purewhite fingers over the hinges and locks like an insect.

"There are three metamasks in there," Bishop Parasimo replied, pushing the case out of her reach. "You have seen one, the one I was wearing when we first met . . . you should remember."

"Yes, I remember . . . let me see."

"The other masks are secrets," he said through tight thin lips. He stretched his right hand fingers and turned his gold ring with his thumb. Bishop Parasimo liked his hands and often spoke to them when he was alone. In public his hands, the right one in particular, often followed his speech as if the two were personal critics of his spoken form and content. In the cloister his hands spoke to each other in shadows on the white walls. His right hand was the most assertive and cultured conversationalist. His right hand had opinions and terminal creeds. He ran one finger on his right hand under his nose and snorted.

Bishop Parasimo was the map reader, directing Sun Bear Sun down the old roads through the small towns to avoid the government mercenaries and the interstate highways where millions of lost souls were walking to nowhere. The postal service truck and trailer roared through Kenyon, Dodge Center, Hayfield, Rose Creek and crossed the boarder between Minnesota and Iowa at Le Roy. The rural roads were deserted, people in small towns were hostile toward those from the cities who had consumed all the fuel and resources with electrical devices. Cities were left to the hostiles and their culture of corruption and consumption. The hostilities of rural people forced evacuees from the cities in search of food to use the interstates on their footmarches south to warmer winters.

"The engine is running hot," said Sun Bear Sun. "I think we need some water for the old postal horse . . . We should stop somewhere soon."

Bishop Parasimo, with his graceful right hand speaking, told him to pull up at a large white frame farmhouse near the creek on the edge of a small town. Sun Bear Sun geared the truck engine down and rumbled to a stop in front of the house.

Bernadette and Devlin, the old farm couple living in the house, were awakened by the roar of the engine. The two shuffled to the front of the house on the second floor and looking out the window saw the bicentennial postal truck on the fallow drive. The doors on the truck cab and trailer opened and out flew seven crows, out leaped four dogs, one glowing, out stepped a mammoth and a giant and a child and an old couple with braids and a woman wrapped in a constellation quilt and a bishop dressed in his ceremonial vestments and velvet dalmatic.

"Mother," said the old farmer turning from the front window toward his third wife, "have we gone . . . Have we left this world for the good circus?"

"The devil sends those clowns and animals here tonight," said Bernadette while she backed away from the window clutching her flannel nightdress against her tense and wrinkled throat. "The devil Devlin . . . The devil!"

The devil comes at night dancing through the blackness under crow wings high wings . . . The devil comes at night dancing under old hair wings . . . Watch the blackness for the scarecrow devils . . . Draw the fingers of the devil through the wings of night hair.

"Blessings upon your lives," said Bishop Parasimo, moving his left hand in the sign of the cross to the farmer and his wife when they answered his gentle knock at their door. "Could you be so kind kind kind as to tell us where we are on this good good good earth?"

"Shun the devil Devlin . . . Shun the blackness of the devil Devlin," warned Bernadette while she drew her knotted fingers through her hair.

"Clowns, are you clowns?" asked Devlin.

"Not as we talk at this threshold tonight."

"Circus, is this the last circus?"

"We are a caravan of freedom seeking tribal pilgrims pilgrims pilgrims, dear father, having lost our places in the old time places in dreams and we seek directions and a little water for ourselves and this fine postal machine," said Bishop Parasimo. His right hand followed his words.

"Shun the devil Devlin."

"Lourdes," said Devlin. "You have brought your lost circus to Lourdes . . . Lourdes, Lourdes, Iowa, place of few virgins now, but the watering is good and clean, never been drunk before from the well."

"Lourdes . . . three times said."

"Shun the devil Devlin," warned Bernadette.

"Mister are you the devil?"

The devil comes at night dancing through the blackness under crow wings high wings . . . The devil comes at night dancing under old hair wings.

"Bless you and your missus back back back there in the wings," said Bishop Parasimo to his right hand. "From the shadows these are not the hands of the devil devil devil now nor does he travel with the pilgrims in this caravan tonight . . . But I know where the dancing devil lives tomorrow."

"Mister where is that tomorrow?"

"Watch his black wings."

"What Cheer."

"What cheer where?"

"What Cheer down the road."

Sun Bear Sun filled the truck radiator and their water containers. The animals ran in the tall grass over the fields behind the house and the clown crows flapped in their blackness and soared high winging down the creek through the trees. The late night air was still like a child holding her breath.

Lilith Mae amused the old farmer woman of the house with stories about birth signs and moon signs and wing signs of the constellations. The old woman ran her fingers through her hair and begged her fortune told and it was told in good rural fantasies of lush gardens and dark servants. Satisfied with their places the circus pilgrims climbed back into the truck and trailer, pulled the doors closed on time behind them and roared out of the drive and onto the road toward morning and tomorrow.

Farmer Devlin dropped the stiff curtains on the circus when the trailer lights disappeared down the road. Then he burped twice and turned back to his loneliness and his grave bed. Bernadette turned out the lights and flew in the blackness of her dreams.

¶ What Cheer Trailer Ruins

Sir Cecil Staples dreams in themes of great rivers dark and deep. Coiled stoutwhite on a leather chair behind his heart shaped desk he is dressed in a shortsleeved tan uniform. Small silver birds are pinned to the epaulets on his shirt. He wears a translucent obsidian pendant on a beaded chain and a diamond ring on his little finger. His bald head, marked with dark pigmentation like tracks from small birds, droops forward on his chest. His upper lip twitches like that of a sleeping desert animal.

Across the narrow carpeted room from the evil gambler, on the eastern wall near the entrance to the black metal altar trailer, are two complete skeletons. Their whitebones touching in fleshless passion. Next to the lusting skeletons are detailed scale models of the What Cheer Trailer Ruins. The ceremonial interstate trucking monument was planned by Sir Cecil in honor of his truck driving mother. The model trailers are arranged in useless concentric circles with two altar trailers upended against the narrow sides of the main black trailer. Inside, mounted on the walls between the model ruins and his desk, are hundreds of wooden and metal traps and rare instruments of torture. The wall behind him is covered with a photographic mural of the southern *misisibi* flowing dark and deep. The pendulum clock next to the skeletons knelled eleven times, seven sun hours late, while his mother hummed her derivative poems to him from the comfortable cab of her truck hurtling across the prairie in his dreams:

new families on the open roads
traveling
running the open roads
rivers and trucks running dark and deep
dark and deep
dark and deep
but we have promises to keep
and miles
and miles of interstate to go
before we sleep
running dark and deep

Sun Bear Sun handled the great postal truck and the caravan of tribal circus pilgrims through the little church town of What Cheer, searching for a sign of the evil gambler, the monarch of unleaded gasoline. The truck roared and rumbled up and down the peaceful streets in the pale green morning, startling good town families from their gentle sleep.

"He will not be living in these little little little stillborn supermarket houses," said Bishop Parasimo, his right hand counting by twos the screen porches and trimmed shrubs of his visual vicinage. "He would not be hiding here ... He would not be hiding!"

"But sure sure sure," said Little Big Mouse, mocking the trine word habit of the bishop. "We are all hiding wherever we live." Her eyes were touching all the houses like stereotropic fingers moving across the surface rows and folds and corners on the block.

"He has nothing to hide but his gasoline," said Bishop Parasimo through firm lips while he gestured to Sun Bear Sun to turn toward the edge of the little town. "He will be on the edge somewhere boasting boasting boasting ... not here with these fair families."

Sun Bear Sun turned the truck and trailer toward the main road entering the town and rumbled down the wide boulevard past abandoned automatic laundries, new and used car dealerships, dead service stations faced with weeds and new wild trees. Near the edge of the town across from several deserted fastfood restaurants there appeared the large sign of the evil gambler:

SIR CECIL STAPLES
The Monarch of Unleaded Gasoline
and
The Mixedblood Horde of Mercenaries
Presenting
LIVING OR DYING FOR GASOLINE
Gamble for Five Gallons
NEW TRAPS AND OLD TORTURES
Follow the Rows of Abandoned Cars to the Altar Trailers
OPEN FOR EVIL BUSINESS

The truck crept over the gravel drive past double rows of cars which had been abandoned without gasoline. At the end of the road near the trailer altars three mixedblood mercenaries waved their rifles. The truck hissed and moaned to a stop. "Out with your hands folded on your fat heads," said two of the mercenaries pulling open the doors. The seven crows and the four animals were the first to emerge from the cavernous trailer into the light of morning. The clown crows swooped and skipped over the rows of cars and circled the trailer altars before flapping low over the startled and confused mercenaries. The boxers ran down the rows of cars pissing on all the tires. Private Jones stretched and smiled and then nodded around the trailers greeting and sniffing the feet and legs of the mixedbloods. He sneezed twice. Pure Gumption shunned the mercenaries.

Using both hands to speak from the top of his head, Bishop Parasimo asked the mercenaries to announce the arrival of the grande caravan of tribal pilgrims to the monarch of gasoline. "And inquire inquire inquire, if you please, as to his willingness to gamble a few gallons of gasoline this fine morning." The three mixedbloods, dressed in diverse combinations of tribal vestments and martial uniforms, bangles and ideological power patches and armbands, watched the hands talking over his head and then looked at each other. Deep furrows of ignorance and intolerance stretched across their unwashed foreheads.

Willie Burke, the Tlingit and Russian mixedblood, had a compulsive need to kill plants and animals and trees. He raised his arms to speak with his hands. The crows saw that his gestures were threatening and swooped on him and scratched his head with their claws. Willie drooled with rage and the furrows on his forehead deepened. When he raised his shotgun toward the crows, Pio Wissakodewinini, the transsexual parawoman mammoth clown, kicked him in the groin with his steel toed boot. Willie crumpled in the middle, his eyes crossed and uncrossed before turning under, and he fell in slow motion with his nose to the gravel. Then Pio pressed his boot on the forearm of the unconscious mixedblood until the bones snapped. Meanwhile, the other two mercenaries were disarmed, one by the snarling boxers and the other by Sun Bear Sun with Little Big Mouse hanging like a marsupial animal from her foot holsters at his side.

Pio turned from the scene in shame and slipped into the darkness of the trailer. His cheeks trembled as he walked. Private Jones followed him tossing his head and sneezing.

"So much for the hired help," said Matchi Makwa. "Now show us to that gambling leader in his pile of weird trailers."

"Wait ... wait! Just one damn minute ... One minute while we question these fools," said Doctor Wilde.

"For what?" asked Matchi Makwa.

"For the location of the gasoline ... No need to gamble," said Doctor Wilde Coxwain as he strolled in a slow circle around the two mercenaries. "Well, well, well, what do we have here," he said flicking his fingers at their bodies. "Some new third world doublecross ... Breathing plastic artifacts from reservation main street ... Would you look at their uniforms, all beads and plastic bone and chicken feathers. My, my, my," he said waving his thin arms, "here stand the classic hobbycraft mannikins dressed in throwaway pantribal vestments, promotional hierograms of cultural suicide."

"For the record ... would you state your names?" asked Justice Pardone Cozener, the short fat horsetrader, tribal mouthpiece and teacher of tribal law. He waited with his fingers tucked under his turquoise studded belt. His hands moved with his stomach as he breathed. "Your names, your names, sumpter mercenaries!" Pardone demanded.

"Cree Casket," said the mixedblood tribal trained cabinet maker with the blue chicken feather vestments.

"Cree casket?"

"Casket is my injun name . . ." He was watching his interrogator curl his toes upward in his shoes and roll from side to side on his fat ankles. "I was trained in the government schools to be a cabinet maker, but all the cabinets were machine made so making custom made wooden caskets made more sense ... Making caskets to fit the corpses, little ones, big ones, wide ones and thin ones. I even made a special one legged casket for a mad medicine man."

"Have you ever been in prison?" asked Little Big Mouse, leaning out from her leather foot holsters.

"Not for long."

"For what?"

"For fucking."

"Dead women in wooden boxes."

"Casket, would you like a living fuck?"

"No!" snorted Casket. "Not on your life."

"Then would you like a dead piece?"

"That would be nice again," Casket replied. "But there have been hundreds here ... The women drive in in packs for a tank of gas and gamble down their lives."

"Tell me, where can we find the gasoline?"

"Somewhere underground somewhere."

"Somewhere where?" demanded Doctor Wilde while he waved his arms at the mixedblood mercenaries. Casket shrugged his shoulders, never looking above his feet.

"Who is this red remount over here with the green and pink stained chicken feathers?" questioned Pardone. He pointed with his chin toward the one with the grin that stretched his fat lips wide across his broken teeth.

"Carmine Cutthroat," Casket answered. "He hears nothing and knows nothing but hand speaking in sign language."

"Then get those hands going and ask him where the gasoline is stored," droned Pardone, who removed his fingers from his belt for the first time to gesture to the feathered mute.

"Do it now, tell him with your hands."

Casket waved one hand in front of Carmine Cutthroat to clear the speaking space and gather his attention for hand to hand conversation. The little casket maker touched his arm, wagged his fingers, and made circles in the air, twitched his cheek muscles, rolled his lips and raised his brows at the mute mixedblood.

"Well, what does he say? Where is the gasoline?"

Casket ignored Justice Pardone and continued his hand to hand conversation until Doctor Wilde grabbed his hands and stopped their talking. Cutthroat was frowning, doubt and misunderstanding spreading across his dark red face like thunderbirds. Then he started, his motions were sudden at first, as if he were critical of the pilgrims, but in a few words his gestures look on the graceful and dramatic movements of ballet dancers.

"Casket, what is he saying?"

The two chicken feathered mixedbloods swooped their gestures like birds and danced over words on phrases in hand. Their hands laughed and clowned together. The pilgrims moved forward to watch and listen. The clown crows stretched their necks. Pure Gumption rolled over in the stiff weeds beside the gravel road and moaned.

"Bishop Omax Parasimo," Pardone called in a formal drone. "Put on your masks and come over here please and translate this hand gibberish so we can find the gasoline ... Can you imagine signing treaties and taking depositions from these two handfucking fools?"

Bishop Parasimo watched for a few minutes. Then, as if his hands had minds of their own, he started picking up on the hand to hand conversation until there were six hands dancing through the secrets and silence of visual space.

"Stop it ... stop it!" screamed Wilde as he waved his arms in wild circles and ran through the circle of hands. "Stop it ... all we want to know is the location of the gasoline storage tank ... Stop that reservation gossiping!"

"Their speech is prairie reservation hand to hand parlance based on the old old old reverent gestures of missionaries and the harsh hand signals of the cavalry," Bishop Parasimo explained.

"Now where is the gasoline?"

"We are getting to that," said Bishop Parasimo, looking down at his idle hands. "You might say these clowns clowns clowns speak the bilingual signs of calvary and cavalry."

"Rather," said Bigfoot as he strutted forward into the circle of hand speakers, "their speech is a handsome hand to mouth finger on the torch." Looking downward, Casket watched his huge feet thump across the gravel.

"Would you get to the gasoline?" pleaded Pardone as he thrust his short fat fingers back between his stomach and his turquoise belt.

The three speakers touched their hands in a circle and then resumed their six handed conversation. Bishop Parasimo spoke over his right shoulder from time to time to Inawa Biwide. Catching words and phrases hand to mouth and flipping them in spoken words overhand out of the silent conversation circle. Carmine Cutthroat . . . Papago and Mescalero mixedblood . . . likes to kill to kill . . . concentrates on the throat . . . uses hands and knives and saws and wire and rope . . . has killed more than three hundred whitepeople . . . less than one third were women . . . likes women . . . lost his voice to seven whitechildren in a park . . . he was sleeping near the wide river where the ponies drink in the spring . . . whitechildren poured hot lead down his throat . . . voice went up in smoke . . ."

"Hand over the gasoline," droned Pardone.

"Hot lead turned him carmine red . . . last word he heard from a whiteman he killed . . . waited until the seven whitechildren were grown men . . . bound them with wire . . . killed them one by one . . . burned their crotch hair with a blowtorch."

"The gasoline . . . the gasoline!"

"Then he burned their ears . . . you can see what he is telling now . . . watch him . . . the genitals and then at last the throat . . . he learned to speak with his hands from the old animals in the mountains . . . Sir Cecil Staples is talking through him now . . . mean man . . . loves him and hates him . . . the best kind of whiteman to know."

"Where is the gasoline?"

"The gasoline for *kitchibiwabik.*"

"The gasoline!"

"There now," said Bishop Parasimo over his shoulder, "watch his hands because he is talking about gasoline . . . Hidden somewhere he thinks . . . he has never seen it . . . has never smelled it . . . he has never heard a word from where it is hiding . . . gasoline does not speak for him . . . he does know where it is in the earth . . . he knows about an old man in the mountains who can find gasoline . . . he could find gasoline but he never drove a machine . . . never had a use for a gasoline machine."

"Shit, all this handfucking for nothing," moaned Wilde. "Well, shit, tell him to throw up his hands and take a wild guess."

"He is telling stories about seeing and knowing the earth with hands and timeless visions," said Bishop Parasimo. "Gasoline eludes those who seek it . . . his advice now, stop looking and what will be seen will be seen."

"Carlos Castenada told him that," said Belladonna.

"Handfucker," sneered Wilde. "Tell the bastards to take their clothes off now . . . strip so we can see that carmine flesh under those chicken feathers." He waved his arms and dipped his head like a water bird.

"Fine idea," droned Pardone.

Wilde and Pardone moved into the conversation circle and pulled chicken feathers from the mixedblood mercenaries. The pink and green and blue feathers floated to the gravel while the mixedbloods continued telling hand stories. Justice Pardone was breathing hard as his vulgar hands swarmed over the dorsal cheeks of the mercenaries. Doctor Wilde deplumed the mixedbloods and then pinched their dark hard nipples.

¶ Words on the Altar

Proude Cedarfair found the two black upturned altar trailers in the center of the ruins. He called to the others and then entered the dark trailer without knocking. Pure Gumption followed him through the double doors.

The skeletons trembled, their bones gleamed in the morning light rushing through the doors. The trailer space was held in hardened screams and the air was parched. Proude waited at the opposite end of the trailer from the evil gambler. Pure Gumption glowed beside him.

The gambler dipped his bald head and wheezed.

When the pilgrims arrived the trailer had the sweet smell of wildflowers. The evil gambler stopped wheezing. He smiled and spoke in melodious tones to the visitors. He told the pilgrims about his trailer monument and ruins. Inawa Biwide moved with caution past the instruments of torture on the walls clicking his tongue at the mechanical traps.

"I seek no one to come and gamble with me but those who would gamble for their lives," the monarch of gasoline explained. His soothing voice had overtones of hissing and echoes of fiendish groans. "I demand nothing but the lives of those who gamble with me for gasoline and lose . . . The losers choose their own means of death.

"The skeletons there near the door were a couple who chose strangulation with wire during a fuck . . . Carmine Cutthroat accommodated their death wish."

The altar trailer filled with dozens of mixedblood mercenaries from his heinous horde. The mercenaries, who had been waiting in the trailer barracks, carried knives and had painted their faces with green and black and brown blotches. Carmine Cutthroat and Cree Casket, featherless and still talking with their hands, were the last to enter the trailer.

"I have spared you all from the horde," chortled the evil gambler as he stood up behind his heart shaped desk in front of the river mural. His shape was almost round. "So that you could stake your lives on gasoline . . . Which of you will be the first to gamble with me?"

"We have not decided," said Belladonna.

"Then how will you decide?"

"We have not decided."

"Five gallons or one of your precious lives," sneered the evil gambler. The sweet air turned acrid with his evil scorn. His rasping laughter and snorting caused the metal birds on his shirt to undulate and escape in flight from the epaulets. "Come . . . who will be the first to challenge me at the dish game? Who will throw the four directions with me? . . . Come, who will be the first to soothe his dark soul with the lust of chance?"

There was silence. Inawa Biwide clicked his tongue turning from the traps. The pilgrims looked at each other. Justice Pardone and Doctor Wilde moved hand in hand toward the back of the trailer, pausing to whisper near the skeletons.

Private Jones sneezed.

The evil gambler coiled back into his leather chair and waited for the pilgrims to respond to his challenge. His pigment tracked bald head dipped as he wheezed through his world of eternal darkness. The timeless underworld swirled in blackness through his blunted vision.

"Tell me stories," Bigfoot said in a teasing tone when the pilgrims began to leave the trailer. "Tell me this is not the second coming or going . . . at least the second morning listening to that bald creep in there."

"We can beat the bastard," said Matchi Makwa.

The pilgrims discussed how the good gambler would be chosen. The methods of selection were all biased. "Goodness should be the measure against evil," suggested Little Big Mouse, "the most good person should be the gambler." Belladonna insisted that the choice be based on chance. The problem was in the meaning of chance. Chance did not have a chance. "Nothing is chance," said Proude. "There is no chance in chance . . . Chances are terminal creeds."

"Numbers, choose numbers," said Sun Bear Sun.

"How?"

"We all pick a number."

"But who is to pick the winning or losing number?"

"How about Inawa Biwide?" asked Rosina Cedarfair.

"No, our chances will not be left to his strange chance," said Doctor Wilde, speaking for himself and Justice Pardone. The two of them were leaning against each other back to back. "We have not considered a competition as a means of selection . . . We could caucus and hold elections or we could nominate and vote our good gambler into action."

"Politics is the opposite of chance."

"Words could be offered," Bishop Parasimo explained. "We could each choose a list of words, the words we most most most appreciate, words that have power and special meaning to each of us and then we could each choose words from each list . . . Suppose we each put together a list of thirteen words, one word for each of us . . .''

"Words are too minded," said Wilde.

"But we each have the same degree of bias in the selection of our words," said Belladonna in defense of the word list. "But how can we choose someone from the word lists?"

"Well," Bishop Parasimo began, raising his hands in comfortable positions to speak with him, "we need but twelve words, because, you see see see, we need not choose a word from our own lists, so it would sound like this . . . now, we each put together a list of twelve words and then we each write one of those words down on the palm palm palm of our hands and clench our fists to keep it a secret until we have all selected our words from the other lists . . ." His hands gestured the values of the numbers. "We take turns each choosing one word from each list list list. Then we mark the words we choose and at the end we throw open our fists and count who has selected the greatest number of secret words . . . The pilgrim with the most secret words will be our good gambler."

"But what if the good gambler loses?" asked Pardone.

"Good question," said Bishop Parasimo. "The pilgrim who gambles, the good gambler, is the pilgrim who loses his or her life, unless of course course course someone should care to volunteer right now to save us all the trouble of choosing the good gambler."

"We are all gamblers," said Matchi Makwa, "but it seems to me we are not all fools."

"It is not foolish to choose a time and place to die," said Proude. "Fools praise chance to avoid the fear of death . . . We must fear the living to leave so much death to chance . . . We are fools with terminal creeds when we gamble with chance."

The pilgrims lined up and wrote their twelve words down in rows on the side of an altar trailer. Sun Bear Sun could not write, the victim of an alternative survival education, so he whispered his words to Little Big Mouse who swung from her foot holsters at his waist and wrote them down next to her list. Instead of telling her his secret word he asked her to number his words so that he could write a number, which he knew how to duplicate, in the palm of his hand. The four animals and seven clown crows lined up to watch the pilgrims writing on the walls of the trailer.

Little Big Mouse wrote her misspelled tree names in a neat pile like fire wood: basswood, *birch,* dutch elm, oak, maple, aspin, catalpa, ceder, cottonwood, magnolia, dogwood, willo.

The misspelled words of Sun Bear Sun were the colors of the rising and setting suns: 1 scarlet, *2 puce,* 3 red, 4 crimsun, 5 wine, 6 pipestone, 7 maroon, 8 cereese, 9 vermilion, 10 carmin, 11 mineum, 12 cardnal.

Zebulon Matchi Makwa wrote the following words in two wide columns: cocksuck, cuntlick, dickslim, nixon, cornhole, father-fucker, balllick, bureau of indian affairs, bottomhump, queersuck, lipcome, *blowpost.*

Benito Saint Plumero presented in a neat row the names of presidents in bold printed letters: grant, monroe, *carter,* jackson, polk, fillmore, taft, coolidge, garfield, cleveland, hoover, truman.

"Carter was the beginning of the end for the little people," said Bigfoot as he printed the names of the presidents. "That southern evangel stuffed the house with commoners and fucked us with his heart and mind . . . Trailed the nation into the temptations of the old believers and reformers but he could not deliver us from our own evil . . . Who has the courage to choose the name carter?"

Bishop Omax Parasimo quoted a Pentecostal hymn for his twelve words: hail, once *despised* jesus, galilean king, thou didst suffer to release us.

"I bring you now the promise of the time when the red man of the prairie will rule the world and not be turned from the hunting grounds," chanted Belladonna Darwin-Winter Catcher. She was quoting a translated speech of Kicking Bear. "The great spirit told me this," she said, "I will cover the earth with new soil to a depth of five times the height of man and under this new soil will be buried all the whites. Kicking Bear knows what is coming down." The pilgrims were not surprised with her list of tribal heroes: kicking bear, crazy horse, sitting bull, spotted tail, red cloud, little raven, *red elk,* ten bears, black hawk, chief joseph, gall, geronimo.

"Listen to what Ten Bears said," she said, clenching her fist over her secret word: "I was born upon the prairie, where the wind blew free, and there was nothing to break the light of the sun. I was born where there were no enclosures and where everything drew a free breath . . . "

"Superserious crap," snapped Matchi Makwa.

Pio Wissakodewinini quoted words from a verse in a century old hymnal published in the *anishinabe* tribal language by the Lake Forest Children of the Church of the Holy Spirit in Illinois. The mammoth wrote the words on the trailer wall and then he spoke them in his parawoman halting voice: kichitau tibicut waseiaziwin ma ayamagut ayad *mary* panizit abinodji nigit umbe anwebiyuk.

Inawa Biwide, the stranger, listed his twelve words which were, save one, variations on the spelling of his own tribal name: inawa, nawai, awain, waina, ainaw, *voices,* biwide, iwideb, widebi, idebiw, debiwi, ebiwid.

Rosina Parent Cedarfair listed some of the names of characters from the beginning of their pilgrimage: sister tallulah, eternal flame, willabelle the survivor, dimetria the cardinal, jacinth the hand washer, caprice the butcher, sophronia the rock freak, *cache center,* first father, father nine, father sixteen, scintilla shruggles.

Justice Pardone Cozener, true to his litigious character and droning voice, listed words from the lexicon of legal language: sovereign, decree, edict, *demurral,* pettifogger, replevin, assumpsit, allegations, forensic, jurisdiction, prisons, simulations.

Doctor Wilde Coxwain, waving his arms and prancing on the toes of his narrow feet, read his list of tribal educators and authors: stoutword deloria, *romancioso momaday,* somewhere silko, lonesome libertus, roadman henderson, visitor vizenor, earthboy welch, twelvewives wilson, redskin rose, ghostwritten antell, arrowshow storm, wholeskin goodsky.

Lilith Mae Farrier was the last to leave the trailer wall. She seemed to have trouble thinking about twelve words that pleased her. She erased several, hesitated on each word, started over, and concluded with this list: cocker, boxer, springer, christopher, douglas, hourglass, banana, *honda,* melvin, uncle, abortion, tomorrow.

Proude Cedarfair wrote the names of the pilgrims: Zebulon Matchi Makwa, Benito Saint Plumero, Belladonna Darwin-Winter Catcher, Inawa Biwide, Sun Bear Sun, *Lilith Mae Farrier,* Rosina Parent Cedarfair, Little Big Mouse, Bishop Omax Parasimo, Pio Wissakodewinini, Justice Pardone Cozener, Doctor Wilde Coxwain. He was complimented and applauded for his list. "Do not choose your own name," he warned.

The pilgrims stood near the trailer wall in a festive mood, chatting about past friends and families, telling stories, unaware for the moment that the federal government had failed, that there was no fuel for public use, that children and old people were abandoned and starving, that groups of urban people were affiliating and organizing around their bizarre and violent needs, and soon, in the middle of the trailer ruins, one of the pilgrims would become the good gambler in a game for death or gasoline. The festive mood was fired with the unspoken fear of death.

"Line up now and choose your words," hailed Bigfoot, in the manner of a circus master. "A word in season is a word for all reasons . . . One and two and three, take your words and see . . . Put your mark after each word on the list, keep that secret word under fist until all the words are chosen." The pilgrims marked their word choices from each list except their own. Each word took on special energies in isolation from gestures and lexicons and written or spoken phrases. Meaning was visual but the power of the word was secret. The excitement of choice was as great as the paradise of the first spoken words of tribal children. The pilgrims said nothing about cuntlick and *blowpost* and the most about the list of tribal writers and educators.

"Words to the wise are words of surprise," said Bigfoot, putting his mark on the name earthboy welch. "Who is this *romancioso momaday?* Is he the one who loves wheeling horses?"

When the last words on the lists were marked the pilgrims waited in silence with clenched fists. In slow motions and inhibited gestures the once festive group moved together in a tight circle. Each pilgrim extended a closed fist toward the center of the circle. Rosina Cedarfair was the first to open her small brown hand showing the word *cache center*. In silence the others opened their hands on the secret words: *voices, despised, mary, birch, blowpost, carter, red elk, 2 puce, lilith mae farrier, honda, demurral, romancioso momaday.*

Bishop Parasimo tallied and recorded the selection of secret words from the hands of the pilgrims. One for himself, *blowpost*, because, he explained, the less offensive words had been selected before his turn.

Three for Pio Wissakodewinini: *cache center, lilith mae farrier* and *voices*. "Lilith Mae is a good person her name is good for me," said the parawoman mammoth in a halting voice.

One for Sun Bear Sun: *birch*.

One for Justice Pardone: *2 puce*.

Five for Lilith Mae, including four names: *red elk, mary, romancioso momaday, carter, and demurral*. "But these are people I love, why are the people I love the secret words?"

Two for Zebulon Matchi Makwa: *despised* and *honda*.

The pilgrims closed their fists and withdrew from the circle leaving Lilith Mae in place. Her face turned pale and then deep red before she fell forward into the gravel with her hand opened and extended. The two boxers were at her side pushing at her cheeks and armpits with their slobbering noses. When the pilgrims moved forward again to assist their good gambler the boxers snarled and showed their teeth between flapping wet lips. While one boxer guarded his mistress the other boxer pushed her with his nose until she rolled over on her back. Her hand was still opened revealing the word *honda* written on her palm. The second boxer inhaled her breath and thrust his nose against her cheeks again and under her chin leaving wet blotches on her dust covered face. Then, while the first boxer pulled her loose fitting dress open and popped her soft nipples into his nostrils, the second boxer licked her limp legs until her muscles twitched. She moaned herself into sexual consciousness and raised the palm of her hand. "Honda, honda, honda, honda . . . " she chanted in a weak voice while the first boxer moved from her breasts to her crotch. The second boxer was so excited that he began humping the first boxer.

"Not now you dumb bastards," Lilith Mae moaned. "Not now . . .

get your noses out of there right now." But it was too late to distract animal passions. The boxers were overexcited from their travels and spurted on her arm and thigh. Inawa Biwide returned from the circus trailer with her ceremonial blanket and constellation quilt. The pilgrims watched her in silence. She wiped her thigh and arm and then draped the quilt with the *kitchi animosh* constellation spread over her right shoulder and shuffled through the gravel in halfsteps toward the altar trailer. "The animal children will protect me from evil." she said over her shoulder as she passed through the doors of evil.

The other pilgrims followed her, but when Proude and Inawa Biwide approached the trailer several mercenaries stopped them at the double doors. The evil gambler was waiting for them. "This game is mine," he said. "You two are not invited to work your magic on me . . . Wait outside with the guards until I have defeated this foolish woman with her hapless constellations . . . Then she will be your fool again as she was when you gave her down to me in your word game."

The evil gambler wheezed and then emitted a high pitched heinous laugh. The sweet odor of ripe apples from his diseased breath lingered in the air when he closed and locked the altar trailer doors.

Inside the circus pilgrims stood around a square table that had been placed in the center of the trailer. Half of the table, the half near the skeletons and the door, was illuminated in a bluish light. The other half of the table, where the evil gambler had taken his place, was shrouded in darkness. The birds on his epaulets gathered the weakness of the light and reflected it back across the table.

The pilgrims moved in silence to the light side of the table where Lilith Mae had taken her seat. She tightened the constellations around her shoulders. The two boxers rested next to her on each side of the chair. She had known evil in her past and was pushing her thoughts with words of confidence that she could spare herself again in the face of evil. She set her mind to luck and chance and being a good gambler. She looked up in the bluish light and smiled. She did not know the rituals of spiritual balance and power.

"It is a good time to begin," she said.

"And so it comes," rattled the evil gambler from the darkness across the table. One gold tooth sparkled like the birds on his shoulder. "Very well . . . You have come to stake your life on five gallons of gasoline . . . I demand the lives of those who gamble and lose. The rules are simple . . . " he said as he placed a large polished flat wooden dish on the table. The dish had deep sides and half of it was placed in the darkness.

"First we have the dish of the earth and these are the four directions or the four ages of man which we will each shake in the dish four times," he said as he tumbled the wooden human figures into the dish. Three fell in the darkness of the dish. One was standing in the bluish light. "The total number of figures that assume the standing position in the dish after four throws each will determine the winner."

Lilith Mae reached into the dish and lifted out one of the figures. She examined the shape and color. The carved facial features of the figure were polished smooth from the wear of the game. The lines of wood grain were dark. The chest of each figure was marked with a disk of color. The colors represented the four directions in the tribal spiritual world. The figure she examined was marked with black for the power of the thunderbirds from the west. The evil gambler turned the dish around until the other figures came into the light. The circus pilgrims leaned over the table and watched the figures in silence.

'Shall we begin?" he wheezed from the darkness.

"So begin!"

The evil gambler picked up the wooden dish and pitched the four figures up and down several times winnowing the four directions. Then he slammed the dish down on the table and there standing in the light were three figures. The figures seemed to leap from the bottom of the dish when it hit the table. The last figure was standing on the dark side of the table.

"Four standing," the evil gambler wheezed.

Lilith Mae first calmed the boxers at her sides and then picked up the dish to take her first turn. She moved the figures around in the bottom of the dish with one hand and then pitched them with the gentleness of a new mother. When the motion of her pitching increased in time the figures were leaping higher and higher in the dish. The circus pilgrims picked up the rhythm in their voices and began to count three four five six seven . . . thirteen and the dish was dropped to the table with a thud. One figure was standing on the table in the light outside the dish. Two figures had fallen in the dish on the dark side. The last figure was standing in the light in the dish.

"You lose the first toss," said the evil gambler with scorn. He flipped down the one figure that was standing outside the dish. "Start the second round."

The good gambler told the circus pilgrims to watch in silence this time while she pitched the figures in slower motion. At a sacred moment of nostalgia in the paradise of tribal dreams when she felt the first feet of the human universe touching the earth she brought the dish down on the table like a padded stick on a painted medicine drum. She was driven with a perfect power. The four figures were standing in the four directions in the light. The pilgrims cheered and applauded her success. The boxers were aroused from the excitement and her perspiration. She took personal pleasure in winning and lost her place in the energies of sacred time.

The evil gambler wheezed his scorn. He groaned and muttered heinous sounds. The space around and over the half lighted table was snapping with the energies of good and evil. The air in the room had turned sour. It smelled of flint and salt and sulphur.

"Fools believe in luck," said the evil gambler as he picked up the dish and in one sudden movement slammed it down with great force on the table. All four directions were standing on the dark side of the dish. Then, beginning the third round of the game, he slammed down the dish again with the same force and muttered and wheezed in scorn. The four directions remained standing in the darkness. "Now show your circus fools what it means to lose . . . one more round in your desperate lives."

Her stomach tingled and her heart thumped in her ears with fear when she raised the four figures in the dish. Lilith Mae smiled at each figure, touching the color of their sacred directions in the cosmic families, and then turned their polished heads in the palm of her hand. She worked through words the creation but her hands perspired and her lips twitched with the heat of defeat. For the first time she stood at the table and moaned in time with her shallow breathing. Then, as the evil gambler had done, the good gambler slammed the dish down in one sudden movement. When she moved closer to count the figures in the darkness she found all four had fallen on the dark side of the dish. She fell backward into her chair and spread her tense fingers across her chest to hold her breathing. With each short breath she whined with fear. She had lost the game. The good gambler would die before morning.

The evil gambler wheezed his evil approval from the darkness. He picked up the dish for the last throw and tossed the figures three times in the darkness while he hissed and wheezed his contempt for the circus pilgrims hovering in the light. The trailer filled with the distant sounds of groaning. He slammed the dish down and the four directions wobbled to the standing position. He was driven and consumed with evil power.

Lilith Mae was transfixed in the bluish light. Her tense fingers touched her breasts like a stranger. She spread her thighs in terror beneath the table and whined the names of her mother and father and all the children of tomorrow . . . all the children in creation.

Bishop Parasimo stood behind her and with care he fitted his talking hands on top of hers and whispered in erotic time, hand over hand across her exposed breasts, until her dark nipples stood against their fingers. She moaned while the boxers licked the perspiration from her inner thighs. The fear of death aroused the pilgrims to the sexual energies of living. The wheezing from the darkness turned to lecherous panting. The table trembled and the figures wobbled and fell in the bowl.

When Pure Gumption passed beneath the table from the bluish light into the darkness she seemed to levitate. A golden light expanded from her space. Her animistic emanation spread like an emollient wreath around the evil gambler who had exposed his frail penis and was masturbating. He squeezed and pounded his stub until a small dollop of evil sperm dribbled over his fingers.

"Fucking evil pervert," snarled Bigfoot. "Look at the old creep sitting over there beating himself off like a machine." But the evil gambler and some of the circus pilgrims could not see the golden wreath of power illuminating the lap of evil.

"Take your last turn," wheezed the evil gambler, while he wiped his hand on his shirt and stuffed his shriveled penis back into hiding. "It is hopeless . . . chance and luck are the games of fools."

When Lilith Mae picked up the dish for her last toss, Pure Gumption moved closer to the table until her wreath of golden light embraced the four directions. She pitched the figures high and then dropped the dish with terrible force on the earth. The sound cracked like thunder and startled the pilgrims. Three directions stood erect in the wreath of light but the fourth direction, the figure of the west, trembled and teetered from side to side and then fell forward into the darkness.

"Haaaaa . . . now what death will you choose?" asked the evil gambler. "You will have until darkness to decide, but remember, little good gambler, your precious life is mine and I will have you before morning. There is no escaping from evil."

"You will never have me . . ."

"Womanfool," snarled the evil gambler. "You were dead before you learned how to live . . . losing with chance you never knew how to live. Is it your precious cunt you protect? The infected folds of your tense dreams, the slime of beasts mixed with your urine? Is it your cunt you will not give me? But I have your life, all of it now, your last chance to live is mine . . . I will have all of you and before your flesh is rotten the horde will have your cold cunt . . . Casket will have you. Does that arouse you now to think of him fucking your cold dead cunt? You will be better fucked dead than alive."

Lilith Mae choked on her breath. Her hair stood strand from strand in static isolation on her head. Her fingernails turned dark, her face wrinkled, she choked and gagged and then when her stomach smacked against her spine in wild spasms of fear she heaved forward on the table and vomited into the wooden bowl. She retched several times, spewing a vile green vomit which oozed around the four figures in the dish. The evil gambler pushed himself from the table, bounced his round shape to the double door and escaped from the altar trailer. Outside the seven circus crows swooped down around his bald head and chased him through the trailer ruins.

Proude Cedarfair could smell ammonia when he entered the trailer. He waited near the door. It was warm from bodies. The trailer smelled of chance and loss, of promises and failures. The pungent odor of false civilizations, foolish terminal creeds and the bare visions of death. Living smells sweet and gives other lives breath. Death has the smell of cities and machines and plastics. There was death and evil in the altar trailer. A fine dark dust was settling on memories. Proude turned and left the trailer without speaking. The crows returned and soared in perfect circles. Perfect Crow, the smallest of the seven, landed on his shoulder. She rattled her wings and stretched her black iridescent neck as she crowed about the monuments of evil and the dangerous hordes.

The circus pilgrims carried Lilith Mae out of the trailer and placed her to rest in the shade of a tree. The two boxers whined about her and licked her pale face clean. The sun had risen to its highest place over the trailer ruins. Proude tipped his head backward into the sun and flew with the crows back to the *misisibi* and the *migis* sandridge. His

120

eyes became black holes from woodland tribal souls. The cedar woods ticked and rustled through the end of summer. He removed his clothes and shoes and gripped the cool sand with his bare feet. Perfect Crow strutted down the clear shoreline stretching her neck to reflect on the water and poking at insects and precious stones. Proude slipped into the water and swam beneath the surface in magical flight. He soared underwater through the colors of the families in the universe ha ha ha haaaa with whales and bears and sacred crows.

"Does the evil gambler fear your power?" asked Matchi Makwa. Proude flew back to the trailer ruins. Matchi Makwa ran his blunt finger under the feathered chin of Perfect Crow. She stabbed at his hand with her black beak.

"We need gasoline," said Bigfoot. "We need gasoline to get the hell out of here . . . The good gambler is done. Proude will beat the evil gambler at his own game."

"Once we win five gallons we can take the rest and move out in these new automobiles," said Doctor Wilde, waving his arms. Justice Pardone stood behind him resting his fat hands on his thin shoulders.

"Beat him Proude . . . beat him for good," chanted Little Big Mouse from her foot holsters at the side of Sun Bear Sun. "Beat him out of his rotten gasoline . . . beat him out of his pants. How come you never did it in the first place? Where were you old man?"

"Yes, where were you during the game?" demanded Doctor Wilde. Justice Pardone tucked his hands in his belt.

Proude lifted Perfect Crow from his shoulder and tossed her into flight. She flapped and dipped in good humor through the trailer ruins. He did not answer the question but when he turned to face the circus pilgrims his face was burning with the rage of bears. When he roared the first time the boxers whimpered and the pilgrims retreated to the altar trailer. When he roared the second time he disappeared into the trees behind the trailer ruins. Inawa Biwide heard the bear roar twice more from the trees. The evil gambler heard the roaring and invited the little stranger into the second altar trailer where he told stories about lust and death.

¶ Outwitting the Evil Gambler

"Mother would be proud. Have you noticed little stranger that there are no insects around here? Not an insect in the entire trailer monument," said the evil gambler. "Mother hated the creeping and crawling of insects and was forever spraying the truck trailer and dipping our clothes in insect poison. Nothing lived on us. She killed more insects in her time than a barn full of bats. In so doing, year after year, she developed a fine toned need to kill and we suffered from the constant poisons.

"Dear mother, she poisoned us all, but she did kill what she wanted to kill. But we inhaled insect poisons all the time we were living together . . . it took my hair and teeth. See," said the evil gambler pulling his lips back over his teeth. "These are false, all but the front two. The real ones were gone before I was seventeen.

"There you sit like the prince of silence listening to the most evil man in the world. My very heart is taken with the power of evil and death. You are sitting with the master of evil power.

"Torture and death. Not the killing of insects like my mother but the death of real people, is an obsession with me. I make the world live right through death . . . Mother is dead. We all killed her when she told us it was time. She wanted to die at the wheel of her beloved truck. So we, there were thirteen children, scooped out a hole big enough to hold her truck. Then we poisoned her and when she drove for the last time into her grave we read her poems and buried the truck with her at the wheel.

"Mother was a poet you know. She loved to write verses and songs for us while we crisscrossed the states from coast to coast . . . been on all the interstates hundreds of times in our family double semitrailer truck. She was a first rate driver . . . The truck was our home, real home, mainstreets for us were the interstates. We lived in the back with whatever cargo we were hauling at the time. We organized our own school and took turns as teachers and students. When mother stopped to pick up hitchhikers she questioned them before offering them a ride. She first wanted to know about their experiences and what they could teach us, say, between Kansas City and Chicago or Denver and Phoenix . . . We had hitching teachers teach us how to sing and dance mime and read the stars and clouds and newspapers backwards . . . One hitcher said the news made more sense backwards. We learned how to plan a revolution and build a windmill for power. One of our teachers, Princess Gallroad, never will forget her name, from Fortuna, North Dakota, lived with us on the truck for two months while she taught us all how to read and then for fun she told us about taxation and economics and how the government worked. At the time of course the government was not working much at all . . . Princess Gallroad was our first sexual experience. Can you imagine coming for the first time on the road with your brothers and sisters watching? No sex is more exciting than incest. No wonder we never wanted to leave the trailer. We had what we wanted on the road. But mother was like a big beaver in the end, she dumped us at interchanges on the interstates one by one. Left in thirteen different states. I was twenty six when she dumped me at a reststop in Iowa. Been here ever since. This is my state.

"When we lived on the truck we never left it, except for movies and those times mother would stop for the night beside a river. The silence of the river water was beautiful. On the truck we drowned out the howl of the wheels with music . . . What I miss most without electric power is music. How we loved music on the road. My favorite tune is the firewords overture . . . The last of the batteries were done several months ago. No more music.

"There were thirteen of us living on the trailer with mother. We were all stolen from different states. Not one of us was the same and because of that we were our own government. Mother stole us and we cared for each other as we arrived in the back of the truck . . . She stole children because she wanted a nice family, all she ever wanted in the world was a family of her own. Nothing more. Before she was eighteen she had borne three children . . . She told us she was in ecstasy with children, but the state welfare people, after the federal reform programs died, took her children away because she was unmarried and because she was pregnant again and never did have a public sponsor. Those welfare witches took her three children and while the doctors aborted the fourth child under state law she was sterilized . . . In time she took to the road and driving trucks. All she wanted was a family. She rustled us from shopping centers across the country.

"Mother treated us all with special respect. She treated us like men, seven of us, giving each of us an honorific title before our names. Mine is sir, others were doctor, reverend, colonel, president . . . she explained that because we could not bleed with the moon and have children, we needed a title to give our lives meaning and respect.

"I was invited to speak all over the country," the evil gambler said, "when I published my book on traps and tortures. They thought I was some kind of royalty. When I told the truth, telling audiences that I was filched by a truck driving poet and raised on an over the road trailer, they thought I was charming and full of wit and an aristocratic. Sir Cecil, tell me tell me what your mother thinks about your studies of sexual traps and tortures, the television interviewers asked me. Can you imagine? There are good reasons to be dishonest in the world when people seldom believe the truth . . . Being honest, as you must know little stranger, is not always being honest. Much depends on the listener . . . The audiences wanted to hear the truth but when I told them dear mother was a child rustler they laughed. She snatched all thirteen of us from shopping centers near interstates and was out of state before most parents knew we were missing. Mother thought the best place to save children from was shopping centers. We never regretted the loss of our real parents. We could have all gone back but who wanted to return to the suburbs? Sister Queen Patricia traced her parents through newspapers and ended up divorcing them and taking to the road again. We learned that biological families are not the center of meaning and identities. We learned from ourselves . . . never had to take the guilt from our parents.

"You are a good listener little stranger," said the evil gambler. "Real mother and father hated each other. He was a smallworld dentist and she was an anthropologist who had a series of affairs with savages while she was doing research on a reservation . . . some research. They were preparing to separate when I was rustled . . . In a year I was declared dead and gone and real parents collected on the insurance . . . I was four when new mother purloined me from the shopping center. Real mother had forgotten she had taken me along while her hair was being done and never missed me for several hours. By then I was playing games in the back of the trailer and soaring across Ohio.

"Mother praised us no matter what we did. When we had fights in the back of the trailer she stopped the truck to celebrate the occasion. We were pleased and praised for all things. She expected nothing from us and praised all that we did together and alone . . . When I was thirteen I killed a person . . . We were at a reststop at the time. When mother found out what I had done she stopped the truck right on the interstate to celebrate the event. She said we should feel no guilt, ignore the expectations of others and practice to perfection whatever you choose to do in the world. She believed that people should do things that gave them pleasure. As it turned out killing gave me a whole lot of pleasure then . . . My business has been to bring people to their death. Until I was nineteen suffocation fascinated me as a form of death. Like an artist I practiced the various means of suffocating people. Later I was attracted to traps and poisons . . . secrets and surprises on the road to death.

"You must be wondering little stranger how many people I have killed. Well, when I reached one hundred deaths I stopped counting. That was more than fifteen years ago now. Since then there have been hundreds more . . . hundreds. Hundreds here at the trailer monument alone. On one occasion I was questioned about the death of three savages on the plains . . . The one time I was close to being arrested. At that time I took sincere pleasure in killing drunken brush savages. I poured motor oil in their mouths until they choked to death on their own vomit. Now I am less interested in perfection . . . less interested in death but I still find good times in balancing the world with evil. Death does not thrill me as it once did . . . Killing people now has lost the excitement it once had . . . Why? Because, I suppose, killing is just too easy now. Look at what has happened to the values of people and the corruption in government. Killing is too easy, thousands of people do it everyday to others and themselves. Nothing new. No surprises. That thin plastic film known as social control hanging over the savage urge to kill was dissolved when the government failed and the economic world collapsed. What reason was there not to kill when money no longer worked? The government and private business, the businesses bigger than government, started this indifference toward death with their pollution and industrial poisons . . . Having lost my hair to insect poisons you must not be surprised that I am so interested in pollution. I learned about slow torture from the government and private business . . . Thousands of people have died the slow death from disfiguring cancers because the government failed to protect the public. The government tortured people and sanctioned killing. There was nothing to hold back the public urge to cause death. The worst part of the government killing people is the indifference. No one even watches or cares. Death comes without knowing or seeing evil. War is better than business pollution, because when death comes in war the power of evil is present. So is the heart of the hunter and the hunted . . . But when the government is the teacher there is no struggle with evil, just a slow unnoticed death.

"When the government failed people first started killing their enemies and neighbors, the people so hated for so long, and then came the public officials. That satisfied most people but others were attracted to the pleasures of death and the power of evil . . . When the values of material possessions were useless without petroleum, when all the motors and gears stopped, when the coin returns no longer returned, there were no common values to bind people together and hold down their needs for violence and the experience of death . . . Death was too simple then. No struggle between good and evil when the good power has failed . . . What does it mean to know evil power when love and the power to do good has died in the hands of indifferent bureaucrats? Being evil and causing death was no longer thrilling. And here you are, the good pilgrims, gambling for gasoline.

"But all is not lost. Our world has turned again to hunting and the hunter . . . The shared fear and instinctive rituals of the hunted and the hunters. We have no survival time going now to plant gardens and wait for them to bloom. Who dares pause near a garden when we are hunted? The best hunters are the best survivors. The gardeners, planners and savers and material dreamers, the grassgrowers and beekeepers are lost in the hunt. The best survivors count their time from secret place to secret place, measuring new hunting games with caution, never turning over their instincts to chance . . . chance.''

Silence.

Inawa Biwide smacked his small dark hands against his thighs while he stood up near the door of the trailer. He stretched his neck and wings like a crow. "Listen to this survival measure about hunters and the hunted," he said to the evil gambler who was wheezing in the darkness.

"Five brothers were hunting when a stranger with evil power visited them," said Inawa Biwide. "It was their vision to know the spirits of the animals they hunted. One of the brothers was moaning and weeping in loneliness. He was in love with images of fine animal people from the tribal past who had abandoned him in the woods because he had tried to steal their masks and spiritual place on the earth. The other four brothers could not stop his weeping. The sound bothered them. When the stranger visited again the brothers asked him for his advice. Without speaking, the evil stranger, who lived on death, moved toward the weeping brother and sucked his brains out through the side of his head. The brother stopped weeping. At first the other brothers were grateful to the evil stranger, but when they discovered that their brother was without brains, they were moved with the furies of winter. The four brothers took faggots of burning wood from the fire and beat the stranger to the ground. When the evil stranger turned his head and wrinkled demilune face upward toward the brothers they dropped the faggots in fear. The eyes of the evil stranger had turned to a solid chrome yellow color and flickered at them like the fires of evil. The chromium eyes were the eyes of evil that lived in death. When the four brothers heard the evil stranger hiss and groan, they ran from the fire. Evil followed them with his chromium eyes searching through the darkness. Millions of moths and insects popped and burst into flaming death dust under his yellow gaze. Trees wilted . . . The brothers ran and evil followed, killing them one by one. His evil eyes would sweep beams of death around the shores of lakes and rivers. One brother, the youngest and the only survivor, crossed prairies and mountains, running for several seasons, until he was stopped by the perfect mirror image of himself in a calm woodland lake. He saw fear and fatigue on his face in the clear deep water. He climbed up a tree that was leaning wide over the water and stood on a thin limb so he could see his image reflecting in the water. The evil stranger hissed and groaned over the hills and through the woods. He approached the lakeshore and saw the last surviving hunter. Evil came closer and snarled that he would stare with all his power to burn a hole through the heart of the hunter. The good image in the water moved as if in mortal fear. Then the hunter, throwing his voice to the water image, pretended to plead for his life . . . I will honor evil power if you spare me my life as a hunter, the hunter said to evil. But the evil stranger hissed and said that evil did not need the honor and praise of hunters and fools. His voice became a terrible roar when he threw his chromium beams on the heart of the hunter in the water. The evil stranger moved closer and closer, the water hissed back but the hunter said nothing. Then the good image mocked the power of evil until evil walked beneath the surface of the water in his lust for revenge and death. The lake burned with a frail yellow light. The good hunter started singing a northern season song. His singing grew more powerful until his voice soared out of time and place into winter. His singing brought the cold and froze the water on the lake. When all the fish and underwater plants in the lake had been killed by the evil stranger, he then turned his death beams on himself and disappeared in a flicker of spring sunlight."

Inawa Biwide blinked his dark eyes and snapped his fingers. The door opened and the trailer altar filled with sunlight. Sir Cecil Staples protected his eyes from the light. On the walls were framed photographs of his interstate childhood and his mother at the wheel of her truck. Her lips seemed to move under the glass in the sunlight. There were pictures of the evil gambler with his brothers and sister and the mercenaries from his mixedblood horde. The sunlight flickered on their frozen faces.

Proude Cedarfair stepped into the trailer and closed the door. The photographs returned to darkness. "I am here to gamble with death. I am here to speak with you about evil and death," he told the evil gambler.

"Splendid," wheezed the evil gambler. "I will assume that one loser must not be enough for the good pilgrims?"

"Would you die for your game?" asked Proude.

"Never!"

"Passionless fears."

"Not fears," wheezed the evil gambler, "but I am not foolish enough to play games with power . . . Lilith Mae was possessed for one toss of the dish but then she lost her good power through her own selfish needs for praise and credit."

"Why did you turn us from the game?"

"You must have power to be walking around with that glowing mongrel," he said from the darkness. "The pilgrims wanted gasoline which is part of the game, but you want to balance the world between good and evil . . . Your game is not a simple game of death. You would change minds and histories and reverse the unusual control of evil power."

"You are a coward."

"Evil power is not an act of courage . . . When the world is ruled with evil there is little to win through insane courage."

"Would you take my life?"

"Insist . . . What is your choice of death?"

"Starvation."

"Starvation?" mocked the evil gambler. "Why would anyone choose starvation from all the interesting and exciting means of death?"

"For the visions from delirium."

"How minded . . . How sanctimonious you tribal woodfreaks are in the real world of evil," wheezed the evil gambler. "Tell me mister proud, is there meaning through suffering?"

"Delirium is timeless," Proude explained. He looked across the trailer to touch Inawa Biwide and Pure Gumption. "Delirium is without measure, it is the absence of the place we were born . . . It is a timeless place to leave but not a measure of death."

"Now tell me what are the stakes?" the evil gambler asked from the darkness. He uncovered a new dish game from a cabinet in the cnter of the trailer. "Where would you like to lose and begin your starvation and delirium?"

"Here at the center."

"Standing?"

"Standing," said Proude. "Tell me will it be my life against yours or my life for the life of Lilith Mae?"

"Not good enough mister good pride," wheezed the evil gambler, "but if you are so sure of your game I will play for the value of your life alone."

"We each take three tosses of the four directions," Proude proposed. "The first toss is for my life against nothing, you have nothing to lose on the first toss. The second toss is for the life of Lilith Mae and the third toss is for my death or your death."

"Agree to this," the evil gambler said after a long pause while he polished the dish. "Your life on all three tosses . . . When you lose on the first I will have your good life. When you lose on the second toss I will have the lives of all the pilgrims . . . You will be gambling with evil for all the lives on one toss of the four directions. On the third toss, which you will never survive to make, I will stake my life against your life . . . One good fool against evil power."

"Agreed . . . Throw the four directions."

"But first," wheezed the evil gambler, "the little stranger and the animal must leave . . . We will toss three times alone and you must agree when you lose the lives of the other pilgrims that you lose your choice of death. No starvation in our game of death."

"Then in return," responded Proude, "when we win your death will be our choice."

The evil gambler waited for Inawa Biwide and Pure Gumption to leave the trailer. He locked the door and returned to the game cabinet. Proude was facing eastward. He smiled and roared in a low bear voice at evil. Sir Cecil Staples wheezed and drooled in the darkness.

The dish was made of fine grained dark burnished wood. The tall bodies of four directions were carved from hard maple. The heads of the figures, the colors of the four directions, were moulded from plastic. The figure with the white head had a deep crease near the temple and around the neck.

Proude was first to pitch the directions in the dish. The trailer smelled of cedar and willow and cottonwood leaves.

"Pride is so certain," wheezed the evil gambler. "And at the end, the end of all games, when we both have the power to balance the world and raise the four directions, we will find a new game because we are after all bound to chance . . . Evil will still be the winner because nothing changes when good and evil are tied in a strange balance."

"Show us your evil power."

Sir Cecil Staples slammed the dish on the center cabinet. The four figures were upright and rigid. "What holds our power together over these directions? What holds us together in this game mister proud . . . What holds us to believe in the rules of our own games?"

"Places in opposition," said Proude as he raised the dish for the second throw. "This one is for Lilith Mae." The four directions remained standing back to back in a tight circle in the dish. the colors of the directions were changed in perfect order: winter opposite summer, south where north should live and morning light into thunder clouds.

"Opposites it is, but you have failed to understand evil," said the evil gambler slamming the dish down the second time. Natural oil spread across his bald head. His ears ticked when he spoke and wheezed. "We are equals at this game of good and evil mister proud. Nothing is lost between equals."

"But we are not equals," Proude responded. "We are not bound in common experiences . . . We do not share a common vision. Your values and language come from evil. Your power is adverse to living. Your culture is death."

"And so we are equal opposites."

"Death is not the opposite of living, but you are the opposite of living . . . Your evil is malignant. The energies to live are never malignant."

"Splendid words . . . Your kindness overwhelms me," wheezed the evil gambler, running his hands across the oil on his bald head. "You are not in a good place to make tribal pronunciamientos."

Proude raised the dish in ceremonial gestures to the four directions while he voiced an honoring message to the morning and the circle of magical dreams. The sacred incense of burning cedar on the cabinet the four figures were balanced and standing wide in the four directions of their color and place in the tribal cosmos.

"What holds us together now is what held the nation together for two centuries," wheezed the evil gambler as he knocked down the four directions. "The constitutional government and the political organizations were deceptive games of evil . . . Personal games became public programs. National games that preserved and protected the causes of evil. . . What happens between us when the game ends is what happened to the government when the political games were exposed . . . nothing! Nothing but the loss of faith among gambling fools. Nothing but chance. Fools and the games with their fantasies that living is more than death and evil is less than goodness . . . Winning is losing."

Sir Cecil Staples picked up the dish for his third and last toss of the game. When he pitched the four directions and brought the burnished dish down in a sudden movement, confident that good and evil were in a strange balance, Proude made a teasing whistle on the wind . . . The dish cracked against the cabinet and the four directions wobbled and fell. All four directions fell forward into the dish.

132

"You have lost the power and the balance of evil," said Proude. "Our game has ended and the pilgrims have not lost their spirit to death and the evil hands of your darkness." Proude picked up the dish and slammed it down seven times in succession. Each time the four figures were standing in the directions of their color and place in the good world.

"Good is an ordeal, evil is not."

"You are still a fool . . . There is no gasoline. Your own selfish needs have brought you here with fantasies of winning gasoline. Do you think I would still be alive with a secret reservoir of gasoline?

"You are all still losers . . . Terminal believers in your own goodness." The evil gambler wheezed and pinched his cheeks while he spoke. The holes on his face turned black. His chromium eyes failed in the darkness. Fourth Proude Cedarfair smiled and then picked up the four directions from the dish and walked out of the altar trailer of evil.

¶ Nineteen Minutes to Paradise

Proude was walking past the black evil altars under late summer when he smelled gasoline and saw a small cloud of smoke rising above the trees. The circus pilgrims were running toward the fire.

"Lilith Mae is burning! She set herself on fire with gasoline!" Belladonna screamed several times as she ran through the circle of trailers.

The gasoline fire moved the pilgrims into perfect silence. The clown crows spread their wings in mourning in the trees. Pure Gumption and Private Jones shunned the flapping flames and trotted into the woods with their heads down low in the fourth world turning beneath them.

In the center of the perfect fire sat the hairless and blackened figure of Lilith Mae Farrier with her hands raised waist high in rigid gestures of hesitation. The blunt flaming faces of the two boxers rested in her scorched lap. The smell of burning flesh inflamed the horde of mercenaries. The horde watched her fingers drip and cheered when her thin forearm burned through at the elbow. The charred featureless figure slumped forward in the weakening flames of lust and revenge.

"But there is no gasoline," said Rosina.

"She siphoned some from the truck," said Matchi Makwa. "Those fucking boxers were in love with her to the flaming end."

While the hardhearted horde of mixedblood mercenaries watched, the circus pilgrims rolled the scorched bodies of the boxers and *abita animosh* into a dark red carpet which had been removed from the altar trailer. In a slow ceremonial procession the pilgrims carried the tube of bloodless burned flesh, like a column of brown funeral ants,

135

through the mercenaries to their circus trailer.

"She gave me her animal blanket," said Little Big Mouse, her little moon face wet with whale tears. "She gave me her animals and sacred stars and then burned down."

Benito Saint Plumero leaped from the back of the circus trailer dressed in his blue ribbon shirt and his finest clown clothes. He popped open his umbrella and spread his feet and sensuous lips in a wide trickster smile. "Load her up now," he commanded. "Sun Bear Sun at the wheel again ... We are leaving this trailer grave as soon as we can with *abita animosh* and her boxers and enough gasoline to make the interstate near Council Bluffs."

"Not enough to Council Bluffs."

"Fuck the distance."

"No gasoline here."

"Driving west on the last drops in the tank."

"Turn the truck around," ordered Bigfoot, dipping his umbrella. "On your mark here until I return." He walked up the road toward the altar trailers. The violet umbrella bobbed like a giant balloon and his huge feet flapped on the gravel raising clouds of dust with each step. His small figure appeared dissociated from his feet as he walked.

Bigfoot first entered the eastern altar trailer where the traps and instruments of torture were displayed. He examined the springs, clamps, cages, snares, traps based on the models of spiders and plants, and selected one of two mechanical neckband death instruments. The narrow flexible metal neckband was notched and fastened to a gearbox and clock spring. When the clock spring was wound it turned several wheels which tightened the sharp neckband. The gearbox, made to fit at the back of the neck, was protected with a locking metal cover. Bigfoot removed the keys from both chronometric neckscrew choker covers.

When Bigfoot entered the second altar with his violet umbrella opened, Sir Cecil Staples, the disgraced monarch of gasoline, was still standing at the cabinet in the center of the trailer. He looked up when sunlight burned through the open doors. He wheezed and his face wrinkled around his chromium gaze.

"The death of evil death," said Bigfoot.

"Damned again with faint praise."

"Can a man be all evil on worn phrases and battered idioms?" asked Bigfoot, placing the chronometric neckscrew choker in the game dish. He clucked his tongue and smiled at the evil gambler.

"Undramatic ... Fear and wonder made."

"Longo intervallo ... Far removed."

"Showing not the white feathers plucked from the internal chicken," wheezed the evil gambler, drawing his hands across his cheeks and over the oil on top of his pigment tracked bald head.

"Rara avis ... a rare bird of ill omen."

"Falling between feathered stools."

"Woe to the conquerees!" exclaimed Bigfoot.

"Flotsam and jetsam plucked ... Evil ruins and the fortunes and tortures of the damned," moaned the evil gambler.

"Benito Saint Plumero here and I have come with my umbrella to your personal altar of evil in this ruins to kill you with this uncommon chronometric neckscrew," he said in ceremonial tones, while raising the instrument from the dish with both hands. "Not for Lilith Mae Farrier the boxerfucker do I praise this neckscrew but in the sacred name of *kitchibiwabik osidaman.*"

The evil gambler leaned his bald head across the cabinet over the dish without speaking. The birds on his epaulets fluttered in the natural sunlight. He wheezed and the fat on his cheeks dipped over the dish like distended organs. Saint Plumero laid the sharp narrow steel band around the neck of the evil gambler and drew the ends through the gearbox until it was tight against his fat flesh. Then he wound the slow chronometric choker spring and set the timer. He locked the cover and thumped the evil gambler on the head with the key. When the evil gambler raised his head from the game dish and looked across the cabinet his face had changed color. Frail yellow beams trailed across the trailer from the evil gaze of the gambler.

"Nineteen minutes to paradise ... The clock is set but should you change your mind and need this," said Bigfoot through his cosmic trickster smile, "I will leave you the magic key to think about ... The key to good living." Bigfoot turned from the evil gaze of the gambler and dropped the gearbox cover key into the dish. He closed his umbrella and thumped out of the altar trailer whistling. The evil gambler picked up the key from the dish and followed the clown to the mail truck and waiting caravan of circus pilgrims.

"Our timeless troubles light as magic air over the evil dust of death," chanted Saint Plumero while he tapped his feet with his umbrella case. "The tables on evil are turned and the road runs with the thunderbirds under pieces of the moon . . . Tell the new world we have counted to four on the faces of evil."

Bigfoot handed his leather umbrella case up to the pilgrims and climbed into the circus trailer where he stood next to his vision *kitchibiwabik osidaman.* Sun Bear Sun started the engine. It sputtered and roared on the gravel drive. The evil gambler followed the postal truck down the road to the edge of the monument ruins where his face turned red around his evil chromium gaze. Thirteen minutes had passed and the neckband was cutting into his flesh. The pilgrims waved and watched the evil gambler reach behind his head and insert the key into the choker cover. He struggled and twisted the key in the lock but the cover did not open.

"This is the one that works in that lock," Bigfoot shouted to the evil gambler from the back of the slow moving trailer. "Follow me evil man and count the minutes . . . fourteen . . . fifteen . . . in four more minutes from where you are now you will find the good key on the road . . . this one," he hollered and then dropped the choker cover key on the road behind the truck.

The evil gambler stumbled behind the circus trailer pulling at the tightening neckband until his fingers were bleeding from the sharp steel edges . . . sixteen . . . seventeen . . . The evil gambler fell on his fat knees several times wheezing in short breaths . . . eighteen . . . The clock spring ticked tighter and tighter cutting the fat flesh on his neck and crushing the cartilage in his throat. The flow of fetid air and evil blood stopped in the fourth world four feet short of the good key on the road.

¶ Burials near Macedonia

The mail truck hurtled westward with the low setting sun over the backroads through Winterset and Orient past poisoned Iowa farms, abandoned tractors, dead animals and wandering families, until the engine sputtered on the last drops of precious gasoline and rumbled to a slow stop in the darkness near Macedonia.

The clown crows were perched on the trailer while the circus pilgrims gathered in silence on the road. They touched each other, spoke of reservation government schools and looked upward to the bright constellations. Primitive warriors thrust their good arrows and swords into the evil hearts of giants across the northern horizons. Pale women rode their horses into the arms of bears. The last world turned cosmic wars into darkness.

"Celestial perfection," said Bishop Parasimo.

"And these stars appear the same to equal fools stranded on deserted roads somewhere else in the universe," said Doctor Wilde. He thrust his arms into the heavens. He threw himself into space against the forces of the earth.

"The road to ruin is in good repair."

"How far to Council Bluffs?"

"One day on foot."

"Tomorrow we will walk," said Belladonna about the obvious. "Measuring our time again on foot and our luck and love with those who have enough to eat."

Big foot walked a short distance up the road and across a field of wildflowers, through a stone sundial, to an abandoned windowless farmhouse. He sat on the front porch and listened to the animals of the night. Pure Gumption moved through the house, glowing and sniffing at the corners with Private Jones at her side. There were powerful odors of sperm, blood bits on genital hair, bread crumbs and particles of skin and vegetables. Pure Gumption continued sniffing until in one sudden breath she stopped at the threshold of a small room near the kitchen in back of the house. Her aura became a golden wreath.

The believers who occupied the house were dead. The couple had moved from the cities back to the homestead of their great great grandparents. While the husband was bound and held in the small room, the local monarchs of the deformed posse comitatus, killed his two children with steel pipes and raped his woman nine time until she bled to death.

Private Jones moved with caution into the small room. He raised his wet nose high and turned to leave. The spirits and small voices of the dead children followed him through the house and out the back door. Against an ancient cottonwood tree the children found their father nailed and wired to the rough bark. His flesh was gone. Pure Gumption moaned and howled and then with the children started digging a hole beneath the tree.

"What is this digging?" questioned Bigfoot.

Pure Gumption and Private Jones snorted and scratched at the dark earth until the white bones of three bodies were uncovered. The children laughed and cried their lost voices back to their bones and shadows. The earth glowed around them in wreaths.

"Look at this," exclaimed Justic Pardone. "Those damn mongrels have uncovered a grave ... Good place to bury the boxerfucker and her two blunts."

"This grave is for *kitchibiwabik*."

"Shit," said Justic Pardone.

"Dog fuckers and bronze fuckers the same."

"A hole is a hole," said Matchi Makwa.

"This hole is for *kitchibiwabik*," said Bigfoot in a firm voice. He jumped into the hole on top of the bones and started digging deeper. The bones howled from the grave. Pure Gumption and Private Jones were backfilling while the grave was claimed for the bronze lover.

When Bigfoot picked up the bones of the children and mother from the hole the two animals turned and snarled at him. Pure Gumption was snapping at the space between them with her teeth exposed. Bigfoot dropped the bones and climbed out of the hole when he saw her aura change from a golden wreath to pale green. The animals filled the hole and sat on top of the grave. Pure Gumption was glowing again.

"Too much for an old bone," said Matchi Makwa.

The circus pilgrims finished digging two new graves and then unrolled the red altar carpet and dumped the charred remains of Lilith Mae Farrier and her boxers into one hole. Into the second grave the pilgrims lowered the green bronze figure of *kitchibiwabik osidaman*. Bigfoot was weeping and moaning as he covered his woman with cold earth. "I will return," he said through his tears. "When there is gasoline again . . . I will return." He slept next to her grave and dreamed of falling with tribal warriors through space.

"*Abita animosh* . . . bless this woman from the good animals who gave me her constellations to keep," whispered Little Big Mouse near the grave of Lilith Mae, "and live under without fear . . . brave animal woman traveling with the real stars now."

"Honda! . . . honda!" shouted Matchi Makwa.

¶ Hlastic Haces and Scolioma Moths

Perfect Crow was strutting on his morning chest. The other six
clown crows were stretching their wings near the fire. The coals were
buried in fine white ash. Proude Cedarfair was the first to awaken.

The first frail light of morning was blooming like tender voices over
the eastern fields and trees and drawing cameos and birthbeads of
moisture from the earth leaves. Proude touched her feathers and
breathed with the morning from his sacred names. The faces of his
father and his uncle, the shaman uncle who gave him his sacred name
tagwagig nessewin and turned him through his first visions, appeared
on his breath. Return to secret energies when sacred places are lost in
the lives of others, his uncle whispered from his breath figure. Return
to inner animal voices and motions in morning breath. Proude soared
through his breath to the *migis* sandridge where he undressed and
swam through the brume to the graves of his fathers in the water. He
slipped beneath the surface, his eyes passing from air to water like
smiles in dreams, and descended in the perfect stillness of the dark
water. When his father did not appear again he opened his mouth and
watched his breath escape in wobbling bubbles to the surface dreams.
Turning under he spread himself over the graves in the weeds on the
bottom. In four deep breaths he inhaled all the water in the lake. In
the oral traditions of whales and past tribal travels he became water
and fish and made the new earth on the backs of sacred turtles.
Proude sat between turtle and otter and the animals on the new earth.
Birds soared through his voices and the clouds were first formed from
sacred cedar smoke. The crows walked through their blackness into
his arms from the water.

Proude rubbed his face and chest with damp leaves and kindled the coals of the fire. While the water heated he soared in the woods behind the old farmhouse with the crows. He found wild mint and spruce leaves and wild cherry twigs for tea. When he returned, Rosina was waiting near the fire. Proude touched her hands and warm cheeks and brushed and braided her dark hair. The two drank tea and shared their silence while watching the morning bloom on leaves and their faces.

"Resurrection morn!" said Bigfoot, opening his eyes and breaking the silence. "Have I ever told you that story?" he asked stretching his fingers at the animals. "Have I ever told you the tale that old John Clement Beaulieu told me? Listen to this ... Clem Beaulieu came back from the war, never mind which war ... back from the war to the reservation with his drunken buddies ... Well, after drinking for several hours late one night, Nearloss Fairbanks was the first to fall over. The tricksters were with them all ... Remembering that the government grave diggers had just finished a fine fresh hole near the old mission for a burial the next day, the drinkers dragged old Nearloss, who was a wounded and decorated hero of the war, but claimed he lost his ears from the vaginal gas in a whorehouse, to the mission and lowered him face up into the grave ... It was a morning like this. I remember the pictures from the telling. Well, the reservation drinkers waited behind trees near the grave for the sun to rise. Sure enough when the sun burned off the ground mist old Nearloss opened his eyes and wagged his head up from the grave and said: Damn those drinking devils ... resurrection morn and old Nearloss is the first to rise."

His telling awakened the other pilgrims who groaned and moaned in response to his stories. The clown crows flapped in flight across the wet grass and disappeared in the cottonwoods.

"Darn that bigfeet ... He wears clown clothes and speaks in clown words," said Little Big Mouse, stretching her miniature blunt toes toward the warmth of the fire. "It feels so good to be alive this morning ... We will meet good people on the road now ... The stars told me that." She moved her moist hands over the constellations on her quilt, walking on her fingertips across the magic space between stars.

The cool morning had turned to hot desert winds in the afternoon while the circus pilgrims walked toward the thunderbirds in the west. The asphalt road from Macedonia to Council Bluffs wavered on thin slips of sunlight at each end of the world. The leaves rattled. Ancient windmills raged against the west.

The farther the circus pilgrims walked the more people there were on the road. It was not the hesitant and withdrawn gestures from other worlds that troubled the pilgrims, but mile after mile in the hot sun there were more cripples and bizarre creatures walking and sitting on the road. When the pilgrims passed the cripples watched them with hesitant vulpine smiles. Dressed in strange clothing of phantoms and angels and dreams the cripples walked little and seldom spoke. Some of them had their faces covered with painted duffel. Others wore dream shirts with various parts of bodies painted on the front.

"I feel like we are walking into an endless tunnel of madness," said Belladonna. She told the other pilgrims not to catch the gaze of the deformed creatures. "Avoid their recognition or the devil will take your image and voice . . . Never let a cripple catch your eye. These cripples are incomplete animals lusting for our whole bodies."

"Look at their sadness," moaned Little Big Mouse from her foot holsters at the waist of Sun Bear Sun. "Look at the loneliness in their faces . . . No one cares for them."

"Evil follows the deformed," exclaimed Belladonna, watching her feet as she walked. "Cripples make unborn children laugh without their parts . . ."

"Squaw rubbish," snapped Matchi Makwa, waving to the cripples as he passed. He seeks most opportunities for public attention, flourishing on the disadvantages in others. The cripples waved back without arms, winked without seeing, frowned without foreheads, smiled and laughed without chins and creeks. Their incomplete bodies lived whole through phantoms and *tchibai* dreams. Matchi Makwa twitched and limped from the silent suggestions of phantoms claiming his sympathetic limbs. His voice echoed from the clicks and clucks and snivels of the cripples who could not speak.

Late in the afternoon near Dumfries the circus pilgrims encountered hundreds of cripples, whole communal families of people with similar disabilities. The blind, the deaf, disfigured giants, the fingerless, earless, noseless, breastless and legless people stumbling, shuffling and hobbling in families down the road. Walking with the cripples were those suffering from various cancers.

First the fish died, the oceans turned sour, and then birds dropped in flight over cities, but it was not until thousands of children were born in the distorted shapes of evil animals that the government cautioned the chemical manufacturers. Millions of people had lost parts of their bodies to malignant neoplasms from cosmetics and chemical poisons in the air and food. The circus pilgrims, all but Little Big Mouse, were silent when passing through the families and support groups of these crippled and deformed with cancer. Little Big Mouse was ecstatic in the presence of cripples and incomplete bodies. She swung from her leather foot holsters with generous gestures, waving, touching and throwing kisses and words of praise. She gave common greetings to uncommon people. "Where are we in the good world?" she asked the passing cripples. "Dumfries, the national capital of all cripples," responded a hairless and noseless woman with pale plastic arms.

"You have a quilt like mine," said Little Big Mouse, pointing toward the hand prints on the dream shawl over the shoulder of the cripple whose plastic arms dangled like broken tails as she passed.

"What happened to your old arms?"

"Lost them in a rain storm."

"Rain storm?" questioned Little Big Mouse.

"Nose gone too under poison rains."

"Rotten poison rain," said Little Big Mouse.

Closer to Dumfries there were more and larger crippled and disfigured families on the road. Little Big Mouse eased the tired circus pilgrims to a stop to watch the procession of deformities. The clown crows soared high above the black road. Pure Gumption and Private Jones pushed through the crowds of cripples. First the blind people and then the limb cripples touched the aura of Pure Gumption for strength.

"Look at the cripples going for the animals."

"Pure Gumption is a healer."

"The blind can feel her warmth passing."

"Cripples are part animal you know," Bigfoot explained in lecture tones, hiding his hands and arms beneath his ribbon shirt. "We were all part fish and animals in the beginning ... our beginning from the seed memories, but over there," he said, pointing with his chin, "see those people with little flipper arms? And those women with cat faces ... Look at the snouts on those people sitting in the road ... Well, for some spiritual or chemical reason those people never developed past the memories of fish and animals in our human past ... Less than whole, less than human."

"Pure bullshit," shouted Doctor Wilde.

"Bullshit indeed," chimed Justice Pardone.

"Cripples are cripples from the chemicals their parents and grandparents drank and smoked and ate ... Simple cases of poisoned genes," Wilde explained. "No call to blame them looks on the faces of animals ... The face of a rabbit is not evil or disgusting ... or incomplete."

"But it is on humans."

"We become our memories and what we believe," said Proude in a deep voice. "We become the terminal creeds we speak. Our words limit the animals we would become ... soaring through words from memories and visions. We are all incomplete ... imperfect. Lost limbs and lost visions stand with the same phantoms."

"Wonderful, wonderful, wonderful," chanted Little Big Mouse as she dismounted. The circus pilgrims gathered under the trees near the road. There they rested and watched the passing cripples and cancer communes.

"These families are beautiful," sighed Little Big Mouse. She waved again and threw kisses and laughed with affection at the passing cripples. "Look at those people with the plastic masks and purple dream shirts ... I want to touch them all and feel their energies," she said clapping her fingertips.

The families of cripples continued to hobble and stumble down the road to and from their capital. Some families with missing limbs wore plastic wings. There were groups with glowing domino hoods marked with hierograms on their missing parts. One small group of men passed in slow dance movements wearing red rubber prosthetic penises thrown over their shoulders and buttoned beneath epaulets.

"The weirds and sensitives would like the looks and lengths of those proud presidents," said Bigfoot laughing while he touched his testicles through his leather trousers.

Little Big Mouse wriggled her fingers at a procession of scolioma moths on the road. There were dozens of them flopping in loops with giant compound eyemasks and double polyphemus wings. She ran after the smallest moth whose wings were attached to narrow sticks controlled by the larger moths following behind. The little moth moved like a puppet without arms.

"Your wings are beautiful," said Little Big Mouse, waving her arms and running beside the puppet moth.

"Our grandmother who lived in a mental hospital made them for all of us," said the puppet moth as her wings flopped and cast huge shadows on the road in the later afternoon sunlight. "She said we would all have fun once in our lives being moths ... She was so right, so right. When the bandits came with the politicians we put on our moth wings and flew out of town ..."

"Birds are so beautiful in flight," said Little Big Mouse running beside the little moth, "but in my heart I have always wanted to be a giant polyphemus moth with big eyes on my wings."

"There are some disadvantages."

"When I was an infant, before I could walk," Little Big Mouse remembered, "my mother made every world I could reach a new shrine. She served me snacks in the shapes of shrines and whispered to me that some day I would fly with the best spirits ... Nothing is random in my world of shrines. My shoes, pencils, collections of stones, plants, buttons, gone now, but all were placed in the special space of shrines." She was dancing down the road as she spoke. "But when I finished shrining, when shelves and hangers are even, I dreamed of flying away like a moth ... I want to dust the shrines with my magic wings and fly into the night across the stars."

"But we never go out as moths at night," said the puppet moth, "because our wings are too large in the dark."

Little Big Mouse asked in a frail and hesitant voice, turning her head to be unsure, "Could I wear your wings for just a little while down the road? It would give me feelings of good power to be within the wings of a moth ... Please!"

The puppet moth without arms and the other larger moths dropped their wings in silence. Then the moths brought their giant eyes together touching antennae. Little Big Mouse was smiling and waiting for an answer when the moths shrieked and attacked her. She backed up, covering her face in fear, and then turned running back to the circus pilgrims. The scolioma moths ran after her twisting their malformed spines to throw stones and clods of asphalt from the road. The crows swooped and crowed down on the wild moths. When the moths stopped their attack, Little Big Mouse turned to face them again. Her face was marked with tears. Puppet moth was standing in front with her unattended wings limp at her sides. "You are perfect and now you want our imagination and visions for your own. . . . We are moths to survive and escape our lives. Perfect people leave so little to the poor and incomplete people in the world."

The scolioma moths turned and flapped down the road in their secrets and good humor. The circus pilgrims were silent. Little Big Mouse mounted and dismounted Sun Bear Sun, wiped her tears, and then she smiled again and waved at new families of cripples.

"Look at the no faces," said Little Big Mouse pointing to nine wanderers wearing permanent transparent plastic faces. Muscles and flesh twitched and quivered behind the plastic facial features. Eyeballs bulged without skin cover. Teeth were exposed like those of hideous skeletons. The plastic faces were formed with short clinical smiles. Some plastic faces had small paper stars attached to the cheeks and foreheads.

"Come here, come over here," Little Big Mouse called. She motioned with her hands. "I want to see the stars on your beautiful faces."

"Not over here you fool."

"No not no faces," said Matchi Makwa.

"Parts of bodies do not make the person whole," said Little Big Mouse. She called to the plastic faces again to come over under the trees. The plastics nodded and marched across the road toward the circus pilgrims. The clown crows were walking in the stiff grass.

"We hound oursels and are going hong again," said one incomplete child through his rigid lips and plastic mouth. Their speech sounds were made without lips. Plastic could not close on words like pepper mouse.

The female plastic faces were moulded into perfect nose slopes with gentle fixed smiles. Little Big Mouse took the little hands belonging to the plastic faces and began to weep. Belladonna looked into the faces of the skin cancer victims and then turned away. She could tell who was smiling and frowning from the combination of muscle movements which were visible beneath the transparent plastic masks. First Doctor Wilde and then Justice Pardone turned from the nine faces and retched.

"Who has done this to you?"

"Skin cancer . . ."

"Skin cancer from the poison rains," said Belladonna. "But who gave you these faces? Who made these transparent sexist faces?"

"We all lik in diherent harts a the country," explained Pastor Joseph Browne through his rigid lips. He had etched his name on his cheek. "Ut we all hwent to the saing doctor hor a new hace hecause a henical hoisons . . . the doctor liked transharent hlastic so here we are now like anatonical nodels.

"Hwen the naton hell ahart we hound each other hor nutual suhort . . . now we are a fanily together. We learned how to read hace nuscles instead a talking without our lits."

The five plastic faced children gathered around Little Big Mouse and touched her face and breasts and constellations. Their cheek muscles twitched when touching the stars.

"I have traveled through space and lived apart from myself with the stars on celestial cheeks like yours," said Little Big Mouse, touching the adhesive gold and red stars on the faces of the children. "I have slept in pieces with the animals of the skies . . . I am the earth child of all the animals."

"More patches on the faces of the disfigured nation," said Bigfoot and then he imitated the speech sounds of the plastic faced speakers. "Or as you would say, nore hatches on the haces as the nation."

While the plastic faces were visiting with the circus pilgrims other wandering cancer communes and families of cripples stopped to listen to the conversations. The smell of putrefaction and cancer sores tingled in the nostrils of the saints. The cripples who were born without normal bodies were more aggressive and hostile than the cancer families. The cancer people were hesitant and pleasant and inhibited about themselves and their emotional expressions. Little Big Mouse continued telling stories about her incomplete lives and perfect shrines from different times and places in the circus trailer and backrooms of the universe. When the number of limbless families increased to a nervous crowd the crows swooped down around the circus pilgrims as a warning. The animals shunned the crowds of cripples.

"Do you love us as we are without balls and elbows?" chanted a clutch of male cripples while Little Big Mouse danced for them. She moved her miniature feet through the grass like her fingers over stars. "My love for you is not measured in balls and elbows," she sang. The cripples cheered and hobbled and wobbled closer to her perfect dancing figure. When she leaped high in the air spreading her constellation quilt like a fine umbrella, the cripples saw a shadow of blond hair between her white clean legs as she descended to earth. Their energies aroused her visual fantasies of animal lust. She swung her hips for the cripples from side to side, flexing her buttocks muscles and then unbuttoning the buttons on her cotton dress until her firm breasts bubbled into view. When the male cripples pushed forward with their penises throbbing and wobbling in the late sunbeams, the crows swooped down again at them crowing and clawing at their heads. Little Big Mouse did not hear the pilgrims pleading with her not to dance for the cripples. She pulled from her mount Sun Bear Sun and danced for the masturbating cripples down the last buttons on her dress. She stood naked before the drooling cripples with her constellation quilt over her small shoulders and then she spread her legs and flexed the muscles in her thighs. For a moment there was silence near the road and then the cripples broke across the escape distance of fantasies and pulled her down on the stiff grass. Little Big Mouse closed her eyes and dreams rolled into a world of beautiful deformities.

Proude stood back and roared in his bear voice from the mountains. He roared four times but the animal lust of the cripples had turned to evil fire. Sun Bear Sun climbed over dozens of crippled bodies. When he was near his little woman in the center of the pile he saw them pulling at her flesh with their teeth and deformed fingers. Others were taking frantic turns thrusting their angular penises into her face and crotch. Little Big Mouse was silent but the cripples moaned and drooled like starving mongrels. The lusting cripples slapped their fists, thrust their beaks, pushed their snouts and scratched the perfect flesh with their claws and paws. Then the savage whitecripples pulled her flesh apart. Her hair was gone from her crotch and head and armpits. Her fingers were broken and removed. Her face was pulled into pieces, her breasts were twisted, her feet and legs were pulled from her body. The cripples gnawed and pulled at her until nothing remained of Little Big Mouse. She was carried away by the whitecripples, heart and brain and undigested food. The cripples carried with them parts of her never known to their own imperfect bodies. Two legless cripples took her legs to keep for magic power. Nothing remained but the constellation quilt and the crushed grass where she had been dancing.

¶ Wheel of Dreams Parish

The Pilgrim Pope was clipping the stout red hairs flaming from his wild nostrils. Bishop Omax Parasimo entered the Wheel of Dreams Parish and appeared in the mirror in the metamask of Princess Gallroad from Fortuna.

Clip, clip, clip. "And who is this little princess?" asked the Pilgrim Pope flicking his nostrils. He was seven feet tall with ears and nose of swine. His head was shaved like that of a tonsured monk.

"Your holiness ... We are but wanderers attracted to your your your sign about becoming a saint," said Princess Gallroad with her hands laced together and her hooded head cocked to the side and aimed at the floor.

"Saint tomorrow ..."

"The sign promised three miracles and offered sainthood your holiness ... Canonization and public veneration overnight."

Clip, clip, clip.

"I am not speaking for myself self self your holiness ... I am but a common hitchhiking fool coming through her simple service of life alone ..."

"What is your name little princess? What are you doing with your hands there?"

"Princess Gallroad ... Nothing your holiness."

"Were you mocking me with your hands?" asked the Pilgrim Pope wiping his fat wrinkled lips with the back of his huge red hand and wrist. His eyes were set narrow with pin hole pupils. His swine nose was creased with red and blue dendrite webs. Smiles and laughter were not familiar to his cheeks and anvil chin.

"Perish the thought your holiness ..." said Princess Gallroad, slipping her hands beneath her duffel cape. "These little shorthand finger gestures mean nothing personal ... talking habits. Consider them neither heard nor seen."

"Saint little princess ... We have enough qualified saints from sacrifices and thankless public service ... What we are looking for now are people with wealth and power ... Something special to keep the dream wheel turning, you know what I mean? We are no longer opposed to honoring those who are corrupt and desperate in their needs for praise and veneration ... Those who need canonization to keep their lies alive ... You get the meaning?"

"But we have little more than our memories and tired bodies bodies bodies to give your holiness."

"What is there to give beneath that crude cape little princess?" asked the Pilgrim Pope. He hoisted his testicles with two red fingers from time to time while speaking.

"Your holiness ... Spare me the language of your sweetest erotic dreams. How plain I am to think of switching from one habit to another."

"Unused and unabused from the rural parishes the old priests once said," said the Pilgrim Pope, hoisting his testicles three times.

Princess Gallroad wore rimless glasses. When she spoke she shifted her weight from foot to foot. Her skin was pale and smooth with deep red lips. "Your holiness . . . Could we serve serve serve the parish and canonize one from our wandering circus?"

"Down here little princess," said the Pilgrim Pope pointing to the floor in front of him. He flipped his red penis from under his cassock. The dark circumcised head bobbed like a shriveled plum on an old winter tree. "Make this hard little princess for three miracles and a saint."

"But your holiness," exclaimed Princess Gallroad drawing her hands from her cape in frantic finger gestures. "You are the softest of the hardest ... But my lips lips lips are not tuned to resurrections."

"Then take it in those gossiping hands of yours," moaned the Pilgrim Pope as he wriggled the red head of his penis with his massive fists.

Princes Gallroad lifted her duffel cape in slow motions past her ankles and knees and then thighs until her proud penis stub was in full view.

"Hosanna ... Here we are with the champion of the breed," said

154

the Pilgrim Pope. He grunted three times in place of laughter and then granted his approval for canonization ceremonies.

Princess Gallroad dropped her cape, folded her hands and shuffled past the Pilgrim Pope around the portable aluminum altar and through the folding chairs. She removed her cape and returned the metamask to his black case.

Bishop Parasimo walked across the street where the other pilgrims were waiting and arranging three miracles with the Four Birds. The birds were Chicken, Owl, Waxwing, and Woodpecker and billed themselves as pantribal curers and healers.

"What are the miracle choices?"

"His choices come in two categories," said the Owl to his plump amanuensis shadow. "Curing or healing others and causing great mysteries of time and place within the celebrant."

"Who will arrange these?"

"With our magic words," said the Chicken. "We will deliver three miracles for canonization with no feathers attached."

"Remember when you run down the list of miracles," Waxwing added, "that the Pilgrim Pope requires that at least one of the three miracles be from healing or curing."

"When will we meet the prospective saint?" the Woodpecker asked. He stretched his neck, thumped the wall with his beak and shivered his feathers into place.

The Four Birds were four mixedblood hustlers and hucksters from prairie reservations down on their luck in the cities. Sleeping together in the summer parks of Council Bluffs the four drinkers were struck with the insight that birds, real park birds, were trusted and treated better than people. Strangers in the parks would turn their backs on the starving tribes to feed and speak with thousands of thankless pigeons and ducks and sparrows. The four took bogus bird visions and wore their feathers to the parks. Dressed in avian vestments the Four Birds sold wigwam superbuck seeds, witching balm, squaw claws, feather charms, *matchi mashkiki*, evil medicine, and bird musk, and told sacred stories about magical flights into the sunset. The Four Birds bottled their medicine from the most polluted rivers in the nation. When the government collapsed the birds feathered the federal drug administration and sold polluted water as a cure for cancer to whitepeople.

Words about the birds spread among birdlovers in the parks and in a few weeks whitepeople were seeking the birds for their power to heal and cure. The Pilgrim Pope met the birds in his search for a cure for nongonococcal urethritis. Trolling in the park one afternoon he invited the birds to serve miracles in the Wheel of Dreams Parish.

"Birds of a feather flock together," said Benito Saint Plumero. The birds turned and shifted their feathers in disgust.

Perfect Crow swooped and crowed past the bird imposters crossing the street to the parish. The clown crows flapped at Waxwing and Chicken and Woodpecker, but their rancor and wrath was directed at Owl. Crowing and rattling their wings the crows dropped their white excrement on Owl. Out of breath Owl ran into the parish to hide but the crows followed. Tormented by the clown crows Owl removed his avian vestments. He was a short stout man with bulging eyes.

The circus pilgrims examined the menu of miracles and intercessions. Following a brief discussion on the attitudes of magical flight, Saint Plumero chose one precognitive dream, one ecstatic vision and curing one woman with breast cancer.

"Delicious order," said Woodpecker.

First miracle: Ten years ago I was lusting for a woman on the edge of the world, Saint Plumero told from his dreams. She said she would give me sex whenever I asked for it if I could reach her in voices and dreams. One night I become solvent in my own hands and atomized through time and space, filling a bottle for her with myself, and then spoke to her through demons until she picked me in the bottle up, popped the lid and out came me in sweet vapors. I took her in lust from the nostrils down to her heels.

Second miracle: I am in love with a woman I met in the park. She is named *kitchibiwabik osidaman,* a woman made from fine bronze. My ecstatic vision is being with her in perfect silence and love. I have killed and traveled in visions to find her. She gives herself to me without questions and she is devoted to me and our mutual attention.

Third miracle: The Four Birds called in their usual bartering congregation of miracle workers for curing and healing ceremonies. A new woman in the stable of extras was instructed to perform her part in the miraculous salvation from the grim grip of breast cancer. The circus pilgrims waited in the back rows of the parish. Saint Plumero, dressed in his finest ribbons and leathers, took his place on the aluminum altar. Pure Gumption and Private Jones were at his side. The vigil candles flickered. When the bells sounded he raised his short arms as he had practiced and called for the sick to come forward with their sickness to be healed. The appointed woman stepped forward to the aluminum altar and dropped to her knees at the huge feet of the healer.

"Where does it hurt my child?"

"On my tits," she said with her head down. She was attracted to the huge feet on the healer. She reached out to touch one.

"What are you doing there?"

Private Jones licked her warm cheeks while she touched the soft leather covering his feet. She lusted for his giant feet.

"Turn over on your back my child," intoned Saint Plumero as he pulled his right foot away from her hands. "Roll over and be healed."

Private Jones sneezed. The woman rolled over and opened her dress exposing her cancerous breasts. The birds moved forward to see but did not know that the woman hired as an extra was not faking the cancer in her breasts. She was waiting to be cured for real on the floor of the Wheel of Dreams Parish with her pendulous breasts under the hands of a trickster and clown.

"Tell her she is healed Saint Plumero."

"You are being healed," said Saint Plumero, squeezing her breasts with both hands while thumbing her nipples erect. "These breasts will be headed and healed forever."

"Enough Plumero ..."

"Never rush to cure," said Saint Plumero, responding to the impatient birds waiting to clear the parish for the next canonization. His hands on her breasts caught up with the deep breathing of the woman.

"Enough on the altar Plumero."

"This is a parish," added Owl without feathers.

Saint Plumero withdrew his hands from her warm breasts when Pure Gumption, who had been glowing between the head and shoulders of the woman, raised the wreath of healing fires in her paws and stood on the cancerous breasts.

"What the hell is that mongrel doing?" questioned Woodpecker from the side of the altar. "Strange people with these mongrels and crows following them around ... We could be cursed with this beatification."

"Hallelujah ... Hallelujah!" Chicken shouted.

"Glowing mongrels ... the both of them."

"That fucking reservation mongrel is curing that woman of something," said Waxwing as she hopped down the aisle toward the aluminum altar. "Who would believe it . . . That mongrel is laying on the paws . . . Tell me great chicken in the coop is this our solucination?"

The woman could feel the wreath and healing fires passing through the paws into her breasts. Her chest was warm and beaming with a golden light around the places where she was pawed. She was healed.

Late in the afternoon the bells knelled from the tower of the Wheel of Dreams Parish. The sounds were sounding four and five and seven. The circus pilgrims and the ceremonial extras were called to the canonization of Benito Saint Plumero. The Pilgrim Pope, dressed in flowing red and violet velvets, had met with the prospective saint in the morning during which time the celebration was rehearsed and a short biographical message was prepared.

"Come one and all from the world to this sacred celebration at the Wheel of Dreams," chanted the Pilgrim Pope in a deep voice.

"The women are with you . . . Lift up your private parts . . . We are gathered together in our baptismal consciousness of sweet death and hard resurrections to consecrate the miraculous intercessions and powers and vision of a selfless man as a new saint . . .

"In the avian canon of the Wheel of Dreams we canonize you in this special hour a new saint in the pilgrim church . . . Saint Benito Saint Plumero.

"This saint sits before you in the humble attitude of great distinctions in the sacred service of visions and dreams and curative powers . . . These miracles are proven for his canonization: This afternoon he laid his paws on the breasts of a venial woman and drove the cancer demons from her flesh . . .

"And so did his distant grandfathers, with special mention of the great man with the red umbrella sailing through the savages, the great Giacomo Constantino Beltrami, who gave himself to bedeviled and backward tribal women in the woods where fools might live again through his veracious flesh . . . These tribal women gave him sons and one was given the mixedblood name of Wee Wee Plumero because he danced hard and carried a feather whisk . . . Several generations later we now know this sacred blood as the venerated and exalted Saint Benito Saint Plumero from the stock of Beltrami . . . Speak to us as a new saint in the power of the avian canon."

Saint Saint Plumero stepped behind the aluminum altar emblazoned with hierogram wheels and vaporous dreams. His huge feet were spread apart on each side of the narrow altar. Looking around the parish he cleared his throat and thanked the world from the bottom of his heart. Tears dripped down his cheeks.

"Let me speak a few words before I begin to speak," said Saint Saint Plumero. "When I first learned the meaning of the word saint I put it in front of my last name, and ever since then I have wanted to be a saint ... A real saint to give my real name real meaning. We were the explorers and mixedbloods of the great beginning and now we are real saints again. Thank you all for making this wonderful moment possible. I promise to serve this honor to the best of my abilities."

The celebrants cleared their throats.

"We have lived in the fellowship of spiritual flight according to the avian canon," said the Pilgrim Pope. "Hovering over the folds and fields of glorious battles between clawing good and charming evil ... Offering ourselves and others through blood and feathers and bread as terminal victims in a vision of soaring death ... But for the illuminating wheel and chance into flight to new places we would shun the morning and turn to darkness ..."

When the Pilgrim Pope had finished speaking Bishop Omax Parasimo gave the circular sign of the sacred wheel. Then the bishop bound the hands of Saint Saint Plumero with narrow bands of soft red cloth.

"Now arise to the sacred dream wheel," chanted the Pilgrim Pope as he pulled aside the drapes which covered the giant wheel at the back of the altar. "Break the ties on your wrists of time and culuture and spin the wheel and where it stops is paradise ... The place where you will travel first as a new saint ... Spin the dream wheel to paradise."

The celebrants stood and cheered.

"Do this in our memories ... He who spins the wheel abides in chance and the fellowship ship ship of spiritual flight according to the avian canon," said Bishop Parasimo in a canorous voice.

"Little princess princess princess take me in time," said the Pilgrim Pope mocking the trine word habit of Bishop Parasimo. "Take me on the wing wing wing ..."

Saint Saint Plumero spread his small hands open breaking the cloth. Then, reaching for the highest knob he pulled the wheel with all his weight. The wheel spun across thousands of places and dreams, slowing down past unknown world words before it stopped on his new paradise named bioavaricious.

"Bioavaricious where?"

"Bioavaricious is in Kansas, good saint," the Pilgrim Pope explained. "No one has ever spun the dream wheel to that place before ... Where it is is down the lawless interstate about a weeks walk from here."

"What are the dreams in that place?"

"Words words words ..."

The Pilgrim Pope led the Four Birds, Owl dressed in feathers again, the celebration extras, the circus pilgrims, the mongrels and seven clown crows out of the parish chanting one final trine amen.

Amen amen ... amen!

¶ Word Wars in the Word Wards

The last fat black flies of summer bounded and buzzed against the heads and faces of the circus pilgrims. The interstate was crowded with families and small groups of people. Some pulled the last of their precious properties in wagons and carts. Beasts of burden lasted less than a few hours on the interstates. Roving mobs of survivor hunters killed animals for food. When violent women chased Private Jones and Pure Gumption for dinner the circus animals were carried in disguises. Private Jones traveled in the foot holsters at the waist of Sun Bear Sun and Proude made Pure Gumption into a comfortable hump on his back. The fear of cannibalism caused the interstate walkers to sleep close together for common protection.

The interstate medians were strewn with discarded furniture and memorabilia the walkers could no longer harness and cumber. From the ruins of personal properties some walkers stopped walking to live in wickiup shelves and berths tilted together and covered with flapping plastic or swatches of carpet. The wickiup people offered various services from their transient berths on the medians.

Wickiup restaurants on the medians maintained hordes to protect their food and supplies. Special clothing, shoes, precious gems and metals, rare books, salt and sugar, chocolate, coffee and tea, well water, drugs and drinkable alcohol were all used as barter. One walker told the circus pilgrims that he had traveled more than a thousand miles eating and sleeping with various families in exchange for diluted alcohol. The circus pilgrims discovered the new meaning of families. Independence for some people was preserved in hunger. Survival on the interstate was more verbal than spiritual, words not silence, more open than closed, less secret, little political. Those who survived the longest knew themselves at least as well as the government investigators once knew them. The toughest survivors never had their internal chickens plucked.

Oral traditions were honored. Families welcomed the good tellers of stories, the wandering historians of follies and tragedies. Readers and writers were seldom praised but the traveling raconteurs were one form of the new shamans on the interstates. Facts and the need for facts had died with newspapers and politics. Nonfacts were more believable. The listeners traveled with the tellers through the same frames of time and place. The telling was in the listening. When the sun had set travelers and moths were drawn to flames. Stories were told about fools and tricksters and human animals. Myths became the center of meaning again.

Parawoman Pio Wissakodewinini eased down like a camel into the deep cool grass at the edge of the interstate and unbound his steaming feet. He carved two holes and buried his feet in the sand beneath the thick garment of grass. The sun slipped beneath his massive shoulders and the laughing cottonwoods. Thin cloud streams carried the last bright light into purple darkness. The circus pilgrims turned to their evening fire. Proude told stories about his father and grandfather and the sovereign nation but no one spoke of returning to the cedar circus.

The clown crows awakened the circus pilgrims before sunrise. The morning light danced over the earth rims. Perfect Crow thrust her beak around the fire and then motioned with her black head toward the interstate. Saint Benito Saint Plumero was on the road alone.

"Bioavaricious . . . He will be there waiting to be surprised when we come," Proude whispered to Perfect Crow who was walking in small circles on his chest. "The crows should follow the new saint to paradise," he said pushing her into flight.

The exit road to the little town of Bioavaricious on the wheat plains was not as crowded as the interstate. The people near the town talked their time through space.

"Listen . . . Listen to the talking," said Matchi Makwa.

"Did you see her there," noted Doctor Wilde, "she was using all she is and owns to state a simple sentence . . . arms, legs, cheeks, head nodding, fingers twitching, ears wagging, she gets her morning exercise from a three line poem."

A wrinkled old man with stiff blades of white hair approached the pilgrims. He had been speaking on himself and lifted his silver cane like a railroad semaphore. The circus stopped. The old man smiled and said, "Welcome to Bioavaricious avaricious avaricious." Then he lowered his cane and continued walking down the road.

"Did you hear that?"

"Sounds like the bishop bishop bishop."

Pointing with three stiff fingers at the end of his tense arm, Doctor Wilde said, "Now, there on that rise ahead, if my eyes are fitting well, do those black blots swirling over the buildings remind you of something?"

"The crows ... the clown crows, the crows must be in paradise," chimed Justice Pardone.

The circus pilgrims walked toward the buildings. The crows were soaring in circles over several figures on a verandah. Private Jones and Pure Gumption, riding in their disguises, were restless when the crows crowed. Turning down a curved road the pilgrims climbed a gentle rise through the willows and sculptured hedge rows around the building guards. There, sitting with three people in uniforms, was Saint Saint Plumero smoking on a stout cigar. Behind him was a large brick government building. Three bronze statues of famous political orators stood on the verandah.

Pure Gumption climbed from her hump and Private Jones leaped from his paw holsters and bounded across the verandah through conversations into the lap of Saint Saint Plumero. The animals whimpered and licked his face. The people in uniform were distracted.

"Well Saint Saint Plumero, tell me the truth now," said Doctor Wilde waving his arms in wild gestures, "is this place on the wheel worth the word paradise?"

"Paradise nothing," Saint Saint Plumero responded while he stood next to the statues. "This is a wild word hospital."

"Never a simple answer ... Saint Saint Saint Plumero," said Bishop Parasimo. His eager hands followed his meaning. "Tell me please what is a word hospital ... simple words."

"Triple Saint Plumero ..."

"Double Saint."

"Double Saint finds a word hospital."

"Words fail me."

The circus pilgrims broke into laughter and wriggled their fingers at each other in forced conversations. Meanwhile the people in uniforms moved from pilgrim to pilgrim catching hands and words. The crows became more daring with the verbal foolishness and hopped from shoulder to shoulder. The people in uniforms were alarmed and could not find words to express their discomfiture.

"Where are you people from?"

"Here here here ..."

"I mean who who are you?"

"Double Saint must know in so many words," mocked Doctor Wilde, who was the most animated with the word games, "and the rest of us are the others."

"Double Saint," pleaded the tall woman in uniform, "please understand me when I tell you that you did not tell us while we were speaking as we have been here on the verandah this morning... You did not tell us about these things that have happened ... These animals and birds now."

"What has happened?"

"These foolish gestures and mindless conversations when what we all want out of our lives is more clearness and meaning to our words to seize the good times from carelessness before living becomes too late for us all again ..."

"For sure."

"What she is attempting to tell you all," interrupted the bald man in uniform, "is one simple fact. Listen to me please while I express what this means to me. We were not prepared with words to consider this conversation with spontaneous appreciation ... These are not problems of the future, mind you, but concern for the moment and at this moment our minds are a bit sore from the confusion... Could we start once again. Now please, Double Saint, would you please take your seat as you were and the others, well, would you all back down the hill for a retake... One last word, please, could we keep our voices down and our hands out of the conversation ... Thank you, please, shall we begin again now?"

The clown crows rode on the shoulders of the circus pilgrims walking backward through the willows down the hill. Matchi Makwa crowded and gathered the pilgrims into a huddle to plan their social behavior. Proude told about the two people in uniforms who came to the cedar nation not willing to speak alone.

"Start up again down there."

"Start again up there when we come."

The pilgrims walked back to the verandah and introduced themselves with formal gestures and handshakes. Private Jones sneezed. The crows wobbled and stretched their necks from the shoulders of the pilgrims. "We have come a long way on the interstate to be with you here," said Proude in a deep voice. "One chance on the dream wheel put us together in this paradise of words. We are grateful for the privilege to be here."

"But we are not there yet," said one.

"Not yet where?"

"There meaning here, meaning we are still working out the models and paradigms and experiments on our language to learn where we are and where we will be, all at the same time that we consider the moment at which we meet and speak," said two.

"This moment we meet is not the moment we met, but we think it is as we speak, because we know what we want to know ..."

"What the fuck are you talking about?"

"Are these fools social workers?"

"What we want to know is what we hear, but this moment, all moments here at the Bioavaricious Regional Word Hospital, are recorded on audio and video tape for future examination and model testing ... We will do studies on these few moments later."

"Words of wisdom," said Double Saint.

"Government thinking," said Pio.

"I am at a loss for words," said Matchi Makwa. "Words cannot describe the feeling that our language is a labor of love against which we rise up and prevail in glorious voices of pride and speak about nothing ..."

The pilgrims applauded his nonsense speech.

"True words words words spoken in due season," said Bishop Parasimo, lacing his hands together in front of his chest. "How good the sound sounds."

The pilgrims dipped and nodded their heads.

"At this word hospital," said three, emphasizing the local specialties, "we find tongues in trees, books in brooks, phrases from the mouths of fish, oral literatures on the wings of insects, sermons in stone, good words here and there, words are all things to all people."

"What does word hospital mean?" asked Inawa Biwide.

The tall woman in uniform gestured to one and two for permission to respond to the question. "This silent pilgrim must sail near the wind words on meaning to ask the bottom line question ... What does word hospital mean? Well, a word is a word is a spoken or printed combination of sounds with meanings determined in the usage of time and social taste. The word hospital means ..."

"We get your meaning," said Matchi Makwa, interrupting the tall woman and slapping the top of his hand several times as he spoke. "But like this, what is it what you folks do here, I mean what does a word hospital do with words in the world?"

"Follow me pilgrims," said one.

"Through this door and we will show and tell what a little old word hospital does for us all," said two. The circus pilgrims followed them into the government buildings where there were dozens of people in uniforms working at desks with recorders and earphones and computerscreens that flashed phrases and words and musical notations. One and two told the histories of word hospitals while the pilgrims were given a tour of the facilities.

"We are futurist facilitators," one explained. "Thirteen years ago the government authorized federal funds for a pilot investigation of public damage to the language ... Since the language is made out of words the business of the investigation became in effect a word for word examination.

"Mindful that we live in a world of political stage whispers, the government expanded the pilot to include more than just the speeches of corrupt presidents and public officials ... We have had solid funding for the past decade to examine words where and when we find them in conflict.

"The government discovered that there was something wrong with our language. The breakdown in law and order, the desecration of institutions, the hardhearted investigations, but most of all the breakdown in traditional families was a breakdown in communication ... This caused our elected officials to create this word hospital and eight others in the nation ... Six of them are new buildings like this one, while two were created in the ruins of the old Bureau of Indian Affairs field offices ..."

"Give me the word ..." said Matchi Makwa.

"The bureau records were included in our analysis of language. You might say we are using the files and reports from the Indian offices as the basic paradigm to determine the causes for the breakdown in language and government services ... The language of the bureau had nothing whatever to do with the reason for its existence."

"What is that machine over there?"

"That is what we call a bioaudience synthesizer," said two. "We now are located in the word ward of symbolic rendering and that machine digests all the words and phrases read into the congressional record."

"Where does it shit?" asked Double Saint. "What I mean to say for sure is where does it shit what it has digested?"

"Humorous thought," said the tall woman in uniform. "Well, so far it has been reading back what it has been digesting in the same political language, which is what we have come to call degenerative grammar ... We are not pleased with the results and will phase that part out soon."

Next the circus pilgrims were escorted to a large room where the central computers were housed. Each machine had a name and number and the employees of the word hospital made personal references to the machine. The machines were humanized while the humans were mechanized. The tall woman explained the rationing of electric power to the word hospital because words were classified as secret.

"This is wonderful," said Doctor Wilde.

"Wonderful!" chimed Justice Pardone.

When Belladonna asked what a dianoetic chromatic encoder was it took the combined explanations of three word hospital officials to explain that the encoder machine was used to code and then reassemble the unit values of meaning in a spoken sentence. "Each word in this sentence, for example," the tall woman said, "would be encoded and given a color value such as red for hot words and cool blue for other words. Each word in the language has a color coded value and chromatic meaning in association with these words. Chromatic deductions on several thousand lines of free verse were turned over to intelligence organizations ... We have also encoded the speeches and writings of radical organizers and terrorists. For example, we have studied the possessive nouns and shifting verbs of Dennis Banks from the old American Indian Movement, the writings of Patricia Hearst and Bertrand Cellanoid. The last chromatic studies were made on the words of Charles Manson, in fact, the machine stopped on one of his prison messages, *dreamers dreaming dreams of dreams dreaming dreamers."*

"What were the deductions?"

"Well, if memories serve me in proper form the results ranged from both color value extremes without significant color configurations to draw conclusions at this time."

"Interesting."

"But the most interesting studies on the dianoetic chromatic encoder involved the printout on the values of meaning during the word wars between various word wards in the word hospital ... Communications first broke down between two word wards and spread like red and orange to officers and other technicians ... There was a sudden epidemic of illogicial negativism. The word hospital was programmed for possible breakdowns. When it happened, all conversations were recorded and fed into the encoder. The results were then announced over the internal bioelectric communication wands between the warring word wards."

"What did the wands tell?"

"It said the word wars were based on the colors of heated words which malfunctioned when cool explanations were understood as negative responses ... What we had was a basic misunderstanding, a thunder storm, you might say we had a good argument."

"This is fascinating!" moaned Doctor Wilde.

"Fascinating!" chimed Justice Pardone.

"Which ward won the word war?" asked Double Saint.

"The neologism and solipsism detection word wards," said the tall woman in uniform. She smiled at Doctor Wilde. Justice Pardone smiled back.

The last stop on the word hospital tour was at a glass enclosed room surrounded with electronic instrument panels. Doctor Wilde Coxwain and Justice Pardone Cozener were volunteered to enter the room for a demonstration of the conversation stimulators. With regenerated bioelectrical energies and electromagnetic fields, conversations were stimulated and modulated for predetermined values. Certain words and ideas were valued and reinforced with bioelectric stimulation.

"Can you hear me in there?" asked one. Justice Pardone and Doctor Wilde were sitting in the silent booth. "Make yourself comfortable and begin discussing anything you wish to, so long as

you both speak and share a common interest. You can begin now . . .
talk."

"What are you going to do to me?"

"Nothing to you mister wild," two said, "but we will attempt to
influence the values and directions of your conversations . . . We will
record words from your speech with the time and stimulation so you
can read the results yourselves. Now, can we begin?"

"This is one fine place . . . You can sound that out again . . .
Fantastic place to research tribal legal reasoning and meaning . . . We
know what that is now . . . What is? . . . Legal reasoning . . . But all
decisions have a chromatic value . . . So what . . . We could teach with
color and not words . . . Who gives a good shit about color in legal
reasoning . . . Judgments could be made in colors . . . We all care
about color values . . . Fuck the color values and fuck the red, white
and blue laws in this place . . . Is this you speaking sweetheart?"

Negative bioelectric stimulation caused the two tribal pilgrims to
disagree. The two in uniform adjusted the instruments to more
pleasant stimulations. "Next we will stimulate a feeling of loneliness
in the conversation and then cause one to speak about his past . . . We
increase the autobiographic stimulator until he responds with
nostalgia and stories."

"Have you stimulated sex?"

"We have avoided that in our research."

"French Kiss Farms . . . So named because the women on the
communal farm french kissed the cows before milking . . . Said the
best milk comes from the best kissed . . . The people there were
animals and birds but the animals were given machine mode names
. . . Carburetor the choking cat . . . Living there was like living in a
continuous conversation . . . If you remember we first met while I was
lodged in the genitalia pilloria for lusting during chores . . . How
could I forget when your beautiful balls were hanging in public view
from that terrible wooden trap . . . You fell in love with my cock and
balls before you saw my face . . . Thinking now about life on the farm
causes me to feel a deep loneliness . . . But our loneliness was a special
happiness . . . Being in love is loneliness . . . Do you remember when
the laugh machine at the farm began to weep . . . It cried for three
hours before we could change the tune . . . The farm was a place of
dispersoned people who lived through conversations and concepts of
themselves . . . The place where selfish needs were spoken of as public

experiences ... Do you remember when all the mind farmers there were taking on new names for animals and birds and we named you the heron ... We named you the stout little woodchuck lawman ... All people and experiences had names ... The houses had names, the barn was called william, the pond was sarah, swim in the sarah, the pump was donald, and the car named the mobile penetralia for those who had to think things out before joining the mind farmers again ... You mean the mind fuckers ... Histories did not exist until words were spoken for time ... Each morning at the farm was the beginning of a new world of words ... The mind farmers lived through superlative verbal visions ... Remember the lambent radiant wheat, the babbling sucking brook, the wonderful, the marvelous, splendid, brilliant, fantastic this and that around them ... It was no place to be alone but a good world to tell about sex and animal fucking ... We felt good with each other there. Doctor Wilde dropped down to his knees beside Justice Pardone and pushed at the fat on his stomach and touched his testicles. When Justice Pardone unzipped his pants the two in uniform flipped the switches and turned the dials until the two pilgrims changed their moods and shunned each other.

"You are selfish with little concern for my feelings ... You are the one who is selfish ... Why do you always disagree with me when we discuss something ... Because you are a stupid bitch ... If you call me a bitch again you can forget about our relationship. The two in uniforms terminated the electronic circuits."

"Did you like the demonstration?"

"Wonderful ... Wonderful!" said Double Saint who had been watching the values on the dials of the stimulators. He whispered to the other pilgrims and then lured the tall woman and the two in uniforms into the booth and locked the door. Double Saint set the dials on argumentation. The circus pilgrims listened for a few minutes and then turned to leave the word hospital.

"The last word in the word wars ..."

Standing hand in hand Justice Pardone and Doctor Wilde announced their mutual decision not to leave the word hospital. The word wards reminded them of their first meeting and love among the mind farmers.

"This is our last chance to be part of the real word," said Justice Pardone, leaning against Doctor Wilde.

"Words are the meaning of living now ... The word is where the world is at now," said Doctor Wilde. "Besides, the government will care for us and feed us here."

"Will the word people care?"

"When we finish stimulating their conversations the three of them will give us their bodies," Doctor Wilde said as he turned the dials from argumentation to the color values of passion and lust.

"Remember this . . ."

"What?"

"Remember, there are no simple answers in a hospital for word wars," said Double Saint. He pinched Justice Pardone on the fat breasts and thumped out of the building with his umbrella popped.

¶ Witch Hunt Restaurant

The circus pilgrims were tired and their muscles were sore from walking on the interstate. The hours passed like centuries under the hot sun and the nights turned in minutes. Even the seven clown crows were listless and careless in flight.

Rosina Cedarfair never complained and seldom expressed her feelings, but when the pilgrims collapsed in the cool grass at a reststop near Ponca City, Oklahoma, she said that distance no longer had meaning in her. "Mind and muscles are so worn down ... Time has lost track of me in this world."

"Not so," said Double Saint reading his wrist watch. "The exact time is three thousand and nine hundred and eight moons since the woodland *anishinabe* first saw a whiteman ..."

"Double Saint," said Bishop Parasimo. "You must never tire of walking and fooling fooling fooling around ... We should have settled for the word wards behind the guards."

Double Saint had ordered the last tribal timepiece from a reservation watchmaker, he explained, as he passed the watch around for the circus pilgrims to see. The tribal watchmaker died in an ideological shootout on the reservation with urban tribal radicals. He had finished nineteen watches before his death. Tribal time is measured with one moon wand, the maker called it a wand. There were also two hour hands. The moon wand measured the moons from the time of the first whiteman, according to the tribe and the first meeting. The conventional hour hands were set within two hours, more or less, of real time. One measure was new tribal time. "And as you know," Double Saint explained, "real time is now about four in the afternoon, which is later than tribal time."

Other families and wanderers left the interstate near the reststop for the same reasons as the circus pilgrims — to rest and find food and water.

The hot winds carried the scent of prairie roses and sage through mauve pillars of the setting sun and into darkness.

On the other side of the exit road from the circus pilgrims two small families of whitewalkers were quarreling. The members of the families spread themselves apart in escape distances. The number of walkers quarreling and the pitch of their voices increased until one whitewalker flashed a stout hunting knife and challenged another whitewalker to fight. Matchi Makwa moved across the road closer to the families and saw the man with the knife thrust and slash in sudden movements. One woman fell forward with blood pumping from a hole in the brisket and the man stumbled backward with blood pulsating between his fingers at his neck. The two victims choked twice and died at the same moment. Without waiting for the flesh to cool the man with the knife removed the hearts of the victims and then carved and sliced the firm muscles from the shoulders and thighs and other parts of their bodies.

"What happened?"

"The man with the knife told the dead one he was going to kill the woman," Matchi Makwa explained while turning from time to time toward the whitewalkers across the road. "He said he was going to kill and eat the woman because she traveled with him several months before and stole his meat supplies ... Seems the man planned to feast on her flesh as restitution. But it was retribution too, because the man said over his dead body, and sure enough, as you saw it was over his dead body ... Now he will feast on the two of them."

"What about the others?"

"Strangers, more or less, from what I heard they had no reason beyond casual conversations to protect the two victims," Matchi Makwa explained. "One time the whitecannibals will not turn down their noses at tribal flesh."

When Matchi Makwa turned again to watch the whitewalkers across the reststop the man with the knife picked up the steaming heart from the dead whiteman and threw it across the road toward the circus pilgrims. "Here," he shouted out of breath, "eat your fucking hearts out." He laughed and turned to wipe the blood from his hands. The heart bounced and quivered before sliding to a stop in the grass. Neither the seven crows, nor the dogs, nor the nine circus pilgrims moved from their places. Eighteen pairs of eyes focused on the heart. Sun Bear Sun imagined the smell of cooking meat until digestive saliva filled his huge mouth. Matchi Makwa would feed it to the animals. Belladonna turned from the heart in tears fearful of evil fixations. Parawoman Pio was fighting back the powerful savage urge to devour the heart raw. He could taste the blood salts and feel the soft muscle slipping between his massive teeth. He swallowed. Proude thought about the death of his fathers and the spiritual power from the hearts of animal.

"We cannot eat this human heart," Proude said. "We cannot take the vision of violence and the violence of the flesh without rituals together in our bodies ... That heart has no power but evil to live in our bodies ... The animals will choose for themselves."

Pio moaned and his mammoth limbs trembled. Sun Bear Sun swallowed and in slow measured steps he walked across the road and talked to the whiteman with the knife. The man paused and then handed Sun Bear Sun a large piece of dried meat. When he returned he explained that the meat was from the biceps of a young woman who had been raped and killed for flesh the month before on the interstate. The meat was prepared. The circus pilgrims were silent. Proude and Inawa Biwide and Rosina and Belladonna and Perfect Crow and Pure Gumption would not eat human flesh. Private Jones and six crows pecked and pulled at the steaming heart.

When the man with the knife finished butchering the two bodies he carried the slabs of fresh flesh to the reststop building. Matchi Makwa and Bishop Parasimo followed the man with the flesh into the building which had been converted from a public reststop to a restaurant and drinking place. There were two large signs over the door of the reststop: *Ponca Witch Hunt Restaurant and Fast Foods* and *The Original Complaint Department Liquors.* Two white-families from eastern cities merged their perverse energies and hordes and seized the federal interstate reststop building for their own bar and fast foods. Three previous occupants were killed when the easterners took the business. Their bodies were dried and served up with stew until the witch hunt families established their own flesh trade.

Inside the circus pilgrims found several picnic tables in the center of the room. Waiters and waitresses were dressed in black. When a table was open the pilgrims seated themselves and read the chalkboard menu: meat stew with wild greens, greens and noodles, breakfast cereals with bread but no milk, water and swamp tea and new wine and beer. *The Original Complaint Department Liquors* was located at one end of the dining room. Over the slab bar was a notice that promised a free drink to the person who could state an original complaint about being alive.

"The thighs must be tough," said Matchi Makwa.

Not until the two pilgrims leaned back in their wooden chairs and looked up did they notice three figures tied and hanging alive above them. The figures were witches captured in the restaurant. The food fascists hung the witches out for a week or two and then cut them down and into pieces for takeout orders. The fascists would not serve the evil flesh of witches in their stew. One witch, the most attractive of the three, was weeping and calling the name of a man who once loved her. The light in the restaurant was dim and the luminescent bacteria embedded in the facial flesh of the witches cast a haunting glow over their faces. Phosphorescence had been the latest development in cosmetics. The food fascists identified women with bioluminescent faces as witches. The food fascists bound the women nude in leather harnesses and poured hot wax in their vaginal and anal openings and in their ears and noses to prevent evil fumes and sex with the devils. Their mouths were filled with cotton and then the witches were hoisted to the rafters. The witches were hanging faces and bellies down with mounds of colored wax stuck to their genital hair. The witches turned in slow motions. Matchi Makwa was attracted to the woman with the luminescent pine trees embedded in her cheeks. Her tears dripped on the table. Matchi Makwa touched the tears with his fingers.

"The time is right for liberations."

"Shall we witch snatch?"

"One is for me to keep," said Matchi Makwa.

"Lust hath no limits," said Bishop Parasimo. Speaking in his canorous cathedral voice, with supporting gestures from his hands, he asked the waiter to explain the meaning of the witches hanging over the table. The waiter looked up as if he had never seen the witches before and shrugged his shoulders. Matchi Makwa marched into the kitchen and in a few minutes returned with the ranking member of the food fascists.

"This is one of the owners," said Matchi Makwa, introducing the woman with deep wrinkles carved into the loose flesh on her face. "This is his grace, Bishop Omax Parasimo, and we would like to know about the witch clowns hanging over us here."

"We do our small part in cleansing the world of evil witches," the woman growled. She looked up at the witches as she spoke. When she sneered the skin of her face slid across her teeth and cheek bones like overripe fruit peel. Nodules of flesh on the sides of her chin dangled like loose testes when she spoke and moved her head.

"We know about witches here . . . This is our business and if witches want to be witches with their poison breath and evil fumes then they better do it somewhere else. We fight off the hordes of evil by night and day," the woman ranted with phlegm rattling in her throat. "We never sleep protecting this place from the glowing faces of their evil kind . . . We seal them with hot wax and hang them up to season and evaporate . . . Why do you want to know?" she asked, swinging her chin testes.

Bishop Parasimo made the sign of the cross.

"Count your blessings your mother was never touched with evil or the sirens from the cities . . . Let me tell you their poison is all over the world. Their fumes ruined this proud nation and gave us the problems we got now . . ."

"Convincing views," said Bishop Parasimo, holding his hands in his lap and speaking with caution. "You have done well as a woman of terminal terminal terminal passions . . ."

"Terminal terminal terminal?"

"Terminal end to the evil evil evil in the world . . . You do have a fine place of business here," said the bishop. "Tell me, do travelers stop in now and then and talk about times past past past when reststops were reststops with clean toilets?"

"We never knew this was a resting place," said the woman. "We took it over from some old women who thought they would rather cook than walk, but when the cook was killed the women moved on counting their simple blessings on the open road."

"Answer me this question," the bishop ventured, raising his hands from his lap to follow his question. "You recognize in me the power power power of a bishop and an exorcist . . . Give me these evil women and I will dispose of them and their evil and bless your fast food."

"No no exorcisms here mister bishop."

"Could we then purchase your witches?" the bishop asked. "Or could we purchase them for a few few few minutes ... You see, we share the same passion against evil and we would like to do our part before the witches die and their fumes of death escape into the sweet sweet sweet air of this good house."

"Well ..." The woman hesitated. The testes on her chin were moving. "Well .. no! Nothing doing, we need them right there on the rafters ... Our customers feel in good hands with the witches bound above them ... Nothing doing mister bishop. Besides, we have them plugged with wax now."

"Lord this woman needs your trust trust trust again," chanted the bishop. He smiled and wiped a sudden sign of the cross over her sliding face and hollow chest. Matchi Makwa burped and walked out of the fascist fast food restaurant.

The other pilgrims listened in silence to the descriptions of the witches and fast food fascists. Not one of the pilgrims resisted the verbal blueprints for the witch libration plans. The restaurant was mapped and framed. The scheme was scheduled for two hours before dawn when the least number of food fascists would be awake. Bishop Parasimo insisted that all his metamasks be worn in the liberation fete. "I have three metamasks masks masks and dominoes in that black case I have carried all this time," said the bishop. "You have seen but two of them. Scintilla Shruggles the face with red hair and Princess Gallroad the hitchhiker ... The third and last last last face will come alive during the nocturnal liberation."

"Supposing these women are real witches?" asked Sun Bear Sun. "The last thing we need now are more witches on the road ... Did the bishop check them out for witch business?"

"Witches have the twisted mouths of gossipers," said Proude. The circus pilgrims were silent. Perfect Crow was sitting on his shoulder.

Proude told stories about hands and wooden figures until the pilgrims dropped from the rims of flowers and the leaves of trees into the dark distance of animal sleep. He soared back to the *migis* sandridge again to swim and talk with the bears and crows. He returned to the burned cedar house. Sweeping cedar ash aside he uncovered a steel door which opened on a secret earth room beneath the house. There he had placed the sacred articles of the cedar fires.

Mitig, wooden, ceremonial charms and bear claws, eagle bones, a raven rattle to call the sun and fire. Then he opened in the secret light the medicine bundles of his father and examined the precious contents. Dropping in each a pinch of cedar incense he closed the leather bundles and covered the earth room with the ashes and charred cedar. Proude roared in his bear voice in the four directions and then returned to sleep beside the fire on the prairie. Rosina watched him appear from the distance. He smiled when she touched his face.

Perfect Crow hopped from chests to buttocks over the sleeping pilgrims two hours before dawn. Proude motioned to the birds and walked back from the road to a small stand of trees. He snipped leaves and grasses and cut thin slivers of bark for tea. The crows bounced from branch to branch near him. When Proude returned to the fire the pilgrims were awake and whispering their final plans for the liberation of the witches. Sun Bear Sun would stand as a sentinel near the entrance. Parawoman Pio the mammoth would move with Matchi Makwa and Bishop Parasimo into the restaurant. The three witches would be lowered from the rafters, unbound and dressed, and then one at a time the pilgrims and the witches would walk out of the restaurant. The gathering point was a few miles down the interstate at the next exit road. The circus pilgrims were dressed and waiting. Three men wore metamasks as women.

Rosina and Inawa Biwide entered the fascist food place first. Sitting at a table near the door the two ordered swamp tea and watched the witches whirling over the center tables. Next Belladonna entered and took her seat at a table on the other side of the room. Proude and Double Saint entered next and sat near Belladonna. Proude walked into the kitchen area and talked to one waiter. The other food fascists were sleeping.

Zebulon Matchi Makwa wore the fine face of Princess Gallroad the hitchhiker with long hair. Pio Wissakodewinini wore the face of Scintilla Shruggles. He moved under red hair with sensuous pride and confidence. Bishop Omax Parasimo wore for the first time the beautiful face of Sister Eternal Flame from the scapehouse of weirds and sensitives. She wore filoplumes on her ears and in her hair. Rosina caught her breath. For an instant she thought the metamask was the real person. The three metamasked women sat at the table beneath the witches. When the waiter returned the three women gave him a complicated order. Shruggles followed him to the kitchen to keep him occupied while Gallroad and Eternal Flame lowered the witches to the table. The harnesses were removed and the witches were dressed in duffel hoods. The witches pulled the wet matted cotton from their mouths and stumbled on stiff legs out of the restaurant. The circus pilgrims and two witches had disappeared into the darkness. While the witch with luminescent pine trees embedded in her cheeks admired the constellation quilt, Princess Gallroad admired her bare stomach and thighs. She touched her firm breasts and shoulders and then pushed her back against the table. When she spread her legs the princess lifted her dress revealing her throbbing penis. The witch clenched the constellation quilt and began to moan. The muscles on her inner thighs twitched. Gallroad took her penis in hand for the grand entrance when she saw the mound of wax moulded to her crotch hair and vagina. Obsessed with her lust she ran into the kitchen past the waiter and returned to the table with a sharp knife which she used to shave the hair from her crotch. When the last black strand was cut she lifted the mound of wax and matter hair like a scalp and tossed it to the floor. Breathless she thrust her penis into her evil warmth. Princess Gallroad and the witch with pine trees were consumed in their own lust and the total spiritual union between good and evil. The two did not hear the waiter call the food fascists to the table.

"No one but the devil would believe this," said the fascist woman with the chin testes. She was holding a knife with a wide blade. "A woman fucking a witch in our restaurant ... Make it good you devils because this is your last perversion in the world.''

Princess Gallroad and the witch did not hear the food fascist and did not feel the knife cutting into their bodies. Their blood mingled with the blood of the universe. In slow motions their bodies slid apart through circles of time over sacred names with good and evil dreams. Gallroad fell to the floor. Their clothes were removed. The skin tight metamask remained in perfect place.

"She has the penis of the devil," said the woman food fascist while the bodies were dragged into the kitchen. The bodies were cut into several parts and stuffed together into a giant handpowered meat grinder. The heads of Princess Gallroad and the witch with luminescent pine trees were mounted on witching sticks and placed at each side of the restaurant entrance. The face of the witch soon slipped from recognition to the ants and black flies, but the metamask face remained innocent and smiling on the outside.

¶ Westward on Witching Sticks

Eight circus pilgrims and two liberated witches were waiting beneath the bridge near the exit road for Matchi Makwa and the third witch with the luminescent pine trees on her cheeks. Wisps of morning light loped across the fields and hills through thin folds on the low clouds.

The pilgrims were silent. The two witches were chattering about their bodies and their futures on the road and in their own time started walking down the interstate.

Tucked beneath the beams under the bridge the pilgrims found a package of photographs with a note attached. The note explained that the owner of the photographs would no longer need them in his memories. Families and friends must wait here for me to return with new words and memories. Share the pictures but return them to the place beneath the bridge. In the name of the love and trust we once shared in this nation, no place, no date, no more living memories, no name. Signed, no name.

The first pictures in the bundle were bucolic scenes . . . A woman and two children standing in front of a sale notice on a small green rural house . . . The woman turned much older than her husband in the following photographs . . . There were three funerals . . . The last photograph showed a grave marker with the names of the woman and her two children . . . I will wander from this stone alone until the memories are gone. The man standing next to the marker was the same whiteman who butchered two people and threw a steaming heart to the pilgrims.

"Something has happened to them," said Sun Bear Sun.

"He ran down with that witch," smirked Belladonna as she packed the photographs back under the bridge beam. "He took that luminous pine tree into a pit somewhere."

"Go back and look look look for him," said Bishop Parasimo to Pio Wissakodewinini. "Wear this metamask again," he added as he handed the mammoth parawoman the face of Scintilla Shruggles. He looked at her and then asked if he could wear the other metamask, the gentle face of Sister Eternal Flame. The bishop agreed and the mammoth trotted in good cheer back down the interstate to the restaurant.

Near the entrance road she stopped and began to wail in a piercing voice when she saw the faces of the witch and Princess Gallroad stuck on witching sticks. She removed her face and then he pounded and pulled the door from the hinges and captured two waiters and one waitress and choked them together until their bodies were limp in his arms. Then he entered the kitchen where he found the food fascist woman with the testes on her chin. The mammoth took her arms in his massive hands and broke them behind her back. When she fainted and fell to the floor he broke her legs and stomped on her back and ribs until he heard the bones separate. Then he pulled up the witching sticks stuck in the heads and carried them like banners back to the pilgrims beneath the bridge.

Pio the parawoman would not speak. He did not permit the bishop, who gathered and packed his metamasks, to remove the face of Princess Gallroad from the rotting head of Zebulon Matchi Makwa.

The circus pilgrims turned from the interstate and walked west-ward toward Salk Fork in Oklahoma. The mammoth carried the heads on witching sticks over his shoulder. During the night he staked them in the earth near his head and the fire. During the third afternoon when the flies were swarming in black circles three times the size of the rotting heads, the mammoth stopped beside the road, removed the face of the Princess and dumped the two heads into a shallow grave. The maggots and ants had eaten the facial features of Matchi Makwa beneath the metamask. Bishop Parasimo cleaned the interior face of the Princess and placed it with the other permanent faces in his black case.

Through Carrier and Cleo Springs and Orienta, Double Saint and

Pio ticked and ticked over the black asphalt road with their witching walking sticks. The people in the little towns locked doors and shunned their passing. The clown crows and animals traveled three times the distance in the same direction in circles through the fields around the pilgrims. In their imperfect circles the birds and animals found water and small bits of food.

Perfect Crow was the first to rise in the morning, walking on the chests of the pilgrims, and was the first to choose a place to rest for the night. The crows were sensitive to the temperature and moisture of the earth and direction of underground rivers and reservoirs. Proude followed the crows and chose the place for the fire. The tribal keepers of the cedar fires, the fires of families and nations, were chosen from the signs of ravens and crows.

"When the tribes forgot about the crows and bears and the cedar fires of our families," Proude said with his back to the orange setting sun, "the tribes died from strange diseases ... The courses of rivers were forgotten and the energies from the heart and the flow of water were confused and changed from morning to evening stars ... The tribes lost their shadows ... The tribes have wandered alone forgetting the voices of the crows and bears bringing back their shadows."

The fire flickered brighter than the setting sun on the faces of the circus pilgrims. Proude dropped cedar incense into the flames and moaned in honoring tones the tribal words and visions for the bear in the shadows of the pilgrims ha ha ha haaaa. The soul of Zebulon Matchi Makwa would not wander on the aimless words of strangers down the interstate. His shadow was brought back to the cedar fire ha ha ha haaaa.

Kitchi makwa, the great bear ... *kitchitwawenima*, honoring the bear ... *agaweteon kitchi makwa*, shadow of the great bear ... *matchi makwa* evil bear name ... *nind ajewina*, I lead him back.

In the silent darkness Proude dropped more cedar incense over the fire. Inawa Biwide inhaled the sacred clouds of cedar smoke. Belladonna watched them and then she waved the smoke over her face and breasts and stomach with her hands. She held a small whistle made from the wing bone of an eagle over the coals of the fire and cedar smoke. The bone was white in her golden hands. Then she dipped her head from the circle and wailed through the sacred tones of the whistle. The mournful cries from the wing whistled soared across the dark earth to eagles on the mountains and to the turtles and bears wandering in the woodland. Pure Gumption moved to her side near the fire and howled in a deep voice with her head turned upward. Their bodies were glowing. Clouds moved from their voices under *binakwigisiss*, the moon of falling leaves.

¶ Conceived at Wounded Knee

Belladonna Darwin-Winter Catcher was singing praise for her tribal prairie father Old John Winter Catcher. He was a man of great Lakota visions . . . "He was *wanblee*, the soaring eagle," she was singing, "and he lived his lives honoring *wakan tanka* and the places in the families made of earth and water and stone . . .

"Frisian blood drove my mother," Belladonna told Inawa Biwide during their walk toward the southwest. "She was tall with golden hair and fire on her breath . . . She was killed writing about the race wars. Too white and too blond to survive third world colors . . .

"Old Winter Catcher gave me this *wanblee* whistle singing his death songs the night before he died. We drove through the darkness because he wanted to enter the next world through Wounded Knee . . . There in the morning when the summer sun stretched over Porcupine Butte and spiritual herds of great buffalo, Winter Catcher told me for the first time that he made me from his spirit, that I was conceived at Wounded Knee during the occupation of the American Indian Movement.

"Dennis Banks, one of the leaders at Wounded Knee, was on the Cheyenne River Reservation seeking the blessings of my father, when my mother, Charlotte Darwin, who was a journalist covering the occupation, found them both at Cherry Creek and asked them for an interview. Banks talked her into driving him through the federal roadblocks to Wounded Knee.

"Winter Catcher was silent. He told me he reached out and touched the golden hair he had dreamed of touching when he was a warrior. He dreamed from the mountains, he said. Mother turned him from his old places in the mountains and he found himself on the road to

Wounded Knee ... Winter Catcher told me how her golden hair glowed in the darkness, how their spirits soared under the stars of the great hunters. I was conceived there on that spiritual battlefield ... Conceived in love where brave people died .. They stayed together and worked at Wounded Knee until the occupation ended and then my mother went back to her home and the newspaper.

"Winter Catcher returned to the mountains ... They had not spoken and did not know how to find each other in the measures of the world. Nine months later, in November, under a moon of the first freezing, Old Winter Catcher was moved again with visions and came down from the mountains to Wounded Knee where he found his woman with the golden hair waiting for him. Their spirits came together again and I was born that night under the stars. I was conceived and born at Wounded Knee. I will return there with the spirit of my father traveling with thunder and eagles."

Belladonna touched Inawa Biwide on the cheek. He turned toward her and saw the fire and loneliness of her dark face. She showed him the *wanblee* whistle and told him, "in the world of evil all that remains of what is sacred are her memories and the eagle whistle ... I have nothing more in the world but his whistle to remind me of the great visions of Old Winter Catcher. He told me to sing with him through this whistle when we were distant or lost ... Singing *alowan alowan,* voices of great praise ... *wanblee wanblee wakan tanka owanka wakan wakan tanka,* the great spirit sacred places of the great spirit ... singing *alowan alowan.*" Raising the *wanblee* whistle to her lips she soared through the clear sounds over the cedar fires to the mountains under the stars of the great hunters.

Inawa Biwide watched her golden face soar through the darkness. When she returned she rested in silence while he spoke toward the fire in a gentle voice about eagles and children ... He told stories about two children walking alone on a beach.

"One child was playing near the edge of the calm water of the great lake with the sacred bones of an eagle ... When she boasted to her little friend and said that she had taken an eagle through his bones to be her husband, an eagle swooped down to the beach and carried his child bride with him to the mountains where he cared for her and brought her beautiful plumes and little birds for food ... But the child bride did not like to eat little birds with beautiful feathers and she changed her mind as children often do in dreams ... She told the faithful eagle that she wanted more and more to eat and when the eagle was out hunting she climbed from his sacred nest down the mountain and across the woodlands to her home near the beach and her waiting parents ... The eagle missed his child bride and soared over the mountains and beaches of the world searching for her ... Then while he soared and soared over the houses near the beach calling for his child bride in a lonesome voice the people in the houses came out to listen and told the eagle that if he wanted to see his child bride he should soar lower with his wings spread wide ... When the eagle spread his powerful wings the hunters from the houses shot and killed him ... The child bride took the wing bones from her dead eagle husband and made whistles to last through all her lives and dreams from the beaches ... When she was older she wandered in the mountains and called the eagles with her *wanblee* whistles to her side during the night."

¶ Terminal Creeds at Orion

Orion was framed in a great wall of red earthen bricks. Behind the earthen wall the blades of seventeen windmills named for the states rattled like strident insects on the hot wind over the panhandle. The circus pilgrims gathered near the main gate in the long lean shadows of the wall to read the application and conditions for admission to the enclosed town.

"Let the bishop read the fine print."

"Getting out worries me," said Sun Bear Sun.

"Listen to this, said Double Saint, visitors are welcome inside the Great Wall of Orion. Within the red walls live several families who were descendants of famous hunters and western bucking horse breeders. Like good horses, we are proud people who keep to ourselves and our own breed. We are amiable families within these walls and choose from time to time certain wanderers to share our food and conversation."

"Get this," said Bishop Parasimo, "it boasts that we should be prepared to eat eat eat and defend our ideas and views on the universe ... Narcissism is a form of isolation."

"Listen to this," said Belladonna. "Listen to this shit, terminal creeds are terminal diseases ... The mind is the perfect hunter ..."

"Not a good place," warned Inawa Biwide.

"What does it say about getting in to eat something?" asked Double Saint. "How do we get through the gate?"

"This is Bishop Omax Parasimo ..." he called into the metal pipe extending through the red wall. He strained his voice. "Is there someone there there there ... This is one of the circus pilgrim clowns ... over."

"We should order what we want," Sun Bear Sun suggested. "This thing is like a restaurant. Tell them to hold the onions ..."

"Give me that damn thing," said Double Saint. "Behind the great red wall ... This is Saint Saint Plumero with a hollow stomach and fantastic stories on the worlds outside these lonesome walls ... over."

"Saint who?" a voice asked.

"Saint Saint Plumero!"

"How many are there out there?"

"Eight pilgrims, seven clown crows, two animals, one that glows, and various good spirits ..." said Double Saint into the pipe.

"Who are these pilgrims?"

"We are tribal mixedbloods with good stories and memories from thousands of good listeners," said Double Saint. "Open the gate and let us in before we knock the walls down ... over."

"Let all the pilgrims speak for themselves."

"Me." - *reader - imt.*

"Trickster and double saint." - *saint Plumero*

"Parawoman." - *Pig*

"Keeper of the cedar fires." - *Proude Cedar fair*

"Mother of secrets and dreams." - *Rosina*

"The great sun of sun bears." - *Sun bear sun*

"Conceived and born at Wounded Knee ..." - *Belladonna*

"The son of everlasting silence." - *Inawate Biwede*

"Smile smile smile on strange faces." - *Bishop Parismo*

"Most unusual ... Peculiar pilgrims," the voice in the pipe said. "Wait where you are and the guards will come to take you through the gate ... We will find families where you can eat but you are too many to stay for the night ..."

In a few minutes the metal portcullis opened and several guards dressed in collegiate band uniforms escorted the pilgrims through the red wall. The dark tunnel inside the gate led to a large room with barred windows overlooking the center of the town. The pilgrims were examined. Information about places of birth, identities and families, education and experience, travels and diseases, attitudes on women and politics and ideologies and other descriptions were recorded.

The red door opened and several hunters and breeders stepped across the threshold with smiles and extended hands. The hunters and breeders looked forward to visitors to keep in touch with what was happening in the world outside the walls, but in the past few months killers and evil demons were lurking at the gates. To protect the families behind the Great Wall of Orion, the elder breeder explained, "we must ask questions about our visitors."

The pilgrims followed the hunters and breeders through the small neat town to one of the largest houses west of the bank and markets. Dozens of people were waiting on the front steps of the house. The pilgrims were introduced again and again and each time asked about their views on politics and news from the world outside the walls. The pilgrims were eager to please in return for the food but were troubled with the rapid questioning and disinterest in answers. Thousands of questions were asked before dinner was served in the church dining room. While the food was being served the hunters and breeders announced that one of the pilgrims would be obligated to speak after dinner. Belladonna agreed to talk about tribal values.

"Food at last," said Double Saint.

"My stomach forgot how to act in front of real food," said Sun Bear Sun as he stuffed several whole potatoes into his mouth with one hand. Onions, carrots, and thin slivers of pork he held in the other hand until his stomach took the potatoes.

The circus pilgrims sat in the church within the red earthen walls and ate and then ate more to avoid answering more questions. Bishop Parasimo was the first to shift the flow of conversation. He asked the hunters and breeders sitting at this table to discuss the meaning of the messages on the outside walls. "What does it mean mean mean narcissism is a form of isolation?"

"Narcissism rules the possessor," said a breeder with a deep scar on the side of his forehead. "Narcissism is the fine art that turns the dreamer into paste and ashes."

"Could narcissism be survival?"

"Never, never!" explained a small boned hunter with thin lips. "Survival is not a possessive reflection ... The turning under in the cold and snow, or the resignation to the forces of evil ... Survival is a keen view, the vision of eagles, the forearm of a bear and the ritual of a spider building his web on the wind ... That is survival!"

"Do the people here here here always ask so many questions?" asked the bishop. He had finished his meal and after wiping his hands and mouth he rested his hands on the table to share in the conversation.

"We cannot live without questions."

"We avoid terminal creeds with questions ... There are no last words to this world," said the breeder with the scar.

"Questions and verbal doubts keep us from the voices of internal violence," said a woman breeder in a western shirt with pearl buttons.

"Internal violence?"

"The violence that comes from shaving conversations too close to agreements," she said with no facial expression. Her lips moved some, but the rest of her face, even her pearl colored eyes, could have been struck from cold stone. "Inside is no place to disagree with ideas ... Inside is no place to be suspicious about the meaning of statements and actions."

"The church would never last last last in your hands," said the bishop. "What I mean is that it would never last through your questions."

"People are the living dead with the unquestioned church in them," the woman with the stone face said. "The church kills people inside with terminal creeds, terminal creeds ... Disliving lightning in the antelope hills."

"Which reminds me," said the bishop, "what does it mean mean mean that the mind is the perfect hunter?" His hands followed and marked a question on the table.

"Your hands are interesting," said a breeder with thin blond hair and a sharp nose bone. "Do your hands ever disagree with what you are saying?"

"With themselves perhaps ..."

"Then your hands must suffer the terminal disease of terminal creeds ... What use are your hands if they never question your view on the sides and shapes of time and experience?"

"I need someone to agree with me me me," said Bishop Parasimo. His humor was tense. "What would the celebrants think if the bishop blessed them and drew the sign of the cross with quarreling hands?"

"They should be quarreling if they bless terminal creeds," said the woman with the stone face. "Did you say the celebrants?"

"Yes, the celebrants."

"Celebrants ... diseases of sheared sheep."

"But sheep have no evil."

"Evil is not a disease ... Evil is a state of being," said the woman. "Sheep are terminal followers with or without evil doing."

"Your brand of survival is making it on hard words behind this red

192

wall ... Your wall is more terminal than the church," said the bishop in his best liturgical voice. To please the listeners he turned his hand gestures in disagreement with his words. "Now how about the perfect hunter, what is your answer to that terminal phrase?"

"The perfect hunter leaves himself and becomes the animal or bird he is hunting," said a hunter on the other side of the table. He touched his ear with his curled trigger finger. "The perfect hunter turns on himself ... He lives on the edge of his own meaning and humor ... The humor is in the contradictions of the hunter being close and distant at the same time, being the hunter and hunted at the same time, being the questioner and the questioned and the answer. The believer and the disbeliever at the same moment of mental awareness."

"Mea culpa culpa culpa," chanted the bishop but his hands did not follow his words. His hands shunned the hunters and breeders. "Spare me the rest of the universe in your contradictions ... May the terminal believers of this good earth spare your voices hiding behind these walls ..."

"The wall saves us from terminal creeds."

"What you need are terminal fools."

"Pitter patter."

The breeders and hunters at the table smiled and nodded and then turned toward the head table where the bald banker breeder was tapping his waterglass. Ting ting ting ding ding dong. Belladonna was sitting next to the banker. Her nervous fingers fumbled with the two beaded necklaces around her neck. Resting his hand on her right shoulder, the banker breeder introduced Belladonna as the speaker and then reviewed the practice of the hunters and breeders challenging the ideas from visitors outside the walls. The families applauded when the banker spoke of their mission against terminal creeds. "Depersonalize the word in the world of terminal believers and we can all share the good side of humor in our own places ... Terminal believers must be changed or driven from our dreams ... Until then we will continue our mission against terminal creeds wherever and whenever we find them." Belladonna could feel the moisture from his hand resting on her shoulder. Then he referred to her as the good spirited speaker who has traveled through the world of savage lust on the interstates, "this serious tribal woman, our speaker, who once carried with her a tame white bird." He released her shoulder when he said her name, Belladonna Darwin-Winter Catcher.

Belladonna leaned back in her chair. The muscles on her chest and thighs twitched from his words about the tame white bird. The banker did not explain how he knew that she once traveled with a tame dove until the medicine man told her it was an evil omen to be seen with a white bird. She turned the dove loose in the woods but the bird was tame and returned to her shoulder. She cursed the bird and locked it out of her house, but the white dove soared in crude circles and hit the windows. The dove would not leave. One night, when she was alone, she squeezed the bird in both hands. The white dove took the pressure for affection and wriggled with contentment in her hands. She shook the dove. Behind the house, against a red pine tree, she severed the head of the white dove with an axe. Blood spurted in her face. The blood stained headless dove flopped alone through the last world into the dark woods.

"We are waiting," said the banker.

Belladonna was still shivering when she stood at the table next to the banker breeder. She fumbled with her beads. "Tribal values and dreams is what I will talk about," she said in a gentle voice.

"Speak up ... Speak up!"

"Tribal values is the subject of my talk!" she said in a loud voice. She dropped her hands from her beads. "We are raised with values that shape our world in a different light ... We are tribal and that means that we are children of dreams and visions ... Our bodies are connected to mother earth and our minds are part of the clouds ... Our voices are the living breath of the wilderness ..."

"My father and grandfathers three generations back were hunters," said the hunter with the trigger finger at his ear. "They said the same things about the hunt that you said is tribal ... Are you telling me that what you are saying is exclusive to your mixedblood race?"

"Yes!" snapped Belladonna. "I am different than a whiteman because of my values and my blood is different ... I would not be white."

"Do tell me," said an old woman breeder in the back of the room. "We can see you are different from a man, but tell us how you are so different from whitepeople."

"We are different because we are raised with different values," Belladonna explained. "Our parents treat us different as children ...

We are not punished because our parents give us the chance to experience limits ... We are never yelled at as children, our parents use their eyes to tell us what we have done wrong ... We live in larger families and never send our old people to homes to be alone. These are some things that make us different."

"What else is so different?"

"Tribal people seldom touch each other," said Belladonna folding her arms over her breasts. "We do not invade the personal bodies of others and we do not stare at people when we are talking ... Indians have more magic in their lives than whitepeople ..."

"Wait a minute, hold on there," said a hunter with an orange beard. "Let me find something out here before you make me so different from the rest of the world ... Tell me about this Indian word you use, tell me which Indians are you talking about, or are you talking for all Indians ... And if you are speaking for all Indians then how can there be truth in what you say?"

"Indians have their religion in common."

"What does Indian mean?"

"Are you so hostile that you cannot figure out what and who Indians are? An Indian is a member of a recognized tribe and a person who has Indian blood."

"But what is Indian blood?"

"Indian blood is not white blood."

"Indians are an invention," said the hunter with the beard. "You tell me that the invention is different than the rest of the world when it was the rest of the world that invented the Indian ... An Indian is an Indian because he speaks and thinks and believes he is an Indian, but an Indian is nothing more than an invention ... Are you speaking as an invention?"

"Mister . . . does it make much difference what the word Indian means when I tell you that I have always been proud that I am an Indian," said Belladonna, "proud ... proud to speak the voice of mother earth and the sacred past of the tribes."

"Please continue ..."

"Well, as I was explaining, tribal people are closer to the earth, the meaning and energies of the woodlands and mountains and plains ... We are not a competitive people like the whites who competed this nation into corruption and failure. We are not competitive because we share our lives and dreams and use little from the earth ..."

"When you use the collective pronoun," asked a woman hunter with short silver hair, "does that mean that you are talking for all tribal people?"

"Most of them."

"How about the western fishing tribes on the ocean, the old tribes, how about including them in your collective generalizations ... Those tribes burned down their own houses in potlatch competition."

"The exceptions are not the rule."

"But the rule has too many exceptions," said the woman with silver hair. "You speak from terminal creeds ... Not a person of real experience and critical substance."

"Thank you for the meal," said Belladonna. She smirked and turned in disgust from the hunters and breeders. The banker placed his moist hand on her shoulder again. "She will speak in good faith," said the banker, "if you will listen with less critical ears. She does not want her beliefs questioned. Give her another good hand." The hunters and breeders applauded her until she stood again to speak. She smiled, accepted apologies for hard questions and started again.

"The tribal past, our religion and dreams and the concept of mother earth, is precious to me ... Living is not good for me if a shaman does not sing for shadows in my dreams. Living is not important if it is turned into competition and material gain ... Living is hearing the wind and speaking the languages of animals and soaring with eagles in magical flight. When I speak about these experiences it makes me feel powerful, the power of tribal religion and spiritual beliefs gives me protection. My tribal blood is like your great red wall ... My blood moves in the circles of mother earth and through dreams without time. My tribal blood is timeless and it gives me strength to live and deal with evil ..."

"Right on sister, right on," said the hunter with the trigger finger on his ear. He leaped to his feet and cheered for her views.

"Hallelujah!" shouted another hunter.

"This is a bad place," whispered Inawa Biwide.

"Powerful speech," said a breeder.

"Truth in beautiful words," said a hunter.

"She deserves her favorite dessert," said a hunter in a deep voice. The hunters and breeders did not trust those narcissistic persons who accepted personal praise.

"Shall we offer our special dessert to this innocent child?" asked the breeder banker of the hunters and breeders gathered in the dining room. "Let me hear it now, those who think she deserves her dessert, and those who think she does not deserve dessert for her excellent speech. Let me see a show of hands for those opposed ... Three opposed. Well, she wins her favorite dessert."

"No dessert please," said Belladonna.

"Now, now, how could you turn down the enthusiasm of the hunters and breeders who listened to your thoughts here. How could you turn down their vote for your dessert. What is the dessert tonight?"

"Sugar cookies."

"Bring the cookies for the speaker of dreams," said the banker breeder. "She will lead us all in our just desserts." The banker breeder put his hot hand on her shoulder again.

The hunters and breeders cheered and whistled when the cookies were served. The circus pilgrims were not comfortable with the shift in moods and excessive praise.

"The energies here here here are strange," said Bishop Parasimo. The hunter with the scar frowned. "What is the meaning of their sudden shift in temperature, what does all this cheering mean?"

"Quite simple, mister bishop," said the breeder with the scar. "You see, when questions are unanswered and there is no humor the messages become terminal creeds, and the good hunters and breeders here seek nothing that is terminal ... So the questioners become celebrants when there is nothing more to learn. Terminal creeds are terminal diseases and when death is inevitable celebration is the best expression."

"Here come the sugar cookies."

"Speakers first ..."

"Here, here, for our mixedblood from the plains, this is a sugar cookie toast to our speaker, a forever toast to her precious tribal past and to the freedom into the present," said the banker breeder. The hunters and breeders cheered her when she nibbled her cookie.

The families smiled when she stood to tell them how much she loved them. "In your smiling faces I can see myself ... This is a good place to live and I admire your courage and your care for the living. Thank you for this special moment on our journeys." The hunters and breeders cheered her again.

"But you applaud her narcissism," said the bishop to the breeder with the scar. His hands were fingering each other and then one hand pulled the fingers on the other.

"She has demanded that we see her narcissism," said the breeder. "You heard her tell us how she saw in our faces her own ... Your mixedblood friend is a terminal believer and a victim of her own narcissism."

"But we are all all all victims."

"The histories of tribal cultures have been terminal creeds and narcissistic revisionism ... If the tribes had more humor and less false pride then the families would not have collapsed under so little pressure from the whiteman ... Show me a solid culture that disintegrates under the plow and the saw?"

"Your views are terminal ..."

"Who is serious about the perfections of the past? Who gathers around them the frail hopes and febrile dreams and tarnished mother earth words?" asked the hunter with the scar. "Surviving in the present means giving up on the burdens of the past and the cultures of tribal narcissism ... No other culture has based social and political consciousness on terminal creeds ... Survival is not narcissism."

"You must be burning at the stake ..."

"All terminal creeds fail ... Economics has taken over the values of the church. If the church could not survive the dollar then tell me how can a tribal culture survive when it sounds like the past took place in the nave of a church?

"Tell me where do the terminal believers gather with their tolerance for the views of others? Your speaker cannot give up her frail bromides without facing the fear of collapsing inward," said the breeder with the scar on his forehead. His voice was harsh. "You see, mister bishop, when we challenge terminal creeds here behind the protection of our great wall, we collapse outward. Outward because we never internalize the blame for ideas that did not work in the real world whenever the world was real. We are not tribal victims seeking those who will punish us for what we believe so that we can be sure we are good believers ...

"Tell me, mister bishop, will you collapse inward, or will you collapse outward? Will you choose the questions and hard words of your collapse, or will the precious words choose you from the burdens of the revised past?"

"Dominus vobiscum ..."

198

"Inward collapses at lightning hills."

"Lightning hills?"

Belladonna nibbled at her sugar cookie like a proud rodent. Her cheeks were filled and flushed. Her tongue tingled from the tartness of the cookie. In the kitchen the cooks had covered her cookie with a granulated time release alkaloid poison that would dissolve in minutes. The poison cookie was the special dessert for narcissists and believers in terminal creeds. She was her own victim. The hunters and breeders have poisoned dozens of terminal believers in the past few months. Belladonna nibbled at the last crumbs, in her effort to be polite, unaware that she would be dead before morning. She smiled and nodded her appreciation to the hunters and breeders.

"But before you and this fine circus resume your pilgrimage," said the banker breeder, "please, as our special dessert speaker, you must sign your name and write a one line thought in our book for us to remember this moment together . . ."

The banker breeder handed her a large leather bound book with a red ribbon. The banker opened the book to the ribbon marker. Belladonna paused to think out her precious line. The circus pilgrims and hunters and breeders waited in silence. Then she took the thick pen and wrote her message. The banker read her message to the hunters and breeders.

"Our hearts soar with the eagles of our people," and then he closed the book on the ribbon marker. The audience cheered her once more. She blew them kisses and then removed one of her beaded necklaces. She slipped it over the stout bald head of the banker. He raised his voice over the cheering and said that the best times were still to come.

The circus pilgrims expressed their appreciation and were escorted out of town under the state windmills and through the portcullis. The sun had dropped beneath the great red earthen wall. The pilgrims walked around the shadows. There were no clouds on the horizon. The seven clown crows hopped and flew and hopped and flew near the pilgrims until it was dark.

"The orange sun still bounces behind my eyes like a bunch of circus balloons," said Belladonna. "The stars are never bright enough to burn through our vision like the sun . . . Hopping down a road with orange balloons . . . And just when I focus on them they float upward and the more I try to catch them in focus the quicker they disappear."

"We shoud have started walking at night when we were on the interstate," said Bishop Parasimo. "It feels good to be alone in the cool darkness without facing the sad faces of all those wanderers."

"Feels like an adventure," said Double Saint.

"My father took me into the sacred hills," chanted Belladonna. "We started when the sun was setting, because Old Winter Catcher had to know what the setting sun looked like before he climbed into the hills for the night . . . The sun was beautiful, it spread great beams of orange and rose across the heavens . . . He said it was a good sunset. No haze to hide the stars. He said it was good and we climbed into the hills . . . I feel like that now, I feel like we are climbing into the hills for the visions of the morning. The morning . . . When the first and last colors of the heavens are turned around."

"So talkative in the dark," said Double Saint.

"Bigfoot . . . Tell me one thing?" Belladonna asked turning and walking backwards. "Have you ever walked up a hill backwards? Have you ever lifted your feet with visions in the back of your head?"

"Never . . . but in dreams. You see, with the size of my feet, nothing abnormal you understand, but with the length and breadth of these beautiful feet," he said looking down at his huge feet thumping on the cool black asphalt. "It is a must to take the world straight out, not to mention hills, in the forward position . . . Have you ever seen a bird walking backwards?"

Belladonna leaped and turned before she landed. She whistled at the stars and the darkness between them while she walked with her head pitched backwards. The crows rode on her shoulders and hopped beside the pilgrims on the road. Perfect Crow hopped and flapped in four or five spurts ahead and then waited for the pilgrims. The crows never hopped backwards.

"Backward flight?"

"We walked up part of the hill backwards," Belladonna said with her head turned backwards. "Then he told me that the world is not as it appears to be frontwards . . . To leave the world and see the power of the spirit on the hills we had to walk out of the known world backwards . . . We had to walk backwards so nothing would follow us up the hill. Things that follow are things that demand attention . . . Do you think we are being followed now?

"When I do this we are walking into the morning with Old Winter Catcher," she said walking backwards down the road. "The first to come into morning with no demands on our attention."

"Another nice thing about walking backwards," said Double Saint

200

while he smacked his hands on his leather covered thighs, "is that when you fall you fall on your ass and not on your face. Ass falling is a lot less embarrassing."

"There go the balloons again," she said turning around. "When will the balloons leave me behind? She waved her arms in the motion of flight and started hopping ahead of the pilgrims. She hopped and flapped like the crows and then, with a high pitched moan, she started running. She disappeared into the darkness. The sound of her feet and breath came back to the pilgrims. Then there was silence. The pilgrims walked for several hours without seeing or hearing her. Their fear increased when they heard her gentle laughter but could not find her. Proude called out to her but she did not answer. When she laughed again her voice seemed miles ahead of them.

Pure Gumption, with Private Jones following at her side, trotted in giant circles through the fields and trees. Her golden aura was visible from a great distance, like a swarm of fireflies appearing and disappearing in the deep dark grass. Pure Gumption stopped and began to howl. When the pilgrims ran toward her glow they found Belladonna on her stomach with her face buried in the grass. Her hands were over her ears. She was trembling in fear.

"We are here," said Proude, putting his hands on her shoulders. Her fear and tension seemed to leave her muscles when he spoke. When she rolled over her once smooth and sensitive face had turned to pale wrinkles and deep lines. Her dark eyes seemed to be pulling inward into darkness, avoiding sight and light.

"The demons were here, the demons were in the grass all around me," she repeated several times in her shrill voice. The pilgrims carried her from the grass back to the road.

"Back to the good road again," she sighed as her feet touched the rough asphalt. Her muscles were more relaxed. She seemed to slide as she laughed harder and harder until the pale wrinkles on her face turned deep red. The pilgrims were silent watching her face change.

"Back to the roads again," she chanted. "Roads are good black lines into the future ... But are there no red lines to follow somewhere? What use are we without colored roads into the unknown?" She spoke in short sentences while she walked in short uneven spurts. Her manner and expressions were strange to the pilgrims. She was a serious person with little foolishness. Double Saint thought that the fear and stress of their travels had broken her strength to survive. She was falling inward from the circles of creation. She was passing through time again over the brim of humor. The pilgrims did not fear her interior journeys, but the demons were waiting on evil. She could not walk with ease.

"We have come . . . to this little night nation . . . in short little steps," Belladonna chanted as she laughed between phrases and dragged her feet on the asphalt. "Short steps . . . short steps . . . dragging our little short steps." Breathless she turned and stumbled backwards down the road.

While the pilgrims carried her to the grass at the side of the road she whispered and laughed between disconnected phrases. "Damn the whitefeet in tribal governments . . . Curses on blonds who travel with the tribes . . . Curse the curses . . . Moan home when the wars are done . . . Moan home . . . Moan home . . . Our fathers love our bodies . . . Magic medicine on our bodies . . . Medicine in our blood and the trees . . . Mind trees and mind leaves changing colors with our time."

The pilgrims comforted her in the grass while she continued talking in short phrases. Proude started a fire to hold back the moisture rising from the earth. Belladonna crawled so close to the flames that she singed her hair. When she was pulled from the fire she laughed and chanted the words," father father fire fire perfect father perfect father fire," over and over again.

Proude heated water and made herbal tea. Belladonna told phrases and laughed. Double Saint said she made "no sense and not listening to meaning made sense." The herbal tea put the pilgrims to sleep before the bishop had finished his lecture on listening. "Sometimes we listen to ourselves so well well well that we have no need for others to listen . . . She is speaking and listening at the same time."

Proude and Inawa Biwide rested beside Belladonna near the fire. She moaned in her half sleep and mumbled unrelated words without moving her lips. The words seemed to speak through her from some unknown power. The night passed in word dreams.

Proude was awakened by Perfect Crow walking across his chest. The first seams of morning light stretched across the eastern horizon. In the distance a rabbit screamed the moment before it died in the talons of an owl. Proude left the circle of the fire and walked into the morning mist across the wet grass. He leaned against the bark of a tree and whispered in honor of the new world. Thin clouds opened to his voice and the earth moved beneath him on the back of sacred turtles.

"Belladonna is near death", Proude told the pilgrims when he returned to the fire circle. "She has been poisoned ... slow poison. Pure Gumption knows what she cannot cure with her power. The poision will take her breath."

"The people behind the red wall ..."

"Those fucking breeders did this to her," said Double Saint. He cursed and threw his hands against the earth. "We should go back and burn them ... fucking whiteperverts."

Belladonna opened her deep disappearing eyes and turned the wrinkles on her face into smiles when she saw the faces of the pilgrims around the fire. Smiling turned her face into sudden expressions of fear. Her vision turned backwards, "from those who harm harm to those without visions and dreams ... Where ghost dancers our mothers are ghost dancers ... Universal dreams their shirts were the shirts," she said backwards in short phrases.

She rested her head near the fire facing her last sunrise. Her facial expressions wavered backwards between fear and humor on whales and hunters. The circus pilgrims listened in silence while she talked backwards. Inawa Biwide touched her cheeks with his hands.

"Our mothers how trance lusted ... Ghost shirts in lust ... Men in their dreams lust no harm comes ... Where are the ones who the ones are conceived ... Conceived prairie in the ghost shirts ... Our mothers mothers."

She was breathing backwards. While she inhaled her chest contracted against her short breaths. Her muscles pulled against familiar motions. The expressions on her face were twisted from recognition.

"Our mothers sold shirt ghosts ... Shirts last year over tribal stores ... Touching store earth ... Over airports ... Eating shirts ... Ghosts."

"Her lips and fingers turned blue."

"Arms numb ... Sold our mothers ghost shirts machine printed ... Breathing gone ... Sold their dreams again ... Harm will come ... Will come to those ... To those ... Sold who ... Dreams who sold their ... Their dreams."

Proude touched her cold lips with his fingers to stop the flow of words backwards. Her breathing came shorter and shorter. The muscles of her face and neck twitched and trembled beneath her loose skin. She said in single spaced words that she was swirling near the center of her death. Then her face muscles stiffened.

Through the warm fingers on her lips she found death bouncing out of reach like small balloon fires in the deep darkness. Walking backwards up the hill were the final halting words she spoke before her breath seemed to catch on the last word hill and stop. On the word hill her muscles relaxed. When the deep wrinkles fell her cervine face returned from fear. Her last words and energies bounced from the morning into the hands of death.

¶ Nijode Bidaban

Proude Cedarfair spread her black braided hair beside her in the cold stiff grass. He dropped cedar incense on the fire and then opened one of his medicine bundles, removing a small rattle and a leather pouch filled with ashes. Rubbing the dark willow and birch and cedar ash into her bloodless checks and forehead he shook the sacred rattle until the sound whispered with the spirits. The animals and birds were drawn together in a close circle to protect her spirit from evil. Her names were unspoken now traveling alone into the deep shadows of the underworld.

Pure Gumption illuminated the circle with her golden aura. Perfect Crow strutted inside the circle with her black wings drooping. The pilgrims were breathing with the slow whispering rattle. Proude chanted in a high pitched voice *wa hi hi hi hi hi nibowin*, death . . . *wa hi hi hi hi nibowin*, death . . . free her spirit. The rattle whispered with the wind from the four sacred directions.

Saint Benito Saint Plumero and Inawa Biwide were singing *wa hi hi hi hi wa hi hi hi hi.* The earth moved beneath them and the morning chased the darkness with the power of their voices on the wind. Pure Gumption and Private Jones howled and the clown crows clucked and chirred with the whispering rattle. Proude was singing *wa hi hi hi hi kitchi gaossed*, great hunter . . . *kigijebawagad*, it is our morning . . . *bimaamog binessiwag*, we are together with the birds . . . *andekwag*, the crows . . . *awessiag*, the animals . . . *anishinabeg nagamon*, songs of the people.

Kitchi gaossed, great hunter . . . *nin wawijenima*, praising him in thought . . . *wabanang*, morning star . . . *nisswi mino manitog*, three fine spirits . . . *weniban*, gone . . . *anishinabeg gijik ishkote*, people of the cedar fires . . . *giweki*, returning to our homes . . . *manitog giweki*, spirits returning home . . . *wa hi hi hi hi* . . . *wa hi hi hi hi.*

Proude touched her stomach with one hand while he shook the rattle near her heart. He pressed his hand against her stomach *wa hi hi hi hi binakwigisiss*, moon of the falling leaves . . . *nagamowin*, singing . . . *tagwagig*, in the autumn . . . *nagamowin*, singing . . . *nin minotagos*, I am heard with pleasure . . . *wa hi hi hi hi* . . . *wa hi hi hi hi.*

Saint Saint Plumero shook the rattle while Proude loosened her clothing. She was wearing a ribbon shirt and trousers tied at the waist with a leather cord. The cord, given to her by her father when he led her backwards up the sacred hills, was decorated with beaded geometric designs of turtles and thunderbirds. Proude raised her shirt to her neck exposing the dark nipples on her breasts and then lowered her trousers to her pubic hair. Pure Gumption moved toward her stomach. She had thickened at the waist. She had conceived the violent seeds from the whitesavages who raped her near the reservation.

Proude was singing *wa hi hi hi hi nagamowin*, singing . . . *nin manitowis*, seen as the spirits . . . *megwe mino binessiwag*, sitting with good birds . . . *dash makwog*, and bears . . . *agawateg*, there are shadows . . . *gigitchitchag*, together with the soul *wa hi hi hi hi.*

The perfect knife blade flashed the colors of the morning fires. Singing to the good spirits of the *kitchi gaossed*, the great hunter *wa hi hi hi hi*, his hands soared over the lost aura on her face and breasts and stomach with waterbirds over water. The seven crows hopped and chirred around the circle.

Proude pressed the point of the blade against her dark skin above her pubic arch. The knife punctured her smooth skin while he was singing. He drew the sharp knife from her pubic arch cutting her flesh in a wide circle from the crest of the ilium upward toward her ribs. Rosina was weeping. She did not understand his need to cut her dead flesh.

Singing *wa hi hi hi hi* while he drew the knife in the other direction from her pubic arch forming an incomplete circle. Then he slipped both of his hands beneath her flesh into her womb. Pure Gumption glowed in her golden aura. Inawa Biwide sounded his plaintive voice through her *wanblee* whistle. Proude sang *wa hi hi hi hi kitchi gaossed*, great hunter . . . *mino manitog*, good spirits . . . *megwe binessiwag dash makwog*, with birds and bears . . . *bisanabiwin*, silence ... *nabe aiaag,* male animals ... *oshki anishinabeg,* new people of the tribes ... *oshki manitog,* new spirits ... *abitawis nadowessi,* half white half Lakota ... *nin pandigawad,* entering their hearts ... *wa hi hi hi hi wa hi hi hi hi.*

Proude lifted the pale wet bodies of twin children from her womb. He raised them through the circle of the circus pilgrims near the fire. He raised them into their good spirits *wa hi hi hi hi* ... He raised them into their living shadows before their nameless death *wa hi hi hi hi* ... These children have lived with *kitchi gaossed,* the great hunter ... Take these twins into the next world to live with the good spirits. The *wanblee* whistle called the winds home.

Holding the twin children, one in each hand, he told the pilgrims to turn in a human circle. Breaking the circle near the cedar fire, he turned to a place east of the fire where three graves were marked on the red earth *wa hi hi hi hi* ... He was singing the children into sacred names, *nijode bidaban,* twins ... *nijode bidaban,* twins with the dawn *wa hi hi hi hi* while the circus pilgrims prepared the graves.

The earth took the shadows of their bodies from death back into the red morning. Proude sat in the middle of the three graves facing the rising sun and singing in a high pitched voice *wa hi hi hi hi.* Rainbows burst from his shoulders over the circle of the pilgrims. The sound of his singing floated on lightstreams from his mouth to the hearts of the two children ... Twins with the dawn ... The dawn loves to rise on the faces of singing children.

Wa hi hi hi hi nagamowin, singing ... *nawaii igiw,* between them ... *nin pandigawad,* entering their hearts ... *nawaii igiw,* between them ... *kagige bimadisiwin,* everlasting lives ... *bisanabiwin wanaki,* silence in a place of peace ... *kagige bimadisiwin,* everlasting lives ... *ho kwi ho ho ho* ...

The first bright beams of morning light turned in the circle of the pilgrims and animals and crows and good spirits of the children ... The sun bloomed over their morning graves marking their shadows and sacred names.

¶ Master Stranger of Lightning

On the banks of the Canadian River near the small world of Peek in Western Oklahoma the circus pilgrims saw bright blue and green coronas over the hills. The river came down through the grass and pine from the high plains of New Mexico and trailed through the red earth under the thunderbirds. The Antelope Hills were blazing with lightning.

Perfect Crow was the first to hear the thunder. "Thunder storms ahead," said Double Saint who had been watching the crows and animals. He sniffed the ozone and rubbed his fingers together to feel the moisture.

"You are the master of the obvious," said Bishop Parasimo. "Perhaps one of the master master master strangers ... Now show us the obvious crossing over the river."

"You have nothing to fear but silence," Double Saint responded. "I have the umbrella now all we need is a boat ... we have done this before, master bishop."

The pilgrims walked along the shore of the river toward the lightning in the hills looking for a crossing place. In nervous fits the crows flapped and hopped on the sand beach and then soared down the water. The pressure in their bones changed with the weather. The pilgrims found a road but the bridge was down. The sign near the road announced that a person known as the Luminous Augur would lead people across the river and over the hills through the lightning.

"Farther down the river."

Near the next bend in the river beside two cottonwood trees decorated with ribbons the pilgrims saw a small dark old woman in a white sailsleeve dress sitting in a folding metal chair. She did not look at the pilgrims when they approached but offered them folding chairs to sit on and share the view of the lightning and great thunderbirds across the river.

"Could you be the auguress?" asked Double Saint, placing his huge feet in the sand against the legs of her chair. He smiled and leaned toward the woman. She was luminous. The air around her space was blue. The old woman neither answered nor shifted her gaze from the lightning. When she did not answer a question about how to cross the river Double Saint tipped her chair with his foot. The nervous crows hopped and chirred when the luminous old woman rolled backwards on the sand. When parawoman reached out to touch her she seemed to draw the tension and fear from his mind and heart out through his hands. He was so relaxed under her gaze that he rolled back on the sand and traveled through his dreams to his childhood home on the reservation peneplain. There he changed his pronouns and touched the world as a woman.

"Does the auguress have a boat?" asked Double Saint when he stopped laughing. She smiled and looked up at him. He avoided her gaze and looked toward the lightning in the hills across the river. The thunder rolled and rumbled with each blue stroke.

"Seventeen strokes per minute in the late afternoon," said the Luminous Augur. When she touched Double Saint on the arm the tension in his muscles rushed to her fingers and he slumped down on the sand in sleep.

"The hills are in perfect balance," said the augur turning toward Rosina who had placed a folding chair next to her. Rosina told about their travels and the dead pilgrims. The lightning flashed and the thunder cracked and rumbled between her phrases.

"We are seeking nothing more than a place to dream again," Rosina told the augur. The nervous crows chirred and pecked at the river sand.

"But dreams are not places," said the Luminous Augur. "The places we have known move in dreams ... Dreams here and the places change."

"Proude knows the earth and trees."

"The red earth has power here ... The lightning leaves the hills in perfect balance with our hearts and the solemn stars."

"How will we cross the river?"

"You should not think about crossing the river," said the

Luminous Augur. She was sweeping her gaze down river as lightning struck the hills. "How will the lightning find you crossing the hills ... It takes three hours to walk through the thunderbirds."

"Walking through the lightning?"

The Luminous Augur pitched her head from side to side in time with the strokes of lightning. Frail blue beams seemed to dash from her vision. "Lightning travels in me ... We are perfect power riding alone through the blue swirling heart of tornadoes."

"Tornadoes?"

"Tornadoes have lifted me across time."

"Does it rain in the hills?"

"Tornadoes give me light and balance ... There is lightning seventeen times a minute in the hills but never rain ... There is wind but no rain."

"Will you lead us through the lightning?"

"Across the river but not into the hills ... There is an old man, a Master Stranger, who lives in a round house made from shattered trees ... Made from cottonwoods and oak trees split and exploded with lightning. He lives near the hardest storms and will lead people through."

"We have nothing but dried food to give."

"He wants nothing but food."

"How does he live there?"

"The lightning ... The lightning keeps him whole and the oak splits protect him from evil and death," said the Luminous Augur. "He believes our lives are electrical ... So he walks between strokes to be alive."

The Luminous Augur sitting in her metal folding chair turned to silence. Peals of thunder shivered on the surface of the dark river water. The clown crows huddled together near the shore. The animals were sleeping. The Luminous Augur pitched her head from side to side and bounced her fingertips together. Rosina was about to speak to her about their home in the sacred cedar when a huge ball of fire came rolling down the river. The wavering blue and green ball skidded from side to side. The crows sounded their warning and flapped and hopped behind a sand ridge. The intense voices of the crows awakened the sleeping pilgrims. Pure Gumption snapped her head awake and growled at the approaching ball of fire. The circus pilgrims were dazzled with the swirling light. The Luminous Augur removed her white sailsleeve dress and walked into the river. The water around her skin was clear and bright. When she reached the middle of the river she turned her head toward the shore. Blue vision beams swept over the pilgrims. The ball of fire passed over her head drawing her out of the water and then she disappeared.

The circus pilgrims waited in silence for her return. Double Saint looked for a sign of the Luminous Augur in the water. While he paced in the sand the river began to recede. The crows walked in the exposed river bottom searching for treasures and bits of food. In less than an hour the dark water receded and revealed a stone path across the river. The Luminous Augur did not return.

"We can wait no longer," said Proude. "The river has opened for us to cross ... The water will not hold back much longer."

The seven circus pilgrims crossed the shallow river. When the pilgrims climbed the bank and looked back the river level had increased and water was flowing over the stone path.

"Look, look, she returned," said Pio.

"She returned from the ball of fire."

Dressed in white the Luminous Augur was again sitting in her metal folding chair. The circus pilgrims waved to her. She pitched her head from side to side.

The Antelope Hills were dark blue and blazing with lightning. The round house of the Master Stranger was located in a crotch between two hills. Lightning sizzled and smacked on the hills but not in the crotch where the Master Stranger lived. The seven crows led the column of circus pilgrims across the fields and into the crotch where lightning struck seventeen times a minute. The red earth was steaming and smelled of ozone. The round house of splintered wood was surrounded with a green and blue corona.

Master Stranger met the pilgrims at the door of his house. Thunder rolled and rattled at his greenish flesh. He wore dark green sunglasses. His cheeks were wide and creased. He was small with a slight twist to his spine which tilted his shoulder and head.

"We are pilgrims from the cedar nation," Proude said to Master Stranger. "We have been on the road for two months. We crossed the river with the Luminous Augur and she told us to speak with you ... She said you could lead us through the lightning..." His voice was interrupted with flashes of lightning and thunder. Master Stranger was silent for several minutes and then said that the Luminous Augur rides in the center of tornadoes.

"But how does she stop river water?"

"River fires."

"How do we go go go through the strokes?"

"Harmless."

"Will you show us through the hills?"

"How much ... how much food?"

"Enough to eat," said the Master Stranger.

Sun Bear Sun unshouldered his pack and placed bundles of dried meat and fruit on the moist grass. The lightning man watched and then took several bundles into his round house. The pilgrims waited but he did not return.

The house smelled of rosehips and burned oak. Slabs of lightning scorched oak were used as wainscoting. A square block bookcase stood in the center of the round house. The stars of thirteen constellations were marked with chips of wood on the dome. The space was decorated with fulgurites, petrified lightning, crude glass tubes from the red earth where lightning struck.

"Fucking cripple took our food."

"He has bark bark bark not meat," said Bishop Parasimo. "While you fools were sleeping I repacked the dried meat and substituted the best with cottonwood bark ... We will have the last last last laugh when he sits down to eat."

The round house began to tremble. Fulgurous beams of blue and green light flashed through the cracks in the slab sides. The circus pilgrims measured this time and decided to lead themselves through the harmonies of earth and lightning from the thunderbirds. "The crows will be first," said Proude, "because the crows can feel the movements of water undergound and hear the places where streamers rise to meet the lightning . . . We will follow the crows."

Less than a hundred feet from the round house a giant bolt of lightning struck so close that their hair was singed and their flesh tingled. The dazzled pilgrims turned back to the round house.

Between the balls of fire Master Stranger appeared in the door of his house. He was smiling. The creases on his wide cheeks were filled with bluish flesh. He stood smiling in silence for several minutes and then said that he would show the pilgrims part way through the lightning. "Half the hills for the bark food ..." he said.

"But you disappeared."

"Pilgrims are so impatient."

"No better time time time than the present ... Lead the way mister fire fire fire balls," said the Bishop who was twitching with stress. The muscles on his face seemed to vibrate. His hands darted and trembled in and out of finger conversations. His jaw and neck jumped from tension and fear. "Pio, Pio, Pio, the three metamasks in this case will be yours to wear whenever you choose if you carry them through the lightning." The mammoth agreed and clutched the black case to his chest. He had dreamed of wearing the metamasks as a woman again.

Master Stranger of lighting, with his twisted spine, shuffled through the moist grass out of his crotch into the hills. The green corona around his head bounced when he walked. The seven circus pilgrims followed in his glowing footprints, covering their eyes to shield them from the bright flashing and sizzling light. The crows rode on the shoulders of the pilgrims.

Master Stranger stopped in the crotch of the fourth and fifth hills. He told the pilgrims he would go no farther. There are three hills remaining before you leave the thunderbirds.

"Feel the water and listen to the streamers ... Lightning is no worse than the old automobile traffic on the interstates," said the Master Stranger.

"We are almost there there there ... What can we give you to take us all the way? Please please please my mind will not last the thunder alone," said the bishop in a tense voice.

The Master Stranger smiled and disappeared at the instant when several bolts of lightning struck the earth around him. Perfect Crow and Proude moved out of the crotch and up the fifth hill into the lightning. The other pilgrims followed. He avoided the paths of underground water. When lightning is thrown from the thunderbirds it seeks the streamers from the underground water trails that rise up to meet above the earth. Proude could hear and feel the streamers rising. He moved across the fifth hill and into the crotch of the next. Lightning flashed around them at every step. When the column of circus pilgrims started up the sixth hill Bishop Parasimo started to moan and then howl in a high pitched voice. He was at the end of the column. The pilgrims turned to see that his face had fallen. His muscles were loose, he was dazed. His eyes were unfocused. Proude

214

stopped the column on the side of the hill but before the pilgrims could turn to help the bishop he started running over the hill into the face of the lightning. His howling voice lingered between the crashing thunderbirds. In the crotch of the seventh hill his voice stopped. He had been struck bloodless three times. His legs ran out from under him, his breath stopped and his blood burned his flesh to a fine white ash. Proude led the pilgrims over the last hill onto the green grass beyond the reach of the thunderbirds.

"We must go back for the bishop," said Rosina.

"No one lives through lightning."

"But he could be numbed."

Perfect Crow and Proude returned to the seventh hill and found the Bishop in an ashen mound with several streamers rising around his remains. The streamers buzzed and cracked around the mound like guardian snakes. Then sizzling bolts of lightning connected in a low whistle with some of the streamers. Proude measured the time between the appearance of the streamers and the strokes of lightning. Dashing between the streamers he dropped cedar incense on the remains. Then he filled a blue cloth with the ashes of the bishop *wa hi hi hi hi hi* and tied the ends of the bundle closed *ho kwi ho ho ho*. Proude leaped from the mounds as bolts of lightning struck the streamers and returned to the thunderbirds. The muscles in his legs tingled. His feet were glowing when he returned to the waiting pilgrims.

"The bishop is dead . . . His remains are surrounded with lightning. We could not remove him," said Proude. He did not tell that he had taken a bundle of ashes. "There are no ceremonies for lightning from the thunderbirds . . . His flesh and bones will turn to ash and rise to meet the thunderbirds in perfect balance . . . His voice will be thunder."

Parawoman was weeping.

Silence.

The setting sun burned orange behind the thunderbirds. Thunder rumbled in the distance. Proude told stories about thunderbirds and the time the first tribes from the cedar nation saw the sun go out in an eclipse. The tribes came together in the darkness of the afternoon and shot flaming arrows at the sun to give it fire again. When the eclipse passed the people of the cedar fires know the sun was alive because of their arrows.

¶ Freedom Train to Santa Fe

Proude Cedarfair gave one medicine bundle to the pentarchical pensioners as fare for six circus pilgrims with seven clown crows and two animals to ride on the freedom train to Santa Fe. The five whiterulers called their slipshod freedom soldiers to attention to receive the magic bundle of tribal secrets.

"How could you do that?" asked Double Saint. He thumped his feet in disbelief. "You can never come back to the center again. The tribes will be done with you now, giving up on yourself."

"You will never touch touch touch the secrets of the earth again," said Scintilla Shruggles speaking in trine words like the bishop. "You will live in shame."

Proude was shunned. What none of the pilgrims knew was that he carried two medicine bundles. The smaller one contained his secrets from the cedar circus and the ashes of the bishop. The second bundle, the one he traded with the whitepensioners for fare on the train, was not sacred. The larger bundle had no power because it had been stolen from a museum. A whiteteacher, fearing that the stolen bundle would emit evil power, delivered it to Proude for safekeeping. Sacred bundles are not evil, he explained, but the whiteteacher refused to touch the stolen bundle of stones, bits of hair, wooden fish, sage and other herbs, fox feet and a small stained ghost dance shirt. Proude returned the ghost dance shirt to a medicine leader on the plains.

"Your power will change," said Sun Bear Sun.

Proude stood alone near the train with the clown crows and animals. He would not speak about the medicine bundles, but when Rosina pleaded with him for an explanation he spoke in a deep voice: "The power of the human spirit is carried in the heart not in histories and materials. The living hold the foolishness of the past," he said. "Good spirits soar with the birds and the sun not in secret bundles."

Rosina removed her shoulder pack and rested against a tree near the freedom train. She touched her cheeks and breasts and looked toward the western horizon. The thin white line between the earth and space wavered in her vision. She was dreaming about her children, their faces bloomed on the horizon; the cedar circus and the woman in the scapehouse of weirds and sensitives. She heard the birds and smelled the fern and mint when she stepped into the warm pool with the scapehouse women.

Coming through the lightning hills the pilgrims then crossed the Washita River near Roll and passed through Cheyenne in western Oklahoma. The pilgrims found the freedom train in New Liberty. The pentarchical pensioners, five short whiterulers in diverse martial uniforms decorated with colorful ribbons and cords, had assembled an old steam engine and thirteen boxcars into a freedom train. The pensioners were veterans from various wars. The whiterulers had enlisted five platoons of mercenaries to liberate the nation from the hands of the elitists. The pensioners accepted passengers to Santa Fe, the place where the new nation and government would be declared.

The five platoons were named for the Texas and Oklahoma birth places of the whiterulers: New Deal, Lone Wolf, Circle Back, Hart Camp and Cloud Chief. Each platoon carried a pennon decorated with five pentacles bound with a chain of human faces and the birthplace names printed in various bright colors. The pentarchical pensioners and soldiers were united in the numbers and shapes of five. The whiterulers issue written orders in pentastich paragraphs and the reorganization plan for the nation is divided into five memorial parts. The pentad plan begins with rigid rules for pure living. The second part calls for sacrifice and obedience. The third part explains the nature of divine rule. The fourth part charts the methods of national economic reorganization and the last part structures the future paradigms of the universe under the divine power of the pentarchical pensioners. The whiterulers blamed the collapse of the government on the elitists, the scholars and educators appointed to federal cabinets and commissions and transaction agencies. The elitists exploited the poor until the poor revolted. When the poor and disadvantaged were elected to legislative offices the elitists were terminated. But the poor were no less corrupt than the privileged. The aspiring poor in the image of the elitists paralyzed the democratic functions of government and terminated services to the public. The new leaders from the lockers of the poor took care of themselves. In declaring a new nation the pentarchical pensioners plan to overthrow fascist power and return the government to whiteworking people. The whiterulers promise monies for transportation and a new government, not in ones and twos, but in fives. Pentamerous committees will govern the new nation.

Rosina watched the sun burn through the thin white line on the horizon. Green discs floated in her vision. Proude built a fire and the pilgrims gathered around in silence. Dozens of other families were waiting for the freedom train. Small fires illuminated their faces.

The pensioners told the waiting families that the freedom train would leave during the night. "Have your bodies greased to move at a moments notice," said the whiteruler from the Circle Back platoon. Double Saint called the pensioner over to the cedar fire and asked him about the steam engine. "Well," he said, looking at the fire and picking his front teeth with a stiff blade of grass, "we had it hidden all these years waiting on the filling stations to go numb. We had it hidden in a cave up near the lightning hills . . . No one would go near there. We planned this freedom train before some of these soldiers were born . . . Three decades on the drawing boards . . . No flight in the night thing here good buddies.

"We got the handle on the way to run this great nation once and for all . . . Santa Fe we got in mind because of the bomb place up in the mountains and because the town ran out of water and all them elitists packed up their lunch counters and turned back to their eastern charms and loopholes . . . Down with the elitists when we take over the government. Down with them educated criminals.

"This is how we are coming . . . Four hundred years after Santa Fe was founded we are going back like the first governors and captain generals to build an empire in the new world . . . To declare a new nation from the old ruins. So, there you have it all in a nut shell.

"The families who are planning to ride the train to freedom give us food and weapons . . . Well, for you, when we seen the four braves and two squaws we softened a bit on the cost of the ride. So we took that medicine bundle for the whole bunch because, well, me and the Hart

Camper and Lone Wolfer, well, putting it one way we got a soft chalk spot in the old chest bone for injuns ... You see, our mothers had a little injun blood from way back in the good old reservation days when squaws knew how to make a man howl across the mountains ... Well, we got a little injun and it takes three to swing the vote, so we put you all on for the price of one ... Not even one, because you get no soup from medicine bundles. But we get some power out of the bundle. We got it hanging for good luck up on the front of the engine."

Four hours before dawn the pentarchical pensioners fired the boiler on the steam engine and called their soldiers and travelers aboard. The first five boxcars were assigned to the five platoons. The remaining eight boxcars were open to travelers. The six circus pilgrims climbed into the third boxcar from the end.

The freedom train hurtled through the darkness across Oklahoma and Texas. Late the next morning the train crossed the border into New Mexico and followed the old Atchison, Topeka and Santa Fe tracks westward. From Clovis the freedom train followed the highway where thousands of people were walking. The whiterulers ordered the train to a stop near the Pecos River at Fort Sumner. The place where eight thousand tribal people, nomads from the desert and sacred mesas, were confined for five years. The place where Colonel Kit Carson was praised and honored for his disgraceful conquest of the Navaho people. He forced the tribes on the long walk to Bosque Redondo where thousands died.

The seven clown crows were the first to leave the boxcar, hopping into flight from the door and then swooping down over the fast moving water. The circus pilgrims climbed down moaning and groaning and shuffled to the river with other families. The pilgrims filled their water vessels and then bathed in the cold shallow water.

"With my eyes closed," said Double Saint, floating in the deepest place in the river, "my body is still moving on that train ... The price of freedom is the same ... Freedom never stands still."

The pentarchical pensioners ordered the pentad soldiers and travelers to gather wood to burn in the steam engine. The soldiers cut trees and pulled up the railroad ties behind the freedom train. Next the soldiers ordered the travelers to fill more than a hundred huge water bags which were carried from the river on poles. The pensioners said there was enough water on the train for the pentad platoons to drink for three months or more. Late in the afternoon the freedom train started again. The steam engine shivered and chugged across the desert through the mesquite and black grama grass. The lurching boxcars filled with the scent of dark sage.

When the sun had set behind the Manzano and Sandia Mountains the whiterulers ordered the freedom train to stop for more wood. The soldiers raided several houses for furniture and took down small wooden buildings. The freedom train continued westward toward Willard where the tracks turned northward toward Santa Fe. The train stopped again near Estancia because the rulers were not certain that there was a shortcut track from Moriarty to Lamy and Santa Fe. The pensioners checked their maps and reconnaissance notes and discovered that the abandoned tracks of the old New Mexico Central Railroad had been restored.

The freedom train continued chugging higher and higher through the blue grama grass and juniper and pinon pine near Handprint and Tangeline and then rattled to a stop near the site of the old mission at Galisteo where the tracks connected again with the route of the Atchison, Topeka and Santa Fe.

The whiterulers voted to wait until the next afternoon before starting again. The cries of animals echoed over the mountains. The circus pilgrims slept in the boxcar.

In the morning the sun slipped and tipped over the top of Glorieta Mesa. On the western horizon the San Pedro and Ortiz Mountains blazed blue in the first morning light. The pilgrims walked into the mountains. The crows swooped and soared ahead of them. The thin air was sweet with juniper and sage. Blue berries dropped in bunches. Looking back the pilgrims saw the freedom train stretched out on the rusted tracks below them. Flames flickered in the firebox of the steam engine. The travelers and soldiers were clumped like rootless weeds near the tracks.

Proude and Inawa Biwide turned toward the mountains and walked higher through the juniper. Late in the morning while the pilgrims were sleeping and telling stories the sound of roaring bears echoed from the mountains to the mesas in the east. The clown crows landed in the trees and remained silent. The wind seemed to wait and listen while the bears roared. The roaring turned to a slow chant and then stopped. The travelers looked up toward the mountains. The soldiers raised their rifles.

Proude and Inawa Biwide returned to the place the pilgrims were resting in time to hear the pentarchical pensioners calling the travelers aboard the train. The soldiers were nervous. Late in the afternoon the whiterulers ordered the soldiers to close and lock the doors on the boxcars. The freedom train lurched into motion across the connecting tracks to Santa Fe. Through the cracks in the siding on the boxcars the pilgrims watched the mountains float across the horizon.

"We have become prisoners on a freedom train," said Proude while he pulled and chipped at the siding in an effort to make an escape hole. "Now like trapped rodents we gnaw at the walls to be free."

The train moved through the dark mountains and then trembled to a slow stop. Before the soldiers opened the boxcar doors the whiterulers explained to the travelers that for their own protection the soldiers would be guarding them. "There are still hostile savages here," said the Cloud Chief pensioner, "and we must protect the first good citizens of our new nation." The doors opened and the travelers were ordered to form teams of five to carry the water bags from the train to the palace. Several shots shattered the darkness when two families tried to escape.

Inawa Biwide led the circus pilgrims with the water bags through the darkness across Santa Fe Plaza. The soldiers directed the travelers with the water through the side entrance into the patio of the Palace of the Governors. The huge water bags were suspended from vigas in the old post office. When all the families were inside the palace, the oldest public building in the nation, the pentarchical pensioners ordered the entrances closed and guarded.

"Why have we become prisoners?" asked Proude.

The soldiers would not speak.

The circus pilgrims were confined to the old documents room in the palace. The adobe room was filled with historical memorabilia. The pilgrims settled in the darkness. The clown crows huddled on the flat palace roof over the pilgrims.

¶ Palace of the Governors

When the sun was high over the Sangre de Cristo Mountains the circus pilgrims were ordered to assemble with the other families in the palace patio. There the soldiers counted heads and then divided the new prisoners into groups of five. An ochre number was painted on the forehead of each prisoner. The circus pilgrims were in prisoner platoon number four under the command of the intense whiteruler from New Deal. Names and numbers were magic and birthplaces were sources of personal power to the pensioners. Touring the museum and historic rooms in the old palace the pentarchical pensioners discovered the grand garments and ceremonial accouterments worn by the old governors. The pensioners assumed their names and their dress with the enthusiasm of historical clowns. Number four, the New Dealer, became known to the prisoners and the soldiers as New Governor Marsh Giddings. The other pensioners became New Governor Cloud Chief Stephen Kearny, Lone Wolf Abraham Rencher, Hart Camp William Pile and Circle Back Lew Wallace. The new governors acted out in voice and gestures a preternatural resemblance to the first territorial governors. New Governor Circle Back Wallace each night closed the doors and the narrow windows in his executive office and pretended to write a book on a plain pine table about Judah Ben Hur.

During the afternoon the prisoner families worked in groups of five. The circus pilgrims worked under guard outside the palace walls. The second day as prisoners the pilgrims hauled water down from a reservoir in the mountains. The crows followed them in flight. The water was carried in huge bags attached to poles. On the third day as prisoners Double Saint loaded abandoned automobiles with water bags and freewheeled and pushed them down the canyon roads to the plaza.

Santa Fe was an adobe ghost town. During the drought the wells dried up and the people moved. The government trucked in water from the north until there was no longer any gasoline. The reservoirs in the Sangre de Cristo Mountains did not hold enough water for the town. Now tribal people were claiming the water from the fresh mountains streams before it flowed into the reservoir.

"This is paradise," moaned Double Saint. "Two months on the road ... Through evil and death we have survived to become prisoners in a weird palace."

"Matchi Makwa and Bishop Parasimo would have planned our escape by now now now," said Princess Gallroad feeling the spirit of the dead pilgrims behind her metamask.

"Old guard face over there has been trained to hear the word escape," cautioned Double Saint. "Watch the fool ... Escape! Escape!" The soldier dipped his rifle in all directions searching for an escaping prisoner.

While the circus pilgrims were assembling in the morning three soldiers caught Private Jones by the ears and tail and carried him to a chopping block in the center of the patio. Several other soldiers guarded the pilgrims while one soldier raised an axe over the head of the animal. The clown crows swooped down and dropped white excrement on the soldiers, but before the crows could return for a second attack Private Jones was dead. The first blow missed his neck and chopped off his paws. One quick second chop severed his head. The soldier, holding the headless Private Jones by the back legs, swung him around until the blood stopped spurting from his neck. Then with precise strokes of a knife the soldier skinned and butchered the animal.

Princess Gallroad wailed and cursed the soldiers. Her curses and metamasks and the peculiar powers of the other pilgrims were discussed during a special meeting of the new governors. Now that we have founded our new nation, the new governors agreed, we must enforce high moral and ethical standards. The prisoners are part of the new nation and must conform to the highest values of our government. Sorcerers and shamans and witches will be punished for their crimes.

The pentarchical pensioners had planned in the beginning to detain the travelers as prisoners. It was for that reason that the whiterulers asked so little fare from the pilgrims. The soldiers and pensioners were agreeable on the rails but now behind the palace walls the new governors were obsessed. The new governors ordered an inquisition into witchcraft and shamanism. Prisoners were questioned, suspicions were confirmed, and charges of evil and diabolism were brought against the pilgrims.

On the fourth night of their imprisonment the new governors questioned the circus pilgrims. Rosina Cedarfair was the first to be called and questioned by the inquisitors. New Governor New Deal Giddings informed the witness that she was within his prison platoon. Then he asked her to talk about her experiences in the past two months. She told them about the evil gambler and the cancer victims with plastic faces and the polyphemus moths and then she explained how the pilgrims had liberated the witches with luminous bacteria and the burial of two unborn children. The inquisitors wrinkled their brows and asked her to be honest and to explain further the liberation of the witches.

"The witches with the luminous designs on their cheeks were hanging in this restaurant ... Well, it was not a real restaurant," Rosina explained. "We lowered the witches and met later under a bridge down the interstate."

"What happened to the witches after this liberation?" asked the New Governor Circle Back Wallace.

"Two of them wandered from the bridge while we were waiting for the others ... and the other witch came back on the end of a stick."

"The end of a what?"

"Her head was stuck on a stick."

"How did it get there?"

"Someone put it there at the restaurant."

"Do you mean to tell us that one of the witches came from the restaurant, that is, her head came from the restaurant, on the end of a stick?" asked New Governor Hart Camp Pile.

"You make it sound so strange."

"How strange was it?"

"Not so strange when you think about some of the things we have seen," said Rosina in a plaintive voice. "We have been walking from the cedar nation for more than two months now and there has been violence and death ... Death and whitepeople punishing and killing each other for no reason ... So when the head of the witch came back on a stick we never thought much about it . . . The heads were buried and we went on walking."

"You speak of more than one head? Were there others?" asked New Governor Lone Wolf Rencher.

"Two heads ... One was the witch and the other was Matchi Makwa. He was one of us, one of the pilgrims from the cedar."

"Was he injun?"

"He was one of us ... from the cedar."

"How did their heads get on the sticks?"

"Someone put them there."

"Who put them there?"

"Pio found them on the sticks next to the restaurant door," Rosina explained. She was nervous. Her face and neck were moist with perspiration.

"Pio who?" asked Cloud Chief Kearny.

"Pio Wissakodewinini ... We call him the parawoman mammoth clown because he is so huge . . . Pio brought the heads back because he found them on sticks."

"Pio, is he the one with the masks?"

"Three metamasks he inherited from the bishop."

"The bishop?"

"Yes, Bishop Omax Parasimo ... He was a fine person. He talked too much with his hands and then gave up and walked into the lightning ... I thought about walking with him then ... We are so tired. So tired!"

"The bishop had three masks?"

"He wore them on special ceremonial occasions."

"Now this mammoth wears them?"

"Pio is a transsexual mammoth and the metamasks of women give him a good feeling about himself. ... Herself, she is much more interesting now with the metamasks. She talks all the time but before, when we were in the cave and then on the postal truck ..."

"On the postal truck?"

"We started out on a postal truck ... Pio would seldom speak. He sort of faded out of the present in spite of his huge size ... But now she feels much better having three metamask to speak through. She was fine until the government cut off her hormone treatments."

"His ... her hormone treatments?"

"Well, he was convicted of rape and the punishment was transsexual surgery. .. They made him a woman as a way to punish him for raping a woman ... He never did the rape but he did like being a woman. The hormones helped him look better but he withdrew from the world when her voice changed again. Now he speaks about himself, or herself, without thinking too much about her shape.''

"He cursed the soldiers this morning."

"We all did . . . These animals," she said pointing to the soldiers standing in the room, "killed our precious Private Jones for no reason. We all cursed the people in this place . . . Once we thought you were people of peace and freedom but now we know you are no different than those whitesavages we met on the interstate."

"Curses are forbidden here at the palace," said New Deal Giddings in a firm voice. He adjusted his borrowed uniform and stretched his wrinkled neck like a chicken. "There will be no witches and shamans permitted in our new nation . . . Governments in the past have fallen because of evil and diabolitics . . . diabolism. The code of our nation calls for severe punishment and banishment for witchcraft.''

"Please tell us about your husband."

Silence.

"Tell us about Proude."

Silence.

"You will be punished if you remain silent and do not tell us about your husband . . . This is an official inquisition and you are under oath to answer all of our questions."

Silence.

"For the last time," said Circle Back Wallace in a gentle tone, "we are honest men and we insist that you tell us the truth about your husband . . . We will not harm him here."

Silence.

The new governors ordered the soldiers to remove Rosina from the inquisition room. Her silence was evidence that she was possessed with evil. The five new governors sat behind a pine table. Hanging behind them on the walls were serious portraits of important persons in the colonial and territorial history of New Mexico.

Proude Cedarfair was called next to appear before the inquisition of the new governors. When he entered the old legislative hall of the palace he could feel the negative energies from the pensioners. Their first questions were cautious and patronizing.

"Cedarfair is a beautiful name."

"Rosina is a fine woman."

"Have you suffered much on your travels?"

"Without grace," said Proude.

"Interesting . . . We come from the back lands of this nation. From the working earth and we have much to learn about this power of the cedar," said Circle Back Wallace. "Could you tell us more about the power of the shaman? The power of good and evil?"

"You ask me about evil . . . You ask me pretending that you are innocent. The power you understand is evil."

"But we have the power and you also have power," said New Governor Hart Camp Pile. "We control the palace and the soldiers and you are a prisoner . . . Now tell us more about your power."

"Prisoners live in a state of grace."

"Do you practice evil witchcraft?"

"Witchcraft is not practiced."

"Rosina told us all about your demonic powers . . . She told us the things you have been doing with witches and shamans," said Lone Wolf Rencher. "There is no reason to hold back information from us now."

Silence.

"Be honest with us now."

Silence.

"Tell us about the cedar nation."

Silence.

"Why did you leave your reservation?"

Silence.

"Were you forced to leave? Removed?"

Silence.

"You are a shaman and practice witchcraft."

Silence.

"You are an evil shaman."

Silence.

"The tribal leaders told you to leave."

Silence.

"You have evil power."

Silence.

"Stop looking at us like that . . ."

"We have heard nothing," said New Governor New Deal Giddings. "It is the order of this official inquisition that the numbers on the foreheads of these evil pilgrims be removed at once . . . Evil will not wear the number of my command."

Proude was removed from the legislative hall. The soldiers escorted him to the documents room where the other pilgrims were detained. There the soldiers scrubbed off the number four from the foreheads of the six pilgrims.

"We will be punished as shamans and demons," said Proude when the soldiers left the room. "Weakness attracts them ... We will be punished tomorrow."

"If you had listened to me in the first place we would not be prisoners now," snapped Double Saint. "Dump the wisdom shit and put your head to escaping."

"The one with the least obvious weakness will reveal our plans to escape," said Proude.

"He means me me me," said Princess Gallroad.

"You and these fucking masks caused the suspicion in the first place ... We are being fingered as evil because of your goddamn masks ... Fucking pervert!" said Sun Bear Sun.

"You people are all sick," said Double Saint.

The circus pilgrims continued their hostile arguments about the inquisition. Double Saint lost his humor and spoke in harsh tones while he paced in circles around the documents room. His huge feet thumped out his rage. Rosina said the inquisition was not unkind to her. Proude asked the pilgrims to be silent. He said the inquisitors were causing them to feel uncomfortable with themselves and to feel shame for not answering their false accusuations. "Mistrusting each other gives them evil power over us," said Proude.

Pure Gumption moved to the corner of the dark documents room where Inawa Biwide was sitting with his back against the wall. He had not spoken since the pilgrims became prisoners. The muscles on his smooth face were tense. He was still mourning the lightning death of the bishop. Pure Gumption was listless since Private Jones was butchered and eaten by the soldiers.

Sun Bear Sun told Inawa Biwide that he shared the same loneliness. He smiled and talked about himself and his father. "Those who walk with a good balance have the best laws within their hearts ... Sun Bear was a proud medicine leader. He believed in the sun and the rattle and the brotherhood of all families of peoples. Father waited and waited for his ideas to become a national movement ... But no more than a few dozen people at a time came to him for his words ... He never liked people who came to learn the rattle alone. Sun Bear gave his energies to those who were learning to serve and teach others ... When I was born he made me the sun, never knew who mother was, he said we were all men of the sun. Said his words had the power of the sun and named me the sun of the sun bear. Go now on your own and make new families of the sun . . . And so here we are together, prisoners in the darkness. The sun of the sun bear is a prisoner in darkness."

Sun Bear said that knowing things "changes nothing. Singing is what changes the world, singing not knowing . . . Mother earth feels the rattle and our feet and voices upon her with the eagles and bears. The heart changes the world not the mouth. Mother earth has had too much mouth on her to listen. Mouth will not change us as prisoners . . . The mouth will not free us from this place. But our hearts will show us freedom . . . Sun Bear told me that the pictures of the earth in our hearts will not change with the mouth. He sent me from the mountains with the message that a nation grows when we take the earth back into our hearts and walk in balance and natural harmonies."

"Even the heart has prisons," said Inawa Biwide.

"The stranger speaks," said Double Saint.

The circus pilgrims heard the bugler sounding the retreat in the palace patio. Prisoners were not permitted to attend the ceremonial salute to the pennons. The whiterulers restated the principles of their new nation and were about to return to the old legislative hall when the clown crows soared over the western wall ánd dropped loads of thick white excrement on the uniforms of the five new governors. The crows crowed and flapped and swooped until the shoulders and heads of the governors were covered like those of park statues. The soldiers waved their rifles and fired dozens of times but the crows escaped over the wall unharmed. The pilgrims heard the shooting but did not know what the crows had done until the soldiers passing the pine door of the documents room uttered their names with disdain. Within minutes the soldiers were ordered to bring another pilgrim to the inquisition room. The soldiers studied the pilgrims in the darkness and then pulled Inawa Biwide to his feet.

The five new governors paced around the pine table in a rage. Their uniforms were stained. The crow excrement had dried deep in the thick material. The soldier ordered Inawa Biwide to sit in a chair in the center of the room.

"Who ordered the crows on us?"

Silence.

"Talk or your head will be gone."

Silence.

"Who told those crows to shit on our uniforms?"
Silence.
"I will ask one more time."
Silence.
"Who did this to our uniforms?"
"The crows," answered Inawa Biwide.
"But who told the crows to do it ... Who?"
Silence.
"Who speaks with the birds?"
Silence.
"Proude Cedarfair?"
Silence.
"That fool with the huge feet?"
Silence.
"Not that masked pervert?"
Silence.
"Damn your evil silence ..."
Silence.
"Than it must be you ..."
New Governor Hart Camp Pile walked over to the stranger and lifted him by the hair from his chair. "Now tell us who wished the crows evil during our ceremonies," he said between his clenched false teeth. Then the new governor twisted the right ear of the stranger until the flesh split and blood ran down his neck. Inawa Biwide moaned in pain. "Now, answer our questions or we will twist of your ears and pull out your eyes ..."
"Did you tell those crows to shit?"
"No."
"Then who did?"
"No one ... We were not there."
"Someone did ... Who was the evil one?"
"No one," answered Inawa Biwide.
"For the last time ... Tell us who caused this?"
"The crows ..."
"The crows! ... The crows!"
"Crows are not told what to do."
"One of those damn perverts told them to shit."
Silence.
While New Governor Hart Camp Pile held the stranger down the other governors lined up in their shit stained uniforms and spat in his

face. When the stranger spat back at them the governors smacked him in the face. Then New Governor Line Wolf Rencher cut his braided hair and severed his ears with three sudden strokes of his knife.

"Pull out his evil eyes."

"The crows have their own power ..."

When the stranger rose up from his chair and roared in the voice of a small bear the governors pounced on him and threw him to the floor and scooped out his dark eyes with their fingers. The soldiers dragged the bleeding stranger back to the documents room with his eyeballs dangling on his cheeks. Faces shimmered in his unfocused vision. Pure Gumption licked his face and ear stubs and eyeballs clean before the pilgrims pushed them back into the bleeding holes. The delicate muscles were ruptured and his eyes wandered without visual control. Rosina cradled him in her arms while Pure Gumption pressed her glowing nose against his face.

Sun Bear Sun was the next pilgrim summoned by the inquisitors to the legislative hall. While he was sitting in the chair in the center of the room answering questions, Double Saint was mashing up the last of his precious vision vine leaves. The pulp was mixed with water. He sipped the hallucinogenic drink and then passed it around in the darkness. The pilgrims sat in a circle on the floor and sipped the thick vision vine drink. Proude refused the drink but he shared time in the vision circle. Double Saint was the first to soar through changing colors. He was chanting on the rainbows slipping under the door and through the crack in the thick abode wall.

"With this vision vine we share our consciousness and speak together with the animals and birds through their voices and singing. We pass through time and voices," chanted Double Saint, "and we will locate our enemies and see this room in all the time it has lived ... Through the visions of insects and the faces of beams of colored light ..."

"The forest is blue in our memories," said Rosina Cedarfair with her head turned up and her eyes wide open in the darkness of the documents room. Inawa Biwide said he was talking "with Private Jones, out of time and place." Then he was in magical flight with the ghosts of other pilgrims over the woodland rivers and cedar fires.

Pio Wissakodewinini was a woman on one side and a man on the other. She he traveled in both minds and double pronouns. She he shared the consciousness of her his double selves . . . "We can feel the power of your thoughts . . . You are traveling through the pine door to the legislative hall."

"Sun Bear Sun is sitting there," chanted Double Saint. "He is sitting with his hands folded over his chest." The pilgrims traveled together from their circle to the inquisition and listened to the questions of the new governors . . . The shit on their uniforms turned to powder . . . Our shared visions are invisible.

"Who told the crows to shit on us?"

"The crows listen to no one."

"How did the witches get on the sticks?"

"Pio found them like that."

"Does Proude have magic power?"

"He knows things . . . He sees spiritual things."

"Does he do evil?"

"Never evil . . . He takes care not to upset the balances of good and evil and the energies of demons," Sun Bear Sun explained. "Proude does not hurt people . . . He has a pure soul."

"Double Saint . . . is he evil?"

"The pilgrims are not evil . . . What reason is there to find evil in what lives . . . When our world is gone the tribes will still be dancing in great circles over the earth."

"When is the escape planned?"

"Tomorrow . . ."

The pilgrims listened in shared consciousness to the inquisition and the honest responses of Sun Bear Sun. Then the pilgrims soared through the patio and over the walls with the seven clown crows. Resting in the cottonwood trees the pilgrims and the black crows flapped and swooped over the abandoned buildings and automobiles and landed on the benches in the plaza. Twelve clown crows rested in the plaza. Time passed as shared visions.

The prison documents room and other rooms in the palace took on lives and shared conversations from the past. "The ballroom is a large, long room, with a dirt floor, and the panels of the interior doors are made of bull and buffalo hide," wrote an officer who had accompanied the first territorial governor to the palace, "tanned and painted so as to resemble wood. There are various other rooms besides the antechamber . . . the guard room and prison on the west end . . . The rear contains kitchens, bake ovens, and ground for a garden, the whole being roomy, convenient, and suitable to the dignity of a governor in New Mexico ..."

Moving through the time of six generations the twelve clown crows were in the palace when the first wooded floors were laid in some of the rooms ... Figured calico covered the whitewashed walls ... The old vigas were replaced when a portion of the earthen roof dropped ... Governor Don Juan Francisco Trevino was discussing the charges against tribal sorcerers and idolators ... Tribal people liberated the prisoners and spared the governor ... The twelve crows did not hear the governor tell that four tribal people had been hanged for their terminal creeds ... The twelve crows watched the flag of the United States unfurl for the first time in Santa Fe right now from the plaza benches on August 18, 1846 ... We are there for this great occasion crowed the twelve crows ... Whitepeople are in uniforms for more than ten generations ... Lusting with intense erotic stimulation the twelve crows are touching each other on the plaza bench ... Who will smoke me now ... Four worlds are swirling through colors through time ... Space turns under and disappears.

The west wall of the documents room is peeling through time return visions ... Beneath the new adobe is a huge fire place and a large smoke hole from the distant past leading to the roof ... Chip the surface vision down to the adobe bricks and pull them out and together we are climbing through the smoke hole over the palace ... One two three four five ... twelve clown crows and Pure Gumption ... Travel with me between these stars where we were born.

Sun Bear Sun is locked in the past without visions answering questions in the legislative hall ... The universal victim is the honest fool answering unanswerable questions.

¶ Backward with the Mission Clowns

The five circus pilgrims followed the main road southwest near the rims and ribs of the sacred mountains down to the Rio Grande. For more than a week the pilgrims walked in silence near the river. The clown crows flew ahead short distances and then waited for the tired pilgrims.

"These people are the kiuwa," said Proude when the pilgrims approached Santa Domingo Pueblo on the east side of the river. Small corn cakes were placed near the adobe walls for strangers but no one greeted them.

The next morning the pilgrims passed San Felipe Pueblo on the opposite side of the river at the foot of black mesa. The sun rising over the mountains burned with the colors of adobe walls and the leaves on the cottonwood and willow near the river.

Late in the afternoon the pilgrims crossed the first bridge over the Rio Grande near Algodones. Hundred of tribal people, with their heads down, were moving across the river into the mountains.

Proude had visions of mythical birds and dancing gods in green and white and yellow and red circles when the pilgrims were near the site of the kuau ruins on the west bank of the river. The old adobe town once had thousands of rooms. Ceremonial frescoes clung to the buried walls. Proude sat with the old people from the pueblo. He was there in their time and place soaring on the mountain winds. Proude was with the old men painting the walls with the colors of the earth and then his visions dissolved with violence and winter dust. The dust came down over the birds and bears from the mountains where the wild wind woman lived in storms.

In less than a week the circus pilgrims passed the Santa Ana and

Zia pueblos north of the river. The Zia kiva was still burning in the memories of the wind and birds and sage. The kiva was still burning from the fires started during the religious wars by the terminal faith healers who came back to the pueblos. Proude could smell the fires and burning flesh on the wind.

At San Ysidro, the place name for whiteangel farmers, the pilgrims turned north and walked near the Jemez River toward Walatowa Pueblo. In the distance the pilgrims saw the red chilis hanging in the sun like giant serpent tongues. Near the pueblo two sacred clowns with corn stalks tied to their hair danced out of the juniper on each side of the trail.

"Your mouths are milking the earth from meaning and your feet are stones," chanted the two sacred clowns in falsetto voices. "Where can you be going with such aimless steps?"

"Who are you you you?" asked Princess Gallroad.

"Penis and precious cunt struck on one cosmic face again," said the clowns to the parawoman in the metamask.

The sacred clowns danced and dipped down the trail like tame mountain doves. Their bodies were painted warm and cold, one red and one white for opposite directions and seasons summer and winter. Around their wrists and waists were warm and cold colored feathers matching their painted bodies. But for their toothless smiles and raucous laughter the clowns could have been the walking dead or avian clown figures from dreams. The seven crows hopped around the clowns. Strutting and thrusting their iridescent black necks around and around the clowns until the clowns stooped and strutted around the crows like crows. The crows huddled on the trail crowing and chirring. The human clown birds chirred and crowed back at the clown crows. When the crows flapped into the juniper and waited in silence like black blotches the sacred clowns doubled over in laughter. The clown crows turned in the trees and ignored their humor. Pure Gumption sneezed. Her golden aura had returned.

"You should be walking backward," said red clown and then the clowns twirled and dipped on the trail.

"You should be walking backward," said white clown. His toothless smile softened the hard gaze on his white face. "Two backward walks make one good forward in the world of fools."

"Belladonna walked backward," said Rosina.

"Backward up the hill," chanted the two clowns. "Backward,

backward up the hill because the place to be is not the place to be or the place you were and the trail to follow forward is not the trail to know ... Backward like grasshoppers leaping and then waiting for directions at an unknown landing landing landing ...

"Time and space between the starting and the stopping makes upward downward and backward forward and noward ..." The two sacred clowns pranced and danced in laughter. Their voices echoed through the trees on the mountains. The two were walking backward in front of the pilgrims.

"Are you from the pueblo ahead?" asked Princess Gallroad.

"The pueblo comes from these," chanted the sacred clowns as two huge penises, one red and one white, emerged from the feathers at their waists. Smiling the clowns walked toward the pilgrims waving the carved and painted penis heads. When the pilgrims did not respond in kind the clowns frowned and clowned. Red clown thrust his wooden penis into the crotch of parawoman and then danced around in silence. Princess Gallroad trembled and hid her face. Moving around and behind Proude the white clown thrust his rough hewn penis between the cheeks of his buttocks. Proude leaped and when he landed he turned and pushed the clown away with his hands. White clown hopped down the trail hooting. The crows swooped on the clowns once and then returned to their perches in the juniper.

"The eagles knew you were saints," said red clown.

"Not saints said the frogs and crickets near the crotch of the earth, these pilgrims are common dust, no more than weed people," said white clown. "Show how deep your roots are running with wandering weeds ... Soon the aimless wings shudder into common dust."

"Places are not places ... Weeds are not weeds ... We are not moving from dreams to dreams," said Proude. "Your strange faces are the dream winds from these mountains ... Laughing from places buried in the dust storms ... Dust storms down from the wild wind woman."

"You speak fine thoughts from the heart paths but who will take your little cock in hand mister proud and lust with you ... Your wife has forgotten the feeling of your rude prize," said white clown.

Double Saint was silent. He traveled on words and laughter with the two clowns. When the sacred clowns waved their wooden cocks, Double Saint was aroused with lust. He unharnessed his massive penis. Standing behind the pilgrims on the trail he worked hand over hand president jackson into a splendid erection. The clown crows chirred and stretched their black wings in the juniper.

"We have seen your journeys on the interstates ... We were walking backward through time and wind while you fools were carried forward into the sunset sunset sunset," the two feathered clowns chanted while swishing in circles.

"The medicine bundle ..." muttered Princess Gallroad.

"Throw the forward world the wind and the crows will catch the smallest shapes ... But not the mammoths ... Not the presidents and masked parawomen," chanted the two clowns. Red clown drew three teasing feathers under the chin of parawoman.

"Free hearts are never caught," said Double Saint while he rolled the tight skin over the purple head of his penis.

"Nor double erections on double saints ..."

"How do you know things about us?"

"We have walked backward in your time."

"How backward?"

"Walking forward but seeing backward ... Seeing in time what we invent in passing ... Birds and animals see behind their motion. Place and time lives in them not between them. Place is not an invention of time, place is a state of mind, place is no notched measuring stick from memories here to there ..." chanted the red and white clowns. Their feathers were shining in the sunlight.

"Who will travel with us to see behind our path?" asked Rosina with her arms folded beneath her breasts. Double Saint was standing behind her with erect president jackson in hand. She could smell his animal lust. Her cheeks were warm.

"That backward connection is standing behind you now," the two clowns chanted and then doubled over in laughter. Pointing and gesturing with their wooden cocks the red and white clowns hopped toward the pilgrims naming the presidents. Rosina shunned their sexual clowning.

The sacred clowns told the pilgrims to follow the course of the river backward through the mountains until their hearts came to the old mission ruins and the warm springs. "Rest there before turning to the desert. Rest there and remember the river flowing backward when following the crows and bears into the desert winter wash."

The red and white clowns hoisted back their wooden presidents and snapped their fingers and disappeared in a crack of sunlight through the junipers. The pilgrims continued walking forward backward northward noward on the river trail to the mission ruins. The setting sun slipped behind the mountains and the trees turned blue. The birds settled in the darkness. The clown crows were hopping near the pilgrims. *Gisiss wawiiesi,* the full moon, the full round moon, was upon the cedar faces walking between the dark mountains.

The pilgrims followed the scent of moist sodium to the warm springs. In the silver darkness the footsore and tired travelers slithered into the warm pool like primordial serpents. The animals of the mountains screamed and howled with lust under the whole moon.

Double Saint moved toward Rosina and touched her breasts and stomach beneath the water. Her wide nipples were erect when he pushed his hard penis into her small hands. She hesitated and then squeezed the throbbing head and touched his tense testicles until his sperm burst beneath the warm water and melted on the surface of the pool. She moved with her nose above water. She was child and fish and dew mother over the warm silver water moons.

Gashkadinogisiss the freezing moon. Winter was closer in the mountains. Hoarfrost covered the earth and mission stones during the night. The five circus pilgrims settled in the ruins of the mission. The walls were thick and made of stone. Proude climbed to the top of the spiral timber staircase where he greeted the sun each morning from the mission tower. He brewed his herb tea and burned blue sage. The spirits from the desert laughed and laughed.

Rosina and Princess Gallroad visited the women at the pueblo and learned how to make yucca baskets and clothing for the winter. The old women of the pueblo showed them how to find water in the desert and told stories about human bears in the mountains.

Proude and Inawa Biwide, who had lost control of his vision and was learning to see with birds, wandered through the azure mountains with the sun and clown crows and sat in silence near the cedar fire at night. Double Saint told stories and lusted after the women in the pueblo. Those two shamans, said the old women, will never speak again from wandering too far into the mountains with the bears.

Rosina was watching the sun dropping over the mountains when Double Saint came behind her and touched her breasts. Her cheeks were warm. Facing the orange horizon he opened his leather trousers and exposed his penis. Forcing her to turn and kneel in front of him he thrust his penis against her soft warm mouth. The huge purple head butted against her closed lips. Then he squeezed the muscles on her chin and when her mouth opened he pushed hard against her lips until the bulbous head slipped past her teeth. He held her head against him with her braids. His penis throbbed in her mouth. With the tip of her tongue she touched the opening on the head. Circling his penis with her tongue her muscles relaxed until president jackson was against the back of her mouth. He moaned when she touched his testicles and then his penis throbbed and spurted and flooded her mouth with warm sperm.

Sister Eternal Flame climbed up the wooded stairs to the mission tower where she was dew mother on her knees sucking on the clown. Sister Flame moved behind Double Saint and placed her mammoth hands around his neck stopping his deep breathing. She squeezed and pressed her thumbs on the back of his neck until he was dead. Rosina felt his penis rise once more and then the president weakened and flopped out of her mouth. Sister Flame released her hold and Double Saint dropped to the mission tower floor. When Rosina looked up and saw Sister Flame she rolled backward with sperm drooling down her chin and emitted a high pitched animal scream. The animals in the mountains were silent.

Rosina awakened the next morning near the fire with Sister Eternal Flame. She had traveled with death during the night. Double Saint laughed and clowned with her through the underground into the next world. Their bodies melted together in water and space.

Rosina looked around the cedar fire. Proude was gone. Inawa Biwide was gone. Pure Gumption was gone. The seven clown crows were gone. The mission stones were covered with hoarfrost. The bears roared from the mountains ha ha ha haaaa.

Next to the fire Proude had placed a pouch of cedar incense, a bundle of sage and a message written on a piece of white cloth. Follow the clown crows to the window on the winter solstice sunrise. Listen to the crows and the bears ha ha ha haaaa.

¶ Winter Solstice Bears

Proude and Inawa Biwide awakened before dawn and spoored the mountain vision bears down the river from the mission ruins. Pure Gumption and the seven crows followed in silence. Voices from the cedar past keened from the dark water. The sacred clowns smiled backward red and white from the blue juniper. Near San Ysidro the two pilgrims turned northwest and walked through tribal reservations.

The next morning the two pilgrims followed the clown crows into the barren mountains. *Manitogisissons* moon of the little spirits. The vision bears roared down the mountains ha ha ha haaaa on the cold night winds.

The two passed near Cabezon Peak, the landmark of the huge volcanic head on the eastern rim of the desert, and stopped on the Rio Puerco. In less than two weeks the two pilgrims followed the river through the cold desert canyons across the continental divide to White Horse. From there the two trailed near the old government road to the west and then north through the washes and arroyos into Chaco Canyon. Proude could hear their breathing when the two passed Fajada Butte. The clown crows called to their echoes down the mesa walls.

"This is the ancient place of vision bears," said Proude as the two passed Chettro Kettle and approached the largest pueblo in the ruins. "*Wanaki* Pueblo Bonito, a place of peace in the village of the heart ... The tribes traveled from here with bears."

The sun was high and bright when the pilgrims arrived. The air in the ancient pueblo was cloudless. The crows flew to the highest mesas and strutted near the rims. Their black wings whistled down and around the air currents over the pueblo ruins. Their crowing rattled between the mesas. Pure Gumption was sitting near a small kiva in her wide golden aura.

Inawa Biwide had learned to see with birds, one eye at a time, turning his head. He trusted more his sense of smell and place perceptions. He practiced walking in darkness and listening to escape distances and the sound and direction of the winds.

Their collective vision came from the mountains near the mission ruins. The two had walked in silence there for several weeks and then one afternoon while sleeping in the sun under the junipers a giant bear came to them and told them to follow their vision of him to the ancient ruins of the pueblos. Dreaming together the two pilgrims traveled in magical flight over the mountains and across rivers and the divide. At Pueblo Bonito the vision bear told the two pilgrims to enter the fourth world as bears. When their bodies changed shapes and began to float through the corner window toward the rising winter solstice sun the crows chirred and hopped through the stone frame. The shadows of the clown crows awakened the two from their bear vision.

"There is the vision window," said Inawa Biwide, pointing toward the southeast face of the pueblo. His words echoed between the massive sandstone mesas and returned to his ear stubs as his bear voice.

The crows swooped through the pueblo windows while the two pilgrims passed from room to room to the window on the winter solstice. There the two waited for the first morning of the winter solstice when the sun reaches the most southern point and rises in the center of the window. The two dreamed and traveled in magical flight over and over with the vision bears from the mission ruins.

Rosina and Sister Eternal Flame visited with their new friends at the Walatowa Pueblo before leaving the mission ruins. The two women visited too long and were given blankets to keep them warm on the winter desert. The two traveled on the same course as the men. The women followed the voices of animals and birds. Listening for bobcats and desert cottontails, hognose skunks and cactus mice to lead them through the parched mountains and mesas across the desert. The two praised the living on the trail. The exotic saltcedar tamarisk and cottonwoods in the washes responded to their touch and voices. Rosina and Sister Eternal Flame spoke to grama grass and greasewood and rabbitbrush. The two dreamed during the cold nights about roaring bears ha ha ha haaa from the mountains.

Near White Horse the two women encountered three tribal medicine men who had been singing in a ritual hogan. It was the last morning of a ceremonial chant to balance the world with humor and spiritual harmonies. Evil had been turned under with the sunrise and their sacred voices. The good power of the dawn was attracted to their rituals. The first breath of dawn was inhaled to balance the world. While the old men were inhaling the dawn, the two women emerged from the desert. The men laughed and laughed knowing the power of their voices had restored good humor to the suffering tribes. Changing woman was coming over the desert with the sun.

Near Chaco Canyon the clown crows flew out to meet them on the trail. Rosina was ecstatic, "the crows are here, the crows are here," she repeated while she waved her arms at them in flight. The crows swooped and flapped and landed on the shoulders and heads of the two women. The old men laughed and laughed and inhaled the dawn again. Perfect Crow nudged Rosina on the cheek while she walked. The women followed the wash to Pueblo Bonito where Pure Gumption was waiting. The two cuddled the animal and the birds and then followed the crows through the small sandstone rooms in the pueblo. In the corner room the two found cedar incense, a medicine bundle, a tribaltime watch and clothing.

That morning when the old men were inhaling the dawn and laughing during the first winter solstice sunrise, Proude Cedarfair and Inawa Biwide flew with vision bears ha ha ha haaa from the window on the perfect light into the fourth world.

Rosina touched the small white otter medicine bundle. The skin was tied with red and blue ribbons. When Sister Eternal Flame reached to open the bundle she was cautioned not to touch or look upon the contents. "His medicine has too much power to know without ceremonies ... Proude will tell us when to open the bundle," said Rosina.

"But he is gone now now now," said Sister Flame. She leaned out the solstice window and watched the crows dropping like black hawks from the mesa rims.

"The crows know where they have gone."

"Pure Gumption will tell ..."

"Tell us little gumption ... Tell us where have they gone now?"

Rosina asked as she cradled the animal in her arms. The small room was filled with a pale light from the golden aura.

The sun was setting over the mesas. Bright red and orange colors wheeled across the horizon. The desert turned cold. Jackrabbits and kangaroo rats leaped through their enormous shadows. Animal voices echoed down the mesas. The orange turned dark blue. The women built a small fire near the solstice window and waited for Proude and Inawa Biwide to return. The window loomed like one star in the constellations of sacred hunters and bears.

During the night while Rosina was sleeping, Sister Eternal Flame untied the red and blue ribbons on the white otter skin and opened the medicine bundle. She examined the contents. Two carved cedar figures. The deep eyes on the carved faces were glowing when she held them over the fire near the solstice window. Next she removed a rattle and wing bones from an eagle and white and blue plumes ... The claws from a giant bear ... Cedar incense and small fur pouches filled with herbal medicines and last she examined three cloth knots. One knot was filled with the ashes of the bishop. Sister Eternal Flame leaned closer to the fire to examine the cedar figures again. Their leer burned her vision.

Rosina awakened before sunrise. The clown crows were huddled in the corner of the room. Near the fire she saw the two cedar spirit figures and the contents of the medicine bundle. Staring out the solstice window she closed the bundle with the figures inside. Then she began to weep until the low winter sun burst in her vision through the center of the window.

Rosina heard the bears roaring ha ha ha haaa. She watched the sun chase shadows over the mesas. The bears roared from the rim of the mesa in the west ha ha ha haaaa. Then seconds later she heard the same roaring from the mesa in the east ha ha ha haaaa. Then the sound of the bears moved to the south and north in timeless flight. The bears were over time in the four directions.

"What is it? Roaring bears?" asked Sister Eternal Flame. Her vision was so weakened from the leering cedar figures that she could stare into the flaming sunrise without blinking.

Rosina took the mammoth parawoman into her small arms. The old men laughed and laughed on the sunrise with humor and tribal harmonies.

Late in the morning the two women were still holding each other in front of the corner winter solstice window. The clown crows flew to the rims of the mesas around the ancient pueblo. Pure Gumption was climbing the ancient stone stairs to the top of the north mesa where the sacred road led to rainbows and the sunrise.

On the third and last morning of the winter solstice sunrise through the pueblo window the two women heard the bears roaring again ha ha ha haaaa. In seconds, faster than birds could soar, the bears roared from the four directions ha ha ha haaaa. When the bears roared from the north there was a pause and then one final roar ha ha ha haaaa that echoed down the mesas and doubled backward through the corner window into the solstice room. The shadows of the two women trembled. Then the roaring trailed into the distance. That night several inches of snow covered the pueblo and surrounding mesas.

In the morning, Rosina found bear tracks in the snow. She followed the solstice bears from the pueblo up the sandstone stairs to the rim of the mesa. During the winter the old men laughed and laughed and told stories about changing woman and vision bears.

AFTERWORD
Louis Owens

"Some upsetting is necessary," Gerald Vizenor has said about his writing. And "upsetting" may be the key word in describing Vizenor's first novel, *Bearheart*. According to the author, the manuscript was "lost" three times in succession by the first three publishers who looked at it. "I think the people probably threw it away," Vizenor says with a coyote chuckle. "They probably read it and thought 'Holy shit,' because it's not anything they would expect on an Indian theme." Vizenor, mixedblood Chippewa—or Anishinaabeg, as the tribal people call themselves—from Minnesota's White Earth Reservation, has made a career as a writer by never giving people what they expect. A trickster, contrary, muckraking political journalist and activist, poet, essayist, novelist, and teacher, Vizenor confronts readers with shape-shifting definitions, inhabiting the wild realm of play within language and seeking, trickster-fashion, to trick and shock us into self-recognition and knowledge.

To read *Bearheart* is to take risks, for no preconceived notion of identity is safe, no dearly held belief inviolable. To teach *Bearheart* is even more dangerous, as I discovered several years ago when I learned that three students in my American Indian fiction course had reported me to a dean. My sin was including *Bearheart* in my syllabus. The three students, all mixedblood women raised in southern California, had known how to respond to the familiar tragedies of Indians—mixedblood or full—played out in novels by other Native American writers. But *Bearheart*, with its wild humor, upset them. Not only was there sexual violence in the novel, but even transsexual Indians. Indians in the novel were capable of cowardice as well as courage, of greed and lust as well as generosity and stoicism. And, according to the students weaned on film versions of Hollywooden Indians, Native American people could never be like that.

In talking with my three upset students, I came to a much greater understanding of Gerald Vizenor's fiction. In the end I realized that it wasn't the novel's irrepressible sexuality, not the violence or bestiality, not the transsexual shape shifting that upset my students. It was the novel's outrageous challenge to all preconceived definitions, what *Bearheart* calls "terminal creeds." The students' carefully nurtured and fragile identities as "Indians" had been dreadfully shaken, identities that had grown out of James Fenimore Cooper and John Wayne and centuries of static definitions of "Indianness" imposed — beginning with the very name itself — upon tribal people by an invading and dominating culture.

Since being hauled on the carpet for teaching *Bearheart*, I have been sure to include the novel in every Native American literature course I teach. It is a brilliant, evocative, essential corrective to all false and externally imposed definitions of "Indian." It challenges all of us, and, like all trickster tales, it wakes us up.

Born in 1934 in Minneapolis, Vizenor seems to have set out from the beginning to discover what it means to be a Native American mixedblood in modern America. One result has been an incredible outpouring of twenty-five books, scores of stories and essays, dozens of poems in magazines and anthologies, and a movie (*Harold of Orange*, 1983), all of which together make Gerald Vizenor both one of the most prolific and, more significantly, one of the most original of American writers.

Unifying virtually all of Vizenor's art is the presence of the trickster, that universal figure so necessary to Native American and world mythology and literature whose duty it is to amuse, surprise, shock, outrage, and generally trick us into self-knowledge. Whether in traditional mythology or Vizenor's fiction, the trickster challenges us in profoundly disturbing ways to reimagine moment by moment the world we inhabit. Trickster tests definitions of the self and, concomitantly, the world defined in relation to that self.

Bearheart, like all of Vizenor's fictions, is a trickster narrative, a postapocalyptic allegory of mixedblood pilgrim clowns afoot in a world gone predictably mad. As the pilgrims move westward toward the vision window at Pueblo Bonito, place of passage into the fourth world, their journey takes on ironic overtones in a parody not merely of the familiar allegorical pilgrimage found in *Canterbury Tales* but more pointedly of the westering pattern of American "discovery" and settlement. "I conceived of it as an episodic journey obliquely opposed to western manifest destiny," Vizenor explains, "a kind of parallel contradiction, of Indians moving south and southwest rather than west. What they're traveling through is the ruins of western civilization, which has exhausted its petroleum, its soul."

Unarguably among the most radical and startling of American novels, *Bearheart* is paradoxically also among the most traditional of novels by American Indian authors. Not only is this a narrative deeply in the trickster tradition, Vizenor's novel also reinforces the crucial Native American emphasis upon community rather than individuality and upon syncretic and dynamic values in place of the cultural suicide inherent in stasis. An intensely ecological narrative as well—again in the Native American tradition—*Bearheart* insists upon the most delicate of harmonies between man and the world he inhabits, and upon man's ultimate responsibility for that world.

The fictional author of this novel-within-a-novel is old Bearheart, the mixedblood shaman ensconced in the BIA offices being ransacked by American Indian Movement radicals as the book begins. Bearheart, who as a child achieved his vision of the bear while imprisoned in a BIA school closet, has written the book we will read. "When we are not victims to the white man then we become victims to ourselves," Bearheart tells an AIM radical with her chicken feathers and plastic beads. He directs her to the novel locked in a file cabinet, the "book about tribal futures, futures without oil and governments to blame for personal failures." To her question, "What is the book about?" Bearheart the trickster answers first, "Sex and violence," before adding, "travels through terminal creeds and social deeds escaping from evil into the fourth world where bears speak the secret languages of saints" (xiii–xiv).

"Terminal creeds" in *Bearheart* are beliefs that seek to impose static definitions upon the world. Such attempts are destructive, suicidal, even when the definitions appear to arise out of revered tradition. Third Proude Cedarfair expresses Vizenor's message when he says very early in the novel, "Beliefs and traditions are not greater than the love of living" (15), a declaration repeated near the end of the novel in Fourth Proude's statement that "the power of the human spirit is carried in the heart not in histories and materials" (217–18). *Bearheart* is a liberation, an attempt by this most radically intellectual of American Indian authors to free us from romantic entrapments, to liberate the imagination. The principal target of this fiction is the sign "Indian," with its predetermined and well-worn path between signifier and signified. Vizenor's aim is to free the play between these two elements, to liberate "Indianness."

With the primary exceptions of Proude, Rosina, and Inawa Biwide, most of the pilgrims in this narrative, to varying degrees, suffer from the illness of terminal creeds. Bishop Omax Parasimo, a believer in the Hollywood version of Indianness, is "obsessed with the romantic and spiritual power of tribal people" (75). Matchi Makwa, another pilgrim (who, along with Lillith Mae Farrier and, briefly, Bearheart himself, appears also in Vizenor's *Wordarrows*, 1978), chants, "Our women were poisoned part white," leading Fourth Proude to explain, "Matchi Makwa was taken with evil word sorcerers" (59).

Belladonna Darwin-Winter Catcher, the most obvious victim of terminal creeds, attempts to define herself as "Indian" to the exclusion of her mixedblood ancestry and, more fatally, to the exclusion of change. When the pilgrims come to Orion, a walled town inhabited by the descendants of famous hunters and western bucking-horse breeders, Belladonna is asked to define "tribal values." She replies with a string of clichés until finally, after trapping Belladonna in a series of inconsistencies and logical culs-de-sac, a hunter asks the question that cuts through the dark heart of the novel and all of Vizenor's fiction: "What does Indian mean?" When Belladonna replies with more clichéd phrases, the hunter says flatly, "Indians are an invention. . . . You tell me that the invention is different than the rest of the world when it was the rest of the world that invented the Indian . . . Are you speaking as an invention?" (195). Speaking as a romantic invention indeed, a reductionist definition of being that would deny possibilities of the life-giving change and adaptation at the center of traditional tribal identity, Belladonna is caught up in contradictions and dead ends and receives her "just desserts."

In a 1981 interview published in *MELUS* (8:1), Vizenor described the "invented Indian," confessing at the same time his own satirical, didactic purpose:

I'm still educating an audience. For example, about Indian identity I have a revolutionary fervor. The hardest

part of it is I believe we're all invented as Indians. . . .
So what I'm pursuing now in much of my writing is the
idea of the invented Indian. The inventions have become
disguises. Much of the power we have is universal,
generative in life itself and specific to our consciousness
here. In my case there's even the balance of white and
Indian, French and Indian, so the balance and
contradiction is within me genetically. . . . There's
another idea that I have worked into the stories, about
terminal creeds. I worked that into the novel Bearheart.
. . . This occurs in invented Indians because we're
invented and we're invented from traditional static
standards and we are stuck in coins and words like
artifacts. So we take up a belief and settle with it, stuck,
static. Some upsetting is necessary. (45–47)

Belladonna is obviously inventing herself from "traditional static standards."

At the What Cheer Trailer Ruins, the pilgrims encounter additional victims of terminal creeds, the Evil Gambler's mixedblood horde. In an experience sadly common to Native Americans, the three killers feel themselves, with some accuracy, to be the victims of white America. Even the Evil Gambler himself is a victim, having been kidnapped from a shopping mall and raised on the road in a big-rig trailer, his upbringing a distillation of the peripatetic Euro-American experience. Being raised outside of any community, Sir Cecil has no tribal or communal identity; he exists only for himself, the destructive essence of evil witchery. From being doused repeatedly with pesticides, he has become pale and hairless, a malignant Moby-Dick of the heartland. He explains, "I learned about slow torture from the government and private business. . . . Thousands of people have died the slow death from disfiguring cancers because the government failed to protect the public" (127). Sir Cecil, the Evil Gambler, is the product of a general failure of responsibility to the communal, tribal, and ecological whole. This failure of responsibility will be further emphasized when the pilgrims meet hordes of deformed stragglers on the highway, victims also of the horrors of modern technology.

When the pilgrims arrive at the Bioavaricious Regional Word Hospital, Vizenor, who had earlier been attracted by the writings of

French critic Roland Barthes as well as others, exploits the opportunity to inject a shot of poststructuralist musing. At the Word Hospital terminal creeds—language whose meaning is fixed, language without creative play—are the goal of the hospital staff. We are told that "with regenerated bioelectrical energies and electromagnetic fields, conversations were stimulated and modulated for predetermined values. Certain words and ideas were valued and reinforced with bioelectric stimulation" (168). This attempt to create an impossibly pure "readerly" prose stands in sharp contrast to the oral tradition defined in a description of life among *Bearheart*'s displaced just a few pages earlier:

> *Oral traditions were honored. . . . Readers and writers*
> *were seldom praised but the traveling raconteurs were one*
> *form of the new shamans on the interstates. . . . The*
> *listeners traveled with the tellers through the same frames*
> *of time and place. The telling was in the listening. . . .*
> *Myths became the center of meaning again (162).*

In the oral tradition a people define themselves and their place in a universe of imagined order, a definition necessarily dynamic and requiring constantly changing stories. The listeners re-create the story in the act of hearing and responding. As Vizenor himself says in the preface to *Earthdivers*, a collection of his prose pieces, "Creation myths are not time bound, the creation takes place in the telling, in present-tense metaphors." Predetermined values represent stasis and thus cultural death.

As they move westward, the pilgrims and sacred clowns meet fewer deformed victims of cultural genocide until finally they encounter the modern pueblos of the Southwest and a people living as they have always lived. At the Jemez Pueblo of New Mexico, the Walatowa Pueblo found in N. Scott Momaday's novel *House Made of Dawn*, the pilgrims encounter two sacred Pueblo clowns who outclown with their traditional wooden phalluses even Saint Plumero himself. The clowns direct Proude and the others toward Chaco Canyon and the vision window where, finally, Proude and Inawa Biwide soar into the fourth world as bears at the winter solstice.

A great deal is happening in *Bearheart*, but central to the entire thrust of the novel is the identification by the author's author, Vizenor, with the trickster, that figure which mediates between oppositions, or as Vizenor himself stresses in the epigraph to his most recent novel, *The Trickster of Liberty*, the figure that "embodies two antithetical, nonrational experiences of man with the natural world, his society, and his own psyche." Citing Warwick Wadlington, Vizenor emphasizes the duality of trickster's role as, on the one hand, "a force of treacherous disorder that outrages and disrupts, and on the other hand, an unanticipated, usually unintentional benevolence in which trickery is at the expense of inimical forces and for the benefit of mankind." For Vizenor, trickster is wenebojo (or manibozho, naanabozho, etc.), "the compassionate tribal trickster of the woodland anishinaabeg, the people named the Chippewa, Ojibway." This is not, according to Vizenor in *The Trickster of Liberty*, the "trickster in the word constructions of Paul Radin, the one who 'possesses no values, moral or social . . . knows neither good nor evil yet is responsible for both,' but the imaginative trickster, the one who cares to balance the world between terminal creeds and humor with unusual manners and ecstatic strategies."

This compassionate trickster—outrageous, disturbing, challenging as he is—is the author of *Bearheart*. In the 1981 *MELUS* interview, Vizenor explained: "When I was seeking some meaning in literature for myself, some identity for myself as a writer, I found it easily in the mythic connections." Central to these mythic connections is trickster, the shape shifter who mediates between man and nature, man and deity, who challenges us to reimagine who we are, who balances the world with laughter. Near the end of *Bearheart*, Rosina and Sister Eternal Flame (Pio in the late bishop's metamask) encounter three tribal holy men "who had been singing in a ritual hogan. It was the last morning of a ceremonial chant to balance the world with humor and and spiritual harmonies. . . . The men laughed and laughed knowing the power of their voices had restored good humor to the suffering tribes. Changing woman was coming over the desert with the sun" (243).

Coming over the desert with the sun, from east to west, is Rosina herself, who, like Proude, has achieved mythic existence through identification with the traditional Navajo deity of Changing Woman here near the end. "During the winter," we are told in the novel's final line, "the old men laughed and told stories about changing woman and vision bears." Translated through trickster's laughter into myth, Proude and Inawa Biwide and Rosina have a new existence within the ever-changing stories, the oral tradition. Contrary to the idea of the Indian as static artifact invented over the past several centuries, adaptation and change have always been central to American Indian cultures, responses that have enabled tribal cultures to survive. For all peoples, Vizenor seems to argue, but for the mixedblood in particular, adaptation and new self-imaginings are synonymous with psychic survival. Those who would live as inventions, who, like Belladonna, would define themselves according to the predetermined values of the sign "Indian," are victims of their own terminal vision. Bearheart's mocking laughter is their warning. As trickster would say, "Some upsetting is necessary."

Gerald Vizenor, a mixedblood member of the Minnesota Chippewa tribe, is a professor of literature and American Studies at the University of California, Santa Cruz. He has also taught at the University of California, Berkeley, the University of Minnesota, and Tianjin University in China. Vizenor wrote the original screenplay for *Harold of Orange*, which won the Film-in-the-Cities National screenwriting award and was also named "best film" at the San Francisco American Indian Film Festival. His second novel, *Griever: An American Monkey King in China*, won the Fiction Collective Prize and the American Book Award sponsored by the Before Columbus Foundation. In 1989, he received the California Arts Council Literature Award.

Vizenor has published several collections of haiku poems; *Matsushima: Pine Island*s is the most recent. Selections of his poems and short stories have appeared in several anthologies, including *Voices of the Rainbow* and *Words in the Blood*. The University of Minnesota Press has published Vizenor's autobiography, *Interior Landscapes*, as well as *Crossbloods: Bone Courts, Bingo, and Other Reports* and *Griever: An American Monkey King in China*. Minnesota has also published his novel *The Trickster of Liberty* and three of his books on the American Indian experience: *Wordarrows*, *Earthdivers*, and *The People Named the Chippewa*.